# THE
# WOMAN
# IN THE
# WINDOW

R.S.CROW

# THE
# WOMAN
# IN THE
# WINDOW

The Other Stories: Book One

This is not a horror story.
This is a story about overcoming fear through friendship.

# Prologue

When fear enters your life, no one wants to be near you. You become repugnant, foul. If you try to tell someone about your fear, your stink only becomes that much more evident. You're like a homeless person, unwashed and filthy, with nothing to offer but wide-mouthed rambling and a short retelling of what you've been through. Beg loud enough, and someone might toss spare change your way just before passing quickly by. These are some of the things they'll offer you:

"You'll be okay."

"You'll get through this."

"It's just nightmares."

"It's only dreams."

But between the words, you can hear what they're really saying. All they want is for you to be normal, to return to the way you used to be back when you talked like them, thought like them, and enjoyed the same things as them. But tell them about real fear, the kind that splits you open and plants unwanted things inside of you, then everyone disappears. You're left alone. So alone, you realize you never before truly comprehended the curse of such a word as *alone.*

But I wasn't utterly alone.

There was the woman in the window.

# – Part 1 –

## *The Woman in the Window*

# 1

I laughed back then. It's strange to remember that.

My friends swarmed me at my locker like a gaggle of geese as I gathered my books into my arms for first period. They chatted on and on about our upcoming prom, gossiping about who was going with who, who asked who, and the leftover singles who should be paired up.

Emma was going with Jared.

Tonya was going with William.

Valeska was going with Hunter.

Courtney was going with Blaine.

As for me, I didn't have a date yet. I was in the *leftover* category. Which, according to all my friends, was a bit of a travesty.

They were busy bodies – my friends – talking loudly, laughing along while we traveled the halls of high school like we owned the building. Before I knew it, I was laughing along too. Then Valeska asked me who I was going with. Before I could even answer, the next thing I knew, I was being passed and lightly shoved from one friend to the next as they tossed me about by my shoulders. They started singing – pretending it was spontaneous – "Oh, Ben! Oh, Ben! You're such a man! You're the man for Sarah!"

They threw their hands out. That was my cue. Spontaneously, I sang with an expression of dramatic longing, "Ben! Won't you take me to prom?" It was ridiculous. The group of us burst out laughing, even as the students around us rolled their eyes or shimmied past to avoid us. I probably would have rolled my eyes too, if I was watching from the outside. I promise – we weren't always *that* obnoxious. But prom was coming up. Our acapella competition was just weeks away. And we were teenage girls in our senior year. We were having the time of our lives.

The bell rang a second time, which meant each of us was going to be late to first period. My girlfriends waved their way off to class, leaving Emma and I to skitter together towards American History. I could tell Emma was pleased with herself. Her grin wouldn't leave her as she strutted along beside me in such a way I knew the whole thing had been her idea. Emma went on to update me about all the rumors she'd recently heard and the mounting evidence that Ben would be asking me to prom any day now. She knew it would happen, was "absolutely positive!" Because Ben had been talking to his friends – who were friends with her friends – and Ben had told those friends that he had finally worked up the nerve to ask a girl to prom.

"That doesn't mean it's me," I said.

"Oh, please," Emma said, waving a dismissive hand at me. She then began counting out the facts. "First of all, it's a girl that Ben has had a crush on for years. Second, he has a lot of the same classes with her. Third, she's pretty. Fourth, she's someone he admires." She tilted her eyes at me.

"And?"

"*And!* It's obviously you!"

"Obviously," I said, rolling my eyes.

"Obviously." She matched my eye roll with one that was even more dramatic.

"Who says I even want to go with Ben?" I asked, pinning my books to my chest just a little more tightly.

Emma spun in frustration, causing the green streak of her dyed hair to toss around before resetting at the corner of her brow, which she then brushed aside. "Sarah, you are the worst liar in the world! You're still blushing," she said as final proof, pointing to my cheek like I had a pimple there.

"Of course I'm blushing," I said. "After that show you just threw at me in the hall, anyone would be blushing."

"You loved it," she stated.

"Did not."

"Not even a little?" She pretended to pout.

"Maybe a little."

"Just a little?"

"Yeah."

"Then why are you smiling?" she teased.

"I smile when I'm embarrassed," I said. "It's my worst character flaw," I said, teasing.

"Your worst character flaw of all!" Emma twirled in front of me. "And Ben is going to ask *you*, Sarah! I swear it! And you *want* him to!"

My smile gave me away for good.

Emma was right, and she knew it. I did want Ben to ask me. Ben was the *only* one I wanted to ask me. But I shook my head. "I don't even care," I said.

"Sarah," was all Emma could say, her smile a little more endearing.

We walked into class. Class had kind of started, which meant kids were still sitting on desks and talking while Mr. Turcotte chalked out some notes on the blackboard. He greeted us after a defeated sigh, "Ladies, thank you for joining us."

"Welcome, Mr. Turcotte," Emma answered as if she had blessed his class with her presence.

"Good morning, Mr. Turcotte," I said. "Sorry we're late."

Mr. Turcotte brushed aside my apology. "Thank you for your concern, Ms. Sarah. Now take a seat, Ladies."

Emma and I sat in our usual spots. Emma continued her attempts to torture me playfully, humming her Ben song verse by verse, while I pretended to not even notice. Mr. Turcotte hushed the room, turning around and lowering his hands like a maestro attempting to regain the focus of a preoccupied amateur orchestra. Somebody snapped their gum. Mr. Turcotte cleared his throat and began disclosing specific details regarding our upcoming test, beginning with his favorite ominous caution, "Be ready for anything, Folks."

I couldn't be ready for anything.

I was thinking of other things.

I was thinking of a song.

Of prom.

And I was thinking of.

Ben.

Ben and I had been friends ever since grade school, back when we didn't even pay attention to or notice things like being a boy and being a girl. We liked each other, sure. But we also enjoyed a very drama-free friendship for years. From middle school through high school, we'd been surrounded by the evidence of friendships which had been ruined by a short-term relationship, which then became an awkward breakup, which then became cold-shouldered attempts to avoid each other in the hall and teary-eyed class attendance. We had seen the warning signs, they were all around us. *Do not cross! Friendship at risk!*

But there was something more than just a friendship between us. The subtle hints were there when we were alone together. A touch of the hand. A brush of body against body. A look. A tease.

And now, after all these years, Ben was going to ask me to prom – according to Emma, I reminded myself. It became an easy obsession in the middle of American History, which consumed me more and more, as Emma's song and Emma's comments opened doors inside of me which I had kept readily and cautiously closed for quite some time.

When would he ask me? I thought.

Would there be other people around, or would Ben try to keep it secretive and special?

Would we go with his friends, or with mine?

Would we share our first kiss during a dance? Maybe after?

Would he kiss me in a nervous sort of way, rushing through in a sloppy-lipped fit of nerves? Or would he take his time, letting me know he'd wanted to kiss me all these years?

My stomach fluttered more and more with each question.

American History ended, and Emma commented, "Sarah, you may want to ease up on that blush."

"It's not –"

Emma laughed, spinning excitedly out through the door and into the hall. "Oh, I know it's not!" Then she skipped away.

The rest of the day came and went. I don't remember much of it. I don't even remember if I even saw Ben or not, and I certainly don't remember being the focus of any more dramatics. Those things don't matter anymore – at least, not as much as I thought they did. My memories of those days come and go in partial pieces, bearing less and less significance over time.

But I remember that night.

My mom had come from work a little earlier than usual, which was a wonderful change from the customary way in which I'd go to bed without even seeing her. We finished our evening together with a movie, cozied up together under one big blanket, knees tucked to our chests as we chatted along throughout the scenes. It wasn't long before an autumn nostalgia took us over, maybe something inspired by the early setting of the sun. I said, "Dad always loved October." My mother said with the hint of a smile, "Yes, he did." We slowly reminisced through memories of my dad, beginning with October, and working our way through Thanksgiving and Christmas, spring and summer, birthdays and other stories which we were suddenly reminded of, back when he was ours and we were his.

I loved listening to the ways in which my mother described him, as though my father might return home any minute to tease us about our movie before heading off to shower.

The movie finished. We said our good nights.

I carried the blanket around me as I went down the hall towards my room, my mother closing the door to her own bedroom after a final, "goodnight." I turned off the light to the hallway before opening my bedroom door. It was dark inside. My bedroom was absolutely freezing, like I had stepped into a refrigerator, and I wrapped the blanket I'd been carrying a little tighter around me. It was my own fault. The window of my bedroom had been left wide open for hours as an open invitation to the cold. I loved it. That feeling of sleeping beneath the pre-wintery air, stuffed beneath the thick layers of heavy blankets as my own body slowly warmed me, leaving my nose a touch of cold. I dropped the blanket I'd been carrying off to the side and pulled on fuzzy socks before climbing into bed where I shimmied myself beneath the covers. I pulled them high to my chin, my body tucked together for warmth.

With my head on the pillow, I gazed out through my open window at the quiet sights of night almost absently. The night was clear. A porch light could be seen in the far corner of the window, barely illuminating a few bushes and the front of a car. And in the center of the window, far off in our neighbor's yard across the street, was an inflated Charlie Brown and Snoopy, side by side, bobbing left and right. I smiled dreamily. Halloween was coming soon, which meant Christmas was right around the corner.

My window went suddenly black.

The outside world vanished.

Confused, I tilted my head to look through the window from a different angle. Nothing changed. Just blackness. I sat up to look at the window directly. Again, nothing changed. I got up from my bed, leaving my warm covers behind and walked through the icy darkness with my arms covering my chest. I stopped in front of the window. I couldn't see through, though I could feel cold air pouring in. I swiped my hand across the blackness.

My fingers brushed through hair.

My hand retreated to my chest, and I clutched it as though it'd been burned. Black strands of hair moved in a streaming flow from the window. The darkness was gone. My neighborhood had returned. The Halloween decorations were visible again. I could hear the small engines of the inflation machines running steadily in a quiet hum.

I slammed the window shut, turning the lock in a drastic motion before hopping back from it. I clambered into bed, blankets pulled up to guard me from a different kind of cold, and kept my eyes pinned warily upon the window, breathing hard breaths. I hardly allowed myself to blink. The minutes passed by. One after another. The blackness didn't return. My mind tossed around ideas on what had happened, on what I had touched. Being on the second floor of the house, such a thing couldn't be possible, could it? Could it really have happened? Hair? Covering my window? No. It couldn't have been what I thought it had been. It was impossible. I had been mistaken. It had been my imagination.

Those lies comforted me. And in the morning, when I discovered a single strand of long black hair on the floor beside my bed – I told myself the strand was mine – and it was the easiest lie I'd ever told.

# 2

Sunday was spent wrapping up homework assignments and getting ready for the week. I was taking all honors classes, which basically meant things were always crazy. When that was all done, I talked on the phone with Emma for forever. After that, I spent some time practicing the acapella songs for the competition. And through all of that, through every second, I waited for a phone call from Ben. Which never happened. By 11:00pm, I was pretty tired, went to bed, and fell asleep quickly.

I woke to a chill. My sheets and blankets were gone. Lying on my back atop the mattress, my body was bare and vulnerable to the frozen air and the cold was like needles on my skin. I was trembling uncontrollably. I could feel the edge of my sheets along my thighs, but when I went to reach for them, I couldn't move my arms. They were rigid, my legs too. I was stiff as a board. The only thing I could move was my eyes. I turned them towards the open window where the sound of the wind ripped through, blowing my curtains violently.

I thought in vain, *I shut my window before bed.*

My sheets suddenly slid down my thighs. I tried to reach for them again, but still couldn't move. Then they slid further. I tilted my eyes towards the bottom of my mattress. Two dark eyes gazed at me. Black hair blew wildly along the pumping gusts that invaded my room. A woman was there. She was on the floor on her hands and knees, curled up like a cat and staring at me. The sheets were in her mouth. She was chewing on them, swallowing them inch by inch down her throat. Soon, the last of my sheets disappeared into the blackness of her throat. She was still staring. Then she tilted her face so she could latch her teeth onto the sheet which was beneath me. She began to chew again, bringing my body closer and closer. I wanted to scream, but my mouth remained sealed shut. I tucked my toes to my feet, cringing. Her tongue brushed my heel.

I woke with a scream.

It had been a dream, I realized.

But I continued screaming.

My bedroom door opened. My mother was there. "Sarah?" she asked, concerned. "What's wrong?"

I sat up, cringing against the cold. My sheets and blankets were gone. "I was having a nightmare. There was a woman. At the end of the bed. She was. Eating my sheets. Pulling me closer. Her eyes. She was going to eat me. Her eyes. I couldn't move. It was terrible." I continued trembling, fixated on the darkness at the end of my bed.

My mother offered soothingly, "Well, it was only a nightmare."

"But it was so real."

"It was only a nightmare," she said, as though facts might help. "Sarah, you're shaking. Let me get your blankets."

"I'm so cold."

"Of course you are. Your window is open and your blankets are on the floor." My mother walked to the end of my bed where the bedding had fallen.

I remained cautious, peering over the end of my mattress as though afraid of dropping off into a hole where the woman had hidden herself. "I must have kicked them off."

My mother lifted the sheets. "Why are they damp?"

"I don't know."

"It must be moisture from the cold," she concluded.

I laid back down as she pulled the sheet and blankets up to cover me. She kissed my forehead. "Let me close your window. You'll catch a cold."

"Thanks, Mom."

"You're welcome. Do you need anything else?"

"I don't think so."

"Are you sure?"

The fear had mostly faded. I laughed at myself. "Yeah. I'm okay. Thanks, Mom."

My mother walked to the door. Her hand was on the knob. "Sarah –"

"Yes, Mom?"

"If you have another nightmare, be careful not scream so loudly, I don't want you to wake the other children."

I asked, "What other children?"

But my question went unanswered as my mother closed the door behind her. I asked, because I didn't yet understand.

# 3

5:45am. Monday morning's alarm buzzed like it had each and every Monday for as long as I could remember. It often early, even too early. This time, the sense of tiredness I felt when I woke up was different. My brain was foggy. My eyes burned. I yawned my way through the entire morning routine, shuffling around sluggishly as I got ready, fumbling at my things and gathering them up awkwardly, like I'd never used my arms before. I said *goodbye* to my mom, and when she told me I looked tired, I said *yep*. If she'd asked why, I'm not sure I would have known how to answer, because at that time, I was adamant about forgetting the dream and the hair and all the other things. There were important things to think about. Things that mattered.

In American History, Emma nudged me and leaned in close enough for me to smell her mint flavored gum which she snapped at. "Did he ask you yet, or nah?"

"Who?" I asked, barely copying notes.

She leaned in a little closer. "Ben."

"No," I said, staying studious as a distraction. "I thought he'd call this weekend, but he never did."

"So, nah?"

"Nah," I answered. I was trying to act nice, but hardly had the energy for that.

"I know he was at some party," she said after thinking it over. "He's been hanging out with Mark, like all the time, for like whatever reason. Mark's always doing something on the weekends, so Ben is too. Maybe Ben should ask Mark to go to prom."

I laughed. Then yawned. Then laugh-yawned. "It's so weird, Ben never mentions Mark to me, and when I ask about the parties, he just blows them off like they're no big deal or like he didn't want to go."

"Maybe you don't know him as well as you think you do," Emma commented.

"We've known each other for years."

"People change though."

"Why are you bringing all this up anyway?"

"Just am. Just talking."

I smiled. "You do love talking."

She winked, snapping her gum again. "You still hope he asks you?"

"I don't know. Maybe."

"Ladies!" Mr. Turcotte interrupted. "That is enough. You may chatter and gossip on your own time."

"Yes, Mr. Turcotte."

"May I continue with my class?"

"Yes, Mr. Turcotte."

Emma and I resumed our note taking. Emma nudged me one more time. I nudged her right back.

The lunch bell eventually rang. I scooped up my things and walked with Emma towards our lockers where we shoved our books away. Before we went our separate ways, Emma said, "Valeska heard that Ben was going to ask a girl today. Have fun." She winked and twirled away.

Her comment wrecked my nerves. As I walked into the busy cafeteria, it felt like I was walking for the first time – or at least being graded on how well I was putting my one foot in front of the other, and I made every effort to be sure not to trip or do something stupid. In preparation for seeing Ben, I gave myself reminders. *It's just lunch. You've sat with Ben a bunch of times. If he asks you, then you'll say yes, and you'll still be friends. If he doesn't ask, so what? You just want to be friends anyway. Being friends is what matters most. Right foot. Left foot. Good.*

I sat at a circular green table in the back corner waiting for Ben to join me. I saw him in line with Mark. They were goofing around and shoving at each other. I wondered if Ben would notice me. I refused to wave. And I dreaded the idea that he would choose to sit with Mark over me. Ben glanced at me. He was the one to wave. My entire heart suddenly amazing and nervous all at once, like it'd come alive unexpectedly. I waved back and smiled, trying to tell my cheeks not to redden. After Ben paid for his lunch, he said something to Mark and Mark went to sit with some other friends. Ben then dropped down next to me with a smile and a "hey."

He was wearing cologne.

Ben never wore cologne. It was something with a little touch of lemon and a little touch of like a woodsy smell. It was mixing in with the smells of the cafeteria – green beans and sloppy Joes. It was adorable. Ben was wearing cologne. And he was wearing cologne for me. I readjusted my hair behind my ears, trying to act casual. My stomach was crazy nervous.

I turned and smiled (but not too big). "Hey."

"How was your weekend?" Ben asked, working to keep his Sloppy Joe together and getting upset when some slopped back down to his tray.

"It was good. Yours?"

"I wanted to go to that party at Hunter's house," Ben said. "Mark said it was going to be lit, but instead, I spent the whole weekend studying and working on papers. Exciting, right? I had no choice though. We're getting killed with exams next week. Plus, I still have to write two essays for college applications. I hate writing those things. You want to tell them all about your accomplishments and how *great* of an applicant you are, but you also don't want to sound like you're bragging or nothing. Know what I mean?"

"Yep. I do."

"Did you send in your essays yet?" he asked.

"Yep. I finished a few of them over the weekend."

"Sounds like your weekend was as exciting as mine."

I laughed. "Yep." Then I said, "I kind of thought you'd call last night," immediately regretting that I did.

"Yeah." He got quiet. I thought maybe he was trying to find the perfect moment to ask me to prom, or maybe he was nervous because there were so many people around us. I wondered if I should ask him. A lot of that whole "boy asks girl" thing was gone (Emma had asked Jared), but being raised traditional was crippling me at that moment.

Thinking it was my perfect chance, I said, "Emma wouldn't stop talking about prom this morning. She's so crazy."

That's when it was supposed to happen. The cafeteria was supposed to go silent. All eyes would turn to us in expectation. And Ben was to ask, *Sarah, will you go to prom with me?*

Okay, maybe not that dramatic. But something close.

"Yeah. About that. You know," he said. "Prom is so overrated."

"Yeah," I said.

But I *didn't* know.

Fiddling with his green beans, Ben suddenly wouldn't look at me. "Yeah, it's overrated." He pierced a single green bean. "And it's no big deal or anything." He ate it. "But I think I'm going to ask Destiny to go with me."

He could have slapped me in the face. "Oh."

"What do you think? Should I ask her? You've always been a good friend, so I need you to tell me the truth."

I had no idea what to say. *Always been a good friend.* Isn't that what mattered most to me. *Always been a good friend.* I suddenly realized just how much I'd been lying to myself about the whole *our friendship is more important* thing. Ben was the one who had been maintaining our friendship. *Always been a good friend.* I was the one pretending to. Now he was asking me – as a friend – if he should ask Destiny. *Always been a good friend.* Because that's what friends do.

It hurt.

"You should definitely ask her. She's beautiful," I said, trying not to cry.

"I know. She really is." He smiled, remembering a moment that had not involved me.

I felt so stupid. Like the stupidest girl in the whole school. I wanted to crawl under the table to hide, stick myself to the bottom with all the dried-up gum. "Yeah, and prom is overrated anyway, like, it's no big deal. You should ask her."

Ben started to unwind. I had done what a good friend should do and encouraged him. He began talking openly and excitedly about Destiny (are teenage boys always so oblivious?). "I've always liked her. But she's so hard to read, you know, with how quiet she can be. But she's super-hot. Anyway, I've liked her since she moved here back in sixth grade. Remember when she did? All the boys liked her. Especially me. But I saw how beautiful she really was, you know, like who she was deep down. And now, we're going to graduate soon, and if I don't ask her, I'll regret it the rest of my life. You know, our lives are about small choices. That's what I read yesterday on my Facebook page. Well, not my page, but Amy's. I felt like it was put there for me. A message or like a sign or something. I know if I don't ask her, I'll regret it. Besides, what's the worst that can happen? She could say, 'no,' sure. But it's okay if she does. I mean, it's not like I really care *that* much. And she's cool, so I don't think it would weird her out or anything. But I think she'll say 'yes.' What do you think? Do you really think I should ask her?"

It took me a moment to realize he'd finally included me in the conversation. But I was still too stunned. "Oh," I said.

He laughed. "*'Oh?'* Really? That's the most intelligent thing you can say right now, Sarah? Is that all you have to offer? *'Oh.'*"

"Sorry." I began placing my unopened yogurt and uneaten sandwich back into my lunch bag.

"But really, do you think I should ask her?"

"Yeah. Sure. Definitely."

"Cool."

I couldn't look at him anymore. I held back the tears that were ready to come spilling out. And as he continued on about Destiny, all I kept thinking was, *I thought you were going to ask me.*

I could tell that he needed another prod of assurance. "You should ask her. She'd be stupid to say, 'no.'"

"I needed that." He smiled and winked. "Thanks."

I told Ben I was going to go to class early. That I needed to talk to Mrs. Lambert about our essay.

"You didn't eat anything," he commented.

I was surprised he noticed anything about me at all.

"I'm not hungry."

"Yeah, that's what I figured. You're acting weird."

"Sorry for acting weird."

"It's fine. I just hope you're not getting sick because I don't want you to get me sick. I need to be at my best when I ask Destiny."

"Yeah."

"Because it's my destiny to be with Destiny." He smirked at his own stupid comment. I wanted to gag. I wanted to hit him with my lunch back. But I smiled instead. I walked away, dropping my lunch bag into the trash as I left the cafeteria.

I was supposed to go to acapella practice after school, but there was no song in me that day. I told Ms. Milsom, our acapella coach, that I couldn't stay for practice because I was feeling sick. She gave me tips on how to take care of myself so that I didn't dehydrate or damage my voice. Then she reminded me that we had a concert in two weeks and I had to be at my best. I had the lead part. Everyone was counting on me. I told her I'd be ready. Then I went home to take a nap and sleep the sadness away.

I remember those vivid details of my conversation with Ben. His minute expressions. That terrible cologne. The way he was oblivious to me in that moment. I remember – not because it still hurts. And not because prom was some drama I never got over. I think deep down, I always hoped I could return to that moment and somehow change how things eventually turned out. You see, I never went to prom. No one asked me to go. Not because I was shy. Not because I wasn't pretty. But because by the time prom came, I had lost my mind.

# 4

I trudged through my mountain of homework while sitting on the couch, legs crossed, blanket over me. A candle on the mantel filled the room with a pumpkin fragrance, providing a seasonal scent that matched the cobweb decorations and plastic spiders near the fireplace my mom and I had set out. I worked through *Macbeth*, deciphering the genius of the dialogue, trying my best to answer the questions Mr. Chuchta had handed out. But I was having trouble concentrating. Every page or two, Ben and Destiny would waltz their way in front of me. I swatted at them, shooing their happiness away. But they'd sway right back, undeterred by my efforts.

My mom wasn't home yet to help me talk through the hurt. She was working two jobs then, her way of paying bills and forgetting how alone she was. So, when Ben and Destiny wouldn't go away, I gave up and decided to take a shower.

The bathroom filled with steam. I let the water run as hot as possible before getting in, and then waited a little longer. I got in, wincing at the heat of the water. The contrast of cool air to hot water was invigorating on my skin, clean. With my hands on the shower wall, the water ran heavy in my hair as I let my thoughts vanish and drift away in the steam. My chest relaxed. My lungs opened. After a while, I felt like I could sing again. With the water streaming over me, I quietly sang verses from the song for our upcoming competition, losing myself in the lyrics and the heat.

I could have stayed there for hours. But the water eventually cooled. I turned the faucet off. Final drips of water fell to my feet. The wide mirror of the bathroom had fogged. I cracked the bathroom door open to thin out the air. Taking my towel from its hook, I bent over to dry my hair. When I did, I caught a glimpse of someone standing in my bedroom.

My heart lurched. I shied behind the door with the towel now covering me. I glanced for another look, just to be sure, peering at a cautious angle through the slim gap between the door and frame. Pale limbs and black hair stood in the corner of my bedroom. They took a step towards me.

I slammed the bathroom door shut and locked it. Shuffling backwards, I hit a wall and crouched to my knees, then tucked myself behind the counter, trembling there like a frightened animal. I had no idea what to do. I was covered in a towel. I was still dripping. I had no weapon, no phone. I watched the doorknob, waiting for it to turn. I had no idea what would happen when it did. I remained paralyzed, stunned. The water dripped down my back and legs.

I heard my mother downstairs. She was home from work.

I stomped on the floor and didn't stop shouting to her until her voice was heard in my room. "Sarah? Where are you? What's wrong? Sarah!"

Throwing the door open, I imagined the other woman standing in the corner. Only my mother was there. I told her someone was in the home, we had to get out and call the police and go, quickly. It didn't take long before my vivid fears convinced her. She said, "okay, okay." I grabbed some clothes and pulled them on as my mother followed me. We went outside and stepped away from the house while we waited for the police to come through the dark empty night.

The cruiser eventually pulled up, almost casually. I had expected sirens and flashing lights. I had expected them to speed their way to us, screech to a stop, concerned for our immediate safety. But the two officers stepped out of the cruiser like plumbers after a long twelve-hour day. While they moseyed up to us, all I could think about was how long it took for them to get to our home. It had been at least twenty minutes. Twenty minutes. Plenty of time for my mother and I to both get murdered a few times each.

The officers spoke to us, asking questions on our front walkway. I explained what I saw. The woman. One of the officers went inside to search the house while the other officer stayed with my mother and I, jotting down notes in his notebook while offering attempts at light-hearted conversation regarding Halloween and the trouble of finding the perfect Halloween costumes for each of his three children.

A little while later, the other officer came back outside. He'd finished his search. He had nothing in his hands, and that seemed strange to me. Maybe I expected him to drag the woman out in cuffs or maybe to tear away her mask to reveal some *Scooby-Do* twist of an ending that would suddenly make sense. Because having the woman in my home made no sense at all. Brushing his empty hands together, as though he'd cleaned up a dusty mess, the officer announced, "The house is clear. There's no one inside."

That didn't make sense at all. For all I had imagined, whether it be the woman walked out in handcuffs or even gunshots splitting the night, the last thing I expected was *nothing.*

I could sense the woman's presence, imagined her standing at my bedroom window, looking down on the four of us in distant amusement. "Please," I begged.

They all looked at me. *Please, what?* they were asking.

"Will you look again?"

The officer hesitated. But he was convinced by how afraid I was, convinced that it mattered to me. "Sure."

"Don't trouble yourself," my mother said.

He looked at me again. "It's no trouble, ma'am."

This time, all of us went inside. My mother and I stayed near the front door, tucked together beneath the entryway light.

The same officer who investigated the first time did so again, clambering back up the stairs with his hand on the rail and his eyes up before him. Footfalls could be heard above us, going from one end of the house to the other, with silent pauses in between as he sifted through a closet or peeked beneath a dresser. Then he came back down, showing us his empty hands again.

I didn't understand. Couldn't comprehend it. How could he *not* have found her? The woman had been so tall, tall as the ceiling.

The adults separated themselves from me and stepped into the kitchen together. I continued to look at the stairs, certain the woman would come for me while my mother and the officers were unaware.

I could hear the whispers from the kitchen. The officers were telling my mother there was nothing else they could really do. My mother was assuring them with a hint of embarrassment, "she's really not like this."

After the officers left, I spent several minutes attempting to convince my mother that I wasn't making it up. The woman was too tall. I had seen her take a step. That's when I saw the way my mother looked at me. Like I was a child again. Like I had disappointed her.

"Let's get some sleep, Sarah," she said. "You need a good night's rest. I know you're stressed with tests and I heard about what happened with Ben."

That upset and frustrated me. While residual fear continued to play at me, making me question myself and what I had seen, suddenly, now, my mother had brought up the one name I didn't want to hear at all. Ben's. Ben. All the ugly emotions from earlier in the day returned. It was like being sick with the flu and then falling down the stairs. I asked touchily, "How do you know about that?"

"Emma's mother called me to let me know. Emma is concerned. And I'm concerned, of course," she added.

"How would anything with Ben make me see a woman in my room?" My voice rose. "Why would anything with Ben make some woman *appear* in my room? How? Tell me?"

"I don't know," my mother said, trying to remain the reasonable one. She began gently pulling at strands of my hair. "But when the officer didn't find anyone, I started thinking about all the pressure that you've been dealing with. Acapella. Tests. College applications. Your father being gone. And then Ben."

"This is so ridiculous." I turned away from her.

"Sarah, the officer didn't find anyone," she reminded me again, trying to sound pleasant and in control, parental.

"It doesn't mean someone wasn't in the home."

"Then why didn't the officer find anyone?" With my back still to her, she put a hand on my shoulder.

"I don't know," I said. "Maybe the woman left while I was hiding in the bathroom."

My mother accepted that with a "Maybe." But I could tell she still didn't believe me.

"You think I made it up."

"No. Not at all. But I think you're tired."

"Being tired and Ben being a jerk aren't going to make me *see* some woman, Mom. I know what I saw." I was pleading with her to see my side as much as she was pleading with me to see hers. I turned back around to face her. "Will you come with me?" I begged. "Please. To look through the house. If the officer didn't find anyone, then we won't either, but I want to be sure. I won't be able to sleep if we don't."

My mother held my hand. "If it will help."

We searched the home. My mother escorted me along, talking gently, but dismissively, as though I were a toddler obsessed with the notion of the Boogieman hiding beneath my bed – placating my ridiculousness. We examined closets. Peeked behind doors. Thumbed our toes through laundry on the floor.

By the time we were done, it was past 2:00am. We found nothing. The both of us were spent. My mother spoke those cliché and predictable words always offered to the fearfully preoccupied: "See, there's nothing to be afraid of." Then she grabbed up a sweater hanging from the corner of my dresser. "This must have been what you saw." She sounded tired, too tired to deal with a gray sweater that had been mistaken for something grim, and she tossed it into the hamper as though she had suddenly vanquished my monster. A monster of cotton sleeves, undone by regular spin cycle.

I did my best to believe her. I did. I began telling myself that maybe it had been my imagination. All the *adults* had told me so. We'd looked everywhere. I *was* tired. I *was* stressed. Ben *was* a jerk. And slowly, I did believe her. Little by little. Second by second. I had been drying my hair, I remembered. The bathroom was filled with steam. I never saw the woman directly. Just glimpses. And the woman was so tall, so abnormal. It must have been my imagination.

My mother saw how disappointed I was with myself. "It's okay, Sarah," she said. "Come here." She pulled me into a hug.

"I'm sorry," I said against her.

"It's okay," she said, stroking my back.

"Promise?"

"Promise."

"Ben is such a jerk," I said.

"Yes, he is."

We both laughed a little.

"I'll see you in the morning, okay?" she asked.

"Sounds good. I love you, Mom."

"I love you, too. Go get some rest."

Every part of me was heavy with exhaustion. I returned to my room, thinking I was still convinced. But I barely slept that night. I don't think I really slept at all. Creeping fright riddled my imagination from every corner and angle, transforming everything in my room into some evidence that the woman was there in the darkness with me. I could see the woman in the corner. I could see her at the end of the bed, her tongue stretching for my toes like an eel in water.

In the morning, the world was less alive. Sounds and colors had been muted. I caught myself four or five times looking over my shoulder, and being startled by close to nothing as an easy paranoia had infested the softer parts of my shaky mind.

My mother asked how I slept. I could see the answer she wanted to hear, so I lied to her and said I slept well. She asked if I felt better, and so I lied again. But when my mother asked if *it was over?*, I said *yes,* because I hoped it was true.

# 5

I was in the woods, running from the woman in the window. I couldn't keep ahead. Her strides were too much. She seemed to glide along the breeze, obstructed only by the branches, which seemed to part for her, even as they whipped at me. I was in the woods. I was crying. Crying and screaming for the woman to stay away. My hair became entangled in a pair of low-forked limbs. I had been trapped. The woman stepped out. There was giggling all around, coming from behind the trees, or maybe it was the trees themselves. I closed my eyes to hide. The woman touched me. Her breath was on my face.

I woke to a gush of warmth. I had peed the bed.

I hopped up in embarrassment. My instant thought: *Mom can't find out.* She had been second-guessing me ever since the police had come to our house that night, asking me why I always looked so tired. And there was always a skeptical look in her eyes. *Has everything been okay?* Translation: *are you still seeing that woman?*

I had to hide the evidence. I peeled the sheets from my mattress, gathering them up into a tight ball. Then I changed into some clean clothes and carried everything to the washer and dryer after a quick glance at my mother's bedroom door. Her bedroom was directly across from mine at the other end of the hall. As I got closer to the washer, I could hear my mom prattling around in her room, her door partially open. I began cramming the first sheet in as quickly as I could. Then the other. I was almost done.

"Why are you washing your sheets?" my mother asked while putting silver earrings in and coming out of her room.

"What?" I asked, pretending I couldn't hear her over the water.

She said a little louder, "Why are you washing your sheets and pajamas?"

"Oh, right. Yeah, I just wanted them clean. It's Wednesday. I always wash them on Wednesday." I still hadn't looked at her.

She walked over and stood beside me. "You're right, Sarah, we do laundry on *Wednesday*. But today is *Friday*, so I just washed everything a couple of days ago."

I laughed. "Oh, right! It's Friday." I really didn't know what day it was and I wished I had thought of a better lie.

"Yes, Sarah." She put the other earring in and shook her head at me. "It's Friday. You know, TGIF. And we did laundry on Wednesday." She flicked a corner of the sheet from the top of the washer so that it dropped into the suds. "Remember, you helped me."

I laughed along as best I could. "I forgot, I guess. That's okay. It's too late now. And it won't hurt to clean them again."

"That's true," she agreed. Then my mother did what I dreaded the most – she lifted my sweatpants from the floor. I didn't know why I hadn't put them in first and I hated that I didn't think of it until it was too late. "What's this dark spot?" she asked. "Is this – Is this urine?" She smelled at the dangling pant-leg from a safe distance as her face contorted at the realization.

"No." I laughed again, this time far less convincing, this time with unmistakable sadness.

"Sarah, you peed the bed," she stated, not knowing what else to say.

My head sank. My arms dropped to my sides. I stood there, wishing she had just left me alone, wishing I was somewhere else.

I could feel the tears coming. I didn't want to say anything because I didn't want to cry. I said as best as I could, "It was an accident."

"But you're seventeen."

"I know."

"You hardly peed the bed as a child," she continued.

"I know."

I just wanted her to comfort me, or leave me alone. "I know, Mom." I took the sweatpants from her and dropped them in, then slammed the lid loud enough to startle the both of us.

"So why are you peeing the bed now?" my mother asked as though it was some new habit I had picked up, something I decided I'd like to start doing.

"Mom, it was one time. And it's not like I wanted to."

"But why?" she pressed. She was ready to go to work. She was ready to stop dealing with my issues, nightmares and calls to the police and bed-wetting. That was my mother at her worst. Wanting answers and reasons, as though no one deserved to have a secret without her permission.

"Mom, please, stop." I turned my back to her, arms crossed over my chest.

"I just want to know why."

I turned back. "Fine! I was having a nightmare and I – I peed the bed!" I burst into tears as the inescapable terror of the nightmare returned, the woman tracing her finger along my side.

My mother pulled me into a hug. "Oh, Sarah, it's okay, it's okay. I'm sorry if I upset you. I'm so sorry. I know you didn't mean to pee the bed. I'm concerned. That's all." The warmth of her body made me feel so much better. I wanted her to stay home. I didn't want her to leave me.

I continued to cry, even as I dabbed away a tear, "I'm such a crybaby lately."

"No, you're not. And it's okay to cry."

So, I cried a little more.

"What was so horrible about your dream?" she asked.

"That woman. It was her. The one from the window."

She did her best to hide her immediate disappointment. "The police didn't find any woman, Sarah," she reminded me.

"I know, Mom. But. I don't know. I think she was, or, I don't know." I knew what I wanted to say, I just didn't know how to say it.

"Sarah, you're scared. Going through a tough time. That's all. Just a rough patch."

"I know. You're right," I said. "It's just. I've been having these nightmares. Every night. But they feel so real, you know. Maybe because I'm so tired or something. So, I try not to sleep at all, or if I do sleep, I don't sleep well. I'm always so tired." I laughed brokenly. "I know it sounds crazy, but sometimes, I don't know when I'm dreaming or when I'm awake."

"Well, they're just nightmares," she offered consolingly. "They can't really hurt you." You see, I never had many nightmares growing up, so, to my mother, this was nothing more than a phase that had caught up to me late, like getting chicken pox as a teenager when everyone else had gotten theirs years ago.

There was no winning. "I know. You're right," I said.

"Well, it's time for you to get ready for school." She checked her watch. "And I'm running late for work." Before jogging down the stairs, she said one last time, "It was just a nightmare, Sarah. Remember that. And hey, TGIF."

"Yep. TGIF," I said, suddenly becoming absolutely and completely disgusted by that simple stupid phrase.

The washing machine swished side to side as I listened and watched from the middle of the hallway, from some strangely meaningful mental and emotional distance that was safe. The rhythmic sound of the machine almost put me to sleep on my feet. I stepped away. "You're right, Mom. They're nothing but nightmares. Each and every night."

I went to school, even though school was beginning to matter less and less each day.

# 6

TGIF. I was tardy for school, which I had never been in my entire life. But I may as well have not even gone, because from class to class, I was no better than an absent pupil. People talked to me. But their words only came and went at a distance. I felt bad for Emma, even as I sank into my hole. I could tell she was worried, but I didn't know how to tell her. Everyone else received nothing more from me than automated responses which were no better than two or three word sentences that may or may not have actually fit the short-lived conversation. Teachers would call on me, waking me back to lectures and discussions. I'd lift my chin. But it would sink again. I was so tired. And I had other things on my mind.

Between classes, friends asked what was wrong. When I said, "I haven't been sleeping very well" the dark circles under my eyes proved I was telling the truth.

"You should get some rest." I probably heard that thirty times.

"I know," was what I said back. It was enough to make people feel better about themselves for asking in the first place.

After school, Emma actually tried to find out more. But when she asked if it was because of Ben, and I didn't give her an outright answer, she just assumed it was actually because of Ben but that I didn't want to talk about it. So, she tried to make me feel better by trash talking Ben until the bus came and picked her up.

It was my own fault. I never had a problem helping my friends through their struggles, but when it came to my own issues, I lived on my own island. Like when my dad and mom separated, no one knew for weeks, not even Emma. And when I finally told her what happened, she was hurt by how long it took me to do so.

I wanted to tell Emma about the woman. I owed it to her. I needed to. But what could she say to help? I also feared the worst, that Emma would respond with something similar to what my mom had been telling me. *You're having crazy-awful nightmares? I'm so sorry! But hey, at least they're only nightmares, right?*

So, I let Emma believe what she wanted to believe.

When I got home from school, I turned on every light in the house. Skimming through the house in the late afternoon, I kept my back to the walls to make sure nothing could sneak up behind me. I was jumpy at unexpected shadows and noises.

TGIF.

I went upstairs before the sun could set. I stopped at the entryway of my bedroom, the open hall behind me. My room felt like it was no longer mine. I could barely step through. Yet the open hallway behind me was just as ominous. I could feel the woman. It was like she was in the walls.

I went to my bedroom window where the cold air flowed in (my mother had opened it for me, knowing it was something I had always enjoyed). I shut it hastily. Latched it. Goosebumps rose up my arms and climbed the back of my neck. I knew it had nothing to do with the cold.

I walked backwards towards the bathroom, keeping my eyes on the window. After shutting and locking the bathroom door, I washed my face in the sink, feeling as though I had aged two hundred years. When I finished, I assured my reflection with a determined nod: "She's...not...real." My reflection mouthed the words. Then she blinked at me.

I climbed into bed, wanting to catch up on sleep, which could easily have taken three or four continuous days. I stared at the ceiling, still doing my best to convince myself that none of it was real.

Why was I in bed? you might ask. It's simple. I didn't know what else to do. The fear made me shortsighted, almost to blindness. Also, I knew that any explanation of why I was awake when my mom got home would make her paranoid, and if I had been sleeping in her bed (like I wanted to), then she would have thought things had gotten much worse. Which would have made her right.

But lying there, every sound stole my attention. If a board creaked, I imagined it was the woman stepping closer. If anything rustled, I imagined her brushing against it. There were sounds and strange buzzing, which I couldn't tell if they were really there, or if my horrid imagination was making them up because it didn't know what else to do anymore. I felt crazed. My – *stop being crazy* voice inside my head – sounded a lot like my mother's. And the more I told myself to stop being crazy, the more crazy I became.

I couldn't do it.

I dragged my bedding downstairs. I snuggled up on the couch. It comforted me. The change. I had made a choice (why hadn't I thought of it earlier?), and I almost felt smart, as though I had outwitted the woman (it sounds so stupid to admit now). Yep! I had foiled the woman in the window by sleeping downstairs, completely outthinking her, causing her to shake a fist of defeat at me from the window. *Darn that Sarah!*

My mother came home after eleven. Her presence centered me, bringing me out of my mind like the gentle tug of a magnet. I didn't want her to know I was awake, so I kept my eyes closed and let the breaths flow deep and even from my nose, trying to mimic how I might look and sound if I was in a deep sleep. My mother dropped her keys onto the kitchen counter, then commented to herself with a hint of frustration, "Why are all of the lights on?"

I was afraid she'd try to wake me. But she stopped when she saw me, then tiptoed to my side. She whispered my name like she was sorry for me. "Sarah. Sleep well. You need it." A kiss was placed on my forehead. Then she snuck upstairs. She even left the lights on for me.

From the comfort of my couch, I thought about the woman in the window – like a homework project to solve – as I considered her invasion into my life. I wondered how long she had been there. Had it been years? Or had it all begun that very first night? I wondered why she came for *me*. Was there something I had done? Something I deserved? I racked my brain over that one question, trying to remember *anything* I may have done to *anyone*. Was I her first, or had she haunted previous children? I didn't think I was her first. It didn't seem likely. She felt so...eternal.

I fell asleep in those thoughts. If an answer or clue ever came, it was something I didn't remember.

In the morning, I woke up in my bedroom, in my own bed. The sheets and blankets had been tucked tight around me, done so with care. Clothes had been laid out on my dresser for the day, a color-coordinated outfit for the day, and my shoes had been placed neatly side-by-side near the door.

When I went downstairs, my mother was in the kitchen. I didn't ask her when she brought me upstairs during the night. I didn't thank her for picking out my clothes. I knew it wasn't her.

My feeling of being tired changed into a different kind of tired.

The hopeless kind.

# 7

During those days in my life, I tried everything that came to mind. Sleeping on the couch. Gluing the window shut. Taping the window shut. I'd have nailed the window shut, if I thought I could have gotten away with it. There wasn't a world of options available to me, and it wasn't like I could move to another home. I was still trying to navigate a balance between survival at night with appearing sane to my mom and those around me during the day. I'd spend days awake, nights awake. I was in a daily fight against exhaustion, watching movies, doing schoolwork, taking walks, even dancing, doing anything to keep my body moving. I'd crash. Then the woman would come. One night, I went to bed with a knife beneath my pillow, a knife from the kitchen. When I woke in the morning, the knife was still there. It was covered in blood. I had no idea whose blood it was. I never did that again.

# 8

William hummed in baritone, laying out the lower melody as the rest of us stood in a semi-circle around him, our voices coming together as one. William made a transition, his throat setting out a heavy steady beat *mmbuhbuhbuhbuhmmmbuhbuh.* The beat picked up pace, raising us out of our somber postures and expressions into something more fluid, fun. Valeska was up next, soft and gorgeous, and she set her voice free, singing the first lines of our modern version of *Ave Maria.* The rest of us snapped our fingers in rhythm. William continued *mmmbuhbuhbuhbuh.* Valeska finished her part, then hummed with the rest of us as Courtney and Tonya repeated their verse, *Ave Maria, Ave Maria.*

Emma's hazel eyes opened. Her voice pierced the room:
*Ave Maria gratia plena*
*Maria gratia plena*
*Maria gratia plena*
*Ave ave dominus, dominus tecum.*
Our song was in bloom. My acapella group lifted me.

Empowered me. Cleansed me of my fear. I was ready to set my voice free, lose myself in the moment, forget the worry and fear that had been mine.

My lips parted. My voice opened. I sang: *We slumber safely till the morrow, Though we've –*

I lurched over, possessed by a sudden coughing fit that curled me to my knees. I could barely breathe. Everyone surrounded me. Hands were placed on my back as they asked if I was okay. Someone patted me. I was choking. Gagging. Tears of asphyxiation rimmed my eyes. Something was in my throat. I reached panicked fingers deep into my mouth and pinched at something near the back of my tongue. I began to draw it out. Strands extended out into the air from my open mouth. But the whole of it remained lodged in my throat. I tugged, wanting it out of me. I almost threw up with my fingers so deep. The thing dislodged and fell from my open mouth. A sticky clump of hair was on the floor. Everyone stared, including me. I wanted to hide it, kick it away. But everyone had already seen, and the glob of hair seemed to be staring at us as much as we were staring at it.

"What the heck is that?" William pointed.

"Oh my god, is that *hair*?" Valeska.

"That is *so* gross!" Courtney.

"Disgusting!" Tonya.

Emma pinched at the wrenched-up hair like it was an uninteresting gigantic spider's nest and flung it into a trashcan nearby where it *thunked*, then slipped to the bottom with a watery *thump*.

I wanted to run away. I wished I'd never gone to school that day, wished I'd never stayed for practice, wished nothing of this was happening to me. Wished I'd never been born. Everyone began asking questions I couldn't answer. I just stood there, dumbfounded. Emma pulled me by the arm and led me into the bathroom. The door shut behind us. Emma yanked a brown paper towel from the container on the wall and began dabbing around my mouth. Then she wiped away my tears with her hand.

Emma held me. "Why are you crying?"

"I don't know. I don't know," I repeated sadly.

"You can tell me."

"I don't know if I can." I couldn't gather up the courage to tell her about the woman.

"Why are you so upset?" she asked.

"Maybe it has something to do with that thing I just coughed up." I laughed miserably through a fresh spell of tears.

"Yeah, what was *that?*"

I almost told her, almost. But I could hear my bizarre explanation in my mind before saying it – about how the woman had been haunting me and that it had been *her* hair in my throat. But that was the problem, it was too bizarre. I wanted to gargle mouth wash until the feeling of her hair left me – maybe even ignore the warning label and swallow a bucket-full.

"Sarah? You can tell me."

"I want to." I shook my head with resolve. "I can't."

"Are you sure?" She asked tenderly, "I'm always gabbing along. But I promise, I can listen too."

I laughed miserably. "I know. I just don't want to think about that thing right now. I just want to forget."

"Are you sure?"

"Yeah."

"But there seems to be something else."

"Maybe it's *everything*. School, acapella. That's what my mom says."

She wasn't convinced.

"I'm going to ruin the show," I said to keep Emma distracted.

Emma laughed sympathetically. "Don't be ridiculous. You'll be fine. You're amazing."

"I'm not."

Emma leaned away to hold my shoulders and look me in the eye. "You're amazing. And besides, we graduate in a few months and all these crazy tests and assignments will be done and you won't have to try so hard to be the smartest girl in the world. Not until college," she teased with a wink. "You'll be fine. I promise."

It was strange, hearing that I'd be fine. It was what I wanted to believe more than anything. "How do you know?" I asked skeptically.

"Because I'm your friend, remember?"

I chuckled, wiping my eyes. "Oh, yeah."

"This isn't like you," she said. "What's going on, really? I mean, you're not yourself. Is it boys, or nah?"

I laughed pathetically. "I wish it *was* boys. But really, I don't want to talk about it."

"Well, if you ever want to talk about it, I'm here, okay?"

"Okay." I grinned weakly. Talking to her made me feel better, even just a little. "Everyone's going to know I was crying." I turned towards the mirror. "Yep." My eyes were bloodshot. Bags had formed beneath them from sleeplessness and crying.

"Crying wouldn't be *my* first worry," Emma said, eyeing the nearby trashcan as a reminder of the one outside the bathroom.

"You think they noticed?" I asked, trying to find some humor in it all.

"You mean that huge wad of hair you puked up? Nah."

"Everyone is going to think I'm so gross."

I knew what was coming. I'd seen it before. Some boy gets so drunk he passes out while crashed out on a couch where he vomits throughout the night. A girl gets her period early, and of course she's in class when it happens. A boy accidentally steps into the girl's bathroom and gets branded a pervert. I didn't know what was going to happen to me – but I knew it would be something close.

"Don't worry about that. People are jerks anyways." Emma hugged me one more time. "Are you ready to go back out, or nah?"

"You mean I can't hide in here forever?"

Looking around at the counters and the mirrors and the faucets and the stalls, Emma said, "I guess we could. But it might get kind of boring."

I let out a short laugh. "Yeah, you're probably right."

We exited the bathroom together. We wore matching compulsory smiles, attempting to shrug it all away. Everyone had gone back to practicing, but their eyes jumped to me as the screeching door announced my return.

"Everything okay?" Ms. Milsom asked.

No one laughed or snorted. No one teased – not yet, at least. They looked concerned more than anything. I was relieved.

"Yep, just a common hair ball. Happens to all of us, right?"

Each of them laughed, just to be nice. I could tell they were relieved I was okay, or at least acting okay. The leading role for the upcoming competition was still mine, and I think they wanted to forget the wooly mammoth-like ball that had been dislodged from my throat and focus on the competition, where we actually had a chance to impress and even win. It was a big opportunity for all of us.

"Are you able to rejoin us and practice?" Ms. Milsom asked.

Emma announced for me, "Of course she is!"

"Good." Ms. Milsom smiled.

We resumed rehearsal. But this time, when I sang, there was no sensation of freedom to attain to or reclaim, my voice was shackled once again by thoughts and fears. When practice was done, I could feel how disappointed everyone was with me.

# 9

Rumors. There weren't many of them. Not at first. But there were enough. Enough aimed at me, as I earned sideways glances from passerby's, fingers pointing at me, chuckles, and the occasional hacking noise from someone pretending to be a cat hacking up a hairball. One morning, Mr. Turcotte handed out tests and then instructed, "Once the test begins, you are to remain seated until you are done. There will be no bathroom breaks, people. No water breaks. No headache breaks. No snack breaks. No selfie breaks. No social media update breaks. So, go to the bathroom now to attend to your needs before the test begins. That includes removing any hairballs." He winked at me in good humor before the class burst out laughing, then he hastily told them all to quiet down, but it was too late.

I crimped out a pained smile to be courteous, doing my best to keep my tears to myself. I chuckled too. If I didn't, I'd only be teased for being too sensitive or not having a sense of humor. Besides, crying only made them meaner.

You know, I had never been that person, that person people paid attention to. Teachers usually liked me because I was a good student with good manners. I had never been in a fight or even been cornered by a bully. I tried to be kind and thoughtful to others, help people with assignments, and all that. I tried to be a good friend, nice to people. Suddenly, I was the butt of everyone's joke.

For the first time in my life, I dreaded going to school.

But I dreaded home even more.

Between those two worlds, I would gladly have chosen to be stuck at school with kids laughing in my face, if it meant escape. The hairball rumor wouldn't be the last rumor that would attach itself to me. And at home, the woman in the window was just beginning.

# 10

I walked home from school, feeling a deep sense of defeat at being a terrible friend. I couldn't manage. I couldn't manage much of anything. My grades were falling fast. Acapella was becoming a disaster. And here I was, walking willingly to my house to where my abuser lived. The woman was always there, forcing herself through every crevice in my life, finding ways to become even more invasive. I tucked my chin against the cold breeze, trying not to think about it as the pebbles at my feet scattered to the grass with my quickened pace as I hurried along.

The trees around me showed the evidence of winter's coming. Their gangly branches trembled in an air that was a wintry gray. The clouds above were gray as well. Everything soon darkened further and further until night crept up all around me at what I knew to be no later than 3:30 in the afternoon. It was as though hours had passed by, as though I'd ventured into a time far later into the night. Up ahead, the lights of my home glowed like lanterns. My mother's car was parked outside of the garage. I jogged the rest of the way, just to be closer to her and to escape the darkness.

Instant relief filled me as I stepped inside the front door. I called out with an added hint of cheer, "Mom, I'm home!"

I received no answer. I hung my jacket on a hook and laid my book bag in the corner, off near my shoes which I had kicked off to the side. My mother's coat and shoes were already in their proper places. I went into kitchen. In the sink were a used plate and used utensils. My mother had eaten without me. I wanted to eat as well, but wanted to find my mother first. Turning at a bend in the wall, I stepped into the living room. The lights were off. But the television was on. From the far wall, bursts of light spread outward from the crackling screen, casting the light of a shattered strobe over the entirety of the room. Static crackled loudly. It was almost deafening. My mother sat on the couch. She was facing away from me, her figure was all black, like a cutout in the light. The light poured over her and the sound didn't seem to bother her at all. Intent upon the sputtering screen, her head was motionless, her gaze stuck.

I stepped around the curve of the couch to say *hi* and ask comically what she found so interesting about the static, but as I did, my smile spoiled on my face. The spattering light pockmarked her, hollowing out her eyes as she turned to me. Her face was emotionless and placid. The discontent light ate at her face like moths at a light. Her mouth opened, as if to say something. Then she patted the couch, signaling for me to come and sit beside her. When I hesitated, she said in a voice that was not quite hers, "Sit with me." Something wriggled in her mouth, but she closed it again before I could see. She patted the couch once more.

I said weakly, "I'm tired. I'm not feeling good."

She nodded at my lie. There was a hint of a smirk on her face. Then she returned her attention to the television screen as I shuffled towards the stairs, wanting to escape to my room where I could at least lock the door. Above me, pattering feet thumped along the ceiling, like children scattering in a game of hide and seek. Fear climbed my throat. I remained stuck at the bottom of the stairs, staring upward, trembling and stuck.

A touch at my shoulder made me fall against the wall as though I'd been struck. My mother was there, her eyes black, having moved soundlessly behind me. I stayed tucked to my fallen position, frozen. My mother pointed up the stairway, her finger stretched out ahead of me to the darkness above. "Go to your room."

Obeying her command, I hurried from her. My nerves were falling apart, even as I tried to stay composed. My legs moved awkwardly, shuffling and fumbling, tripping up the stairs. My arms stayed wrapped around my torso in cautious fear, as though holding together my insides. I clambered to the top of the stairs. The long darkness of the hall stretched out ahead of me. I flicked at the light switch, just for some measure of comfort. It did nothing. I did so again, but still, the lights remained off. At the other end of the hall, the outline of my bedroom door suddenly glowed a dull yellow. I stood there, trapped. There was nowhere I wanted to go, expect out of the home. My mother began walking up the stairs.

I moved through the blackened tunnel, intent upon avoiding my mother. Near my bedroom door, my fingers shook in the air as reached for the knob. Blaring light caused my eyes to shut. When I opened them again, I saw a lantern hanging near the entrance, burning brightly.

Something was wrong. Everything was wrong. But my mother was behind me, coming down the hallway, pointing ahead. I stepped inside and pressed the door shut, hoping my mother would be appeased.

This was not my room. The gray wooden ceiling had a slant to it, like the hard angle of a roof. Permeating the air was the smell of mold and old sheets and a strange smell I didn't recognize, though it made me think of a barn. The floor was splintered and wooden, not carpeted like my own. There were no windows to be seen. And the room was long, much longer than mine. Two rows of beds were lined on each side of the room, the headboards of which met at the slant of the ceiling. There were eight beds total. The beds were small. I noticed suddenly that they were filled with bodies. Children were there, lying beneath the covers as though tucked in for the night, with gray woolen blankets having been pulled up to their chins, toes pointed upward. Each of them was covering their eyes with their little hands, as though each of them were hiding.

I remained by the door, the lantern near my shoulder. One girl peeled apart two fingers to peek at me. She was scared, and she warned in a trembling whisper, "Get in bed. Hurry."

The sound of approaching steps was coming down the hallway. I thought at first my mother was returning, but the footfalls were someone else's, dutiful and deft. The flame inside the lantern wavered, as though brushed by a breeze, causing shadows to wave around the room. I feared the light would go out. Waking me from my petrified trance, another child said with a voice that was tiny and sad, "Get in bed. Or she'll punish us."

Two empty beds were stationed at the far end of the room. I went to them and climbed into the one on the left, simply because it seemed to be the furthest from the door. I pulled the blankets up to my chin, toes pointed up, and placed my hand over my eyes, mimicking the other children in an effort to hide among them.

The door creaked open. An arm stretched inside, reaching for the lantern. Long fingers, longer than any I'd ever seen, turned at the valve until the flame shrunk and died out. Before the door was shut again, the woman whispered into the bedtime blackness, "Shhhhhhhhhhh." A lock turned.

We were left there. I breathed in the old smells of the wool blanket that itched at my chin and cheeks, listening to the gasps of the other children, each of them fearful and quiet, not wanting to disturb the woman or summon her attention back to the room. I could hear my breaths as well. I sounded just like them. I began to cry, restraining my sobs as best I could.

"Please stop," a voice begged.

Another child whispered, "We don't want to be punished."

I did my best to obey, smothering my mouth with my own hand. Silent tears dripped down my face to the musty pillow beneath my head. When I awoke, I had returned to my own bed. There were no other beds, no children. There were visages of what I had seen all around me though, as though the nightmare had somehow interlaced with my reality, like two translucent photos placed on top of each other to form one distinct image. I couldn't move, afraid that if I did, I'd reawaken the alternate reality I had experienced, so I called out to my mother, yelling louder and louder until she finally came.

"What's wrong?" she asked from the doorway, eyeing me as I lay wrapped in my covers. She knew.

"I was having a nightmare," I began. "But it wasn't just a

nightmare, Mom. There were other children. They were as afraid as I was. But they actually lived in that room. There was a woman. It was the same woman, Mom. The woman in the window." I pulled in a deep breath, and when I did, the smells from the other room invaded my nose. "I can still smell the other place! I can still smell it! Do you understand? Stop looking at me like that, Mom! Please stop. Please stop."

My mother came and sat at the side of my bed. "I don't know what to say, Sarah. If you're having nightmares, then they're nightmares. Even if they seem real, they're just not. There isn't a woman. And if there is, she's only in your dreams. She can't *really* hurt you."

"Maybe she can, Mom."

"Then why hasn't she already?" she asked as though it should have inspired some hope.

"I – I don't think she wants to yet," I attempted to explain. "I think she enjoys making me afraid."

"Why would anyone enjoy seeing someone else afraid?" she asked as though such a notion was kept to the world of movies where outlandish characters wore black tuxedos and curly mustaches.

"She just does," I said.

"It sounds like a nightmare to me. Look around you, Sarah. You're here, in your room. If it was real, wouldn't you still be *there,* in that other place? Wouldn't this woman of yours be here, in this home? Wouldn't this woman of yours leave some evidence?"

"Stop saying *that*!"

"What?" she was distraught and confused.

"*This woman of yours!* Just stop!"

"Okay, okay. I'm sorry."

"It's fine. Just don't say it again."

"I won't." She patted my hand in promise. "But again, Sarah, wouldn't there be some way we'd know she was real and not just in your nightmares?"

"I – I don't know." She was right, but she wasn't.

"You'll get through this, Sarah. You will. These nightmares will end. They can't last forever." She shook her head, and I knew it was difficult for her as well, seeing what was happening to me.

"What can I do to help?"

"I don't know. I guess, just believe me."

"Believe what? That there's a woman in your dreams who can actually hurt you?" She looked confused again.

It was just that simple. "Yes."

"*Sarah,*" she said, as though I'd asked for a unicorn for my 18th birthday and it was time for me to grow up. "How about this? I'll believe that you're having nightmares – nightmares that are vivid and awful. And that you'll get through this." She'd found a reasonable middle ground for us to agree on.

"No," I said. "It's not enough. I need you to *believe* me, Mom."

She shook her head subtly. "I don't know if I can. But I'm trying. I think about you and about what's been going on, with the nightmares and the woman, and it, well, it has me concerned."

"I'm the one who's going through this, Mom."

"But Sarah." My mother made a pained expression. "There's no woman. Not in real life."

"Yes, there is, Mom! How can you say you're trying to believe me when you won't believe what I tell you?"

"Sarah. Please. Your room is on the second floor." She presented her hand out towards the window, showing me how high up we were. "That woman would need a ladder to get up here. And she'd have to be able to unlock the window from outside. It's just not possible."

I hated my mother's lack of belief, and yet, in a strange way, it felt good to talk about it. I tried to maintain my composure while I explained, "The first night, when I touched the woman's hair in my window, I heard owls and could see trees when she stepped away. It was as if there was a different world, the world she comes from, I think. And in the nightmares, they're so real, I can *feel* them. Like, I'm not really sleeping, but I'm not really awake either. And then sometimes, I'm in other places, but those feel real too, even though I've never really been to them. And then in this dream, the one last night, it was the worst. The other children felt like they were real children. When they talked to me, *they* were talking to me. It wasn't my imagination making up things for them to say."

I had been so engulfed in my explanation, I didn't realize my mother had started crying. On instinct, I stretched for her and asked, "What's wrong?"

"What's happened to you, Sarah? You were never like this. What happened to school and acapella and spending time with your friends? I get calls from your teachers now. They're concerned. They say you haven't turned an assignment in for weeks. You haven't followed up with any colleges, even though they want you to commit so you can attend next fall. They've all accepted you, you know. But all you talk about is this woman." She stopped herself from saying *this woman of yours.*

"I guess all those things don't matter when you're running for your life!"

My mother oriented her body to face me completely, then shook my hands in hers, trying to will me back to reality. "Sarah! It's not real! She's not real!" She threw a hand at the window again, as though the empty glass in that instant was proof that a woman had never been there at all.

"Then what is it, Mom? If it's not real, then what is it?" I yelled.

"It's – it's got to be something else." She then asked, "Did you read that article I put in here the other day?"

My stomach tightened. "You mean the one about schizophrenia?"

"Yes."

I smirked sadly. "I'm not crazy, Mom." She was hurting me more than she could ever know.

"I know you're not, I know." She brushed my cheek. "And I don't want to jump to conclusions. But she – this woman – she can't be real. It's just not possible. Look at it from my perspective. You say this woman has been in your room, but again, there's no way she could get up here. Think about it. There's no way this could be real."

"I don't want to believe it either, Mom. But it's real. And it's horrible. You don't know what it's like to be so afraid every second of the day. You don't. At night, I do my best to stay awake. But you can't stay up forever. And right before I fall asleep, there's this tiny bit of hope that she won't come. That she'll leave me alone. Then she doesn't."

"I'm not saying they don't *feel* real, Sarah. But there has to be an explanation. I mean, have you ever believed in all of the other things kids believe in, like Santa or the Easter Bunny?"

"Maybe a little, when I was a lot younger."

"Sure, of course. But not as you got older. And why did you stop believing?"

"I don't know. I guess I just knew they weren't real."

"Okay, so maybe this is your imagination simply going through a growth spurt or something."

"I never stopped having an imagination, Mom."

"I know you still have an imagination." She chuckled dryly. "I'm not saying *that*. But maybe your imagination is just really growing right now. They say the adolescent brain goes through these intense periods of development."

I still wanted to find that middle ground. So did she. "If I agree to believe that, that it has something to do with my brain growing, will you stop thinking I'm crazy."

"I never thought you were crazy, Sarah."

"You definitely said I should consider the possibility."

"That's not what I meant. But I wanted you to stop thinking it was really happening, you know, like really happening. In real life."

"Oh, great then."

"No need to be sarcastic, Ms. Sarah."

I brushed her hand away as she touched my nose playfully. When she did it again, I couldn't help but smile. It felt like we were ourselves again, just for a moment. It was nice.

Wanting to be a good daughter, I said, "Sorry for being such a mess lately." I wiped my eyes. "I'm sorry. I am."

"Oh, Sarah –" my mother pulled me into her arms "– there's no reason to apologize."

"Mom?"

"Yes, Sarah?"

I hesitated. "Can I sleep in your room tonight?"

She didn't say anything right away. "Sure. But just for tonight."

"Thanks, Mom."

"Sure."

"And Mom?"

"Yes?"

"I love you."

"I love you, too."

# 11

Talking to my mom didn't solve anything, but it felt good to talk. I felt like I was a soda bottle that had been shaken and I was about to burst, and talking had relieved some pressure. I slept in her room that night. The woman never came. But I had to return to my own room after that. After a few more nights of not sleeping and not talking about it with anyone – the overwhelming pressure returned and I was a soda bottle again fit to burst. I found myself twitching sometimes and crying at the drop of a hat. I needed relief again, even a little. I called Emma.

I had prepared myself all afternoon for how I would explain everything to her, along with all the possible responses I'd get back, from flat-out rejection on one end all the way to apologetic disbelief on the other. But I had to do it. And it couldn't be just vague hints, like *so, there's been this woman in my window, and yeah, it's terrible – so, how about Thanksgiving break coming up?*

I had to do it while I still had the nerve to be honest. I called her on the phone. Pacing my room, I told Emma about the haunting of my life, beginning with the hairball that had been in my throat and backtracking to the first night just before Halloween.

Emma didn't say much. But when she did, she said the absolute perfect thing in all the world. "Want to stay at my house tonight, or nah?"

It was wonderful. "Are you sure? Your mom won't mind? Last time I spent the night she got super angry because we kept her up talking."

"Believe me, my mom won't even care. Besides, she's got like a new boyfriend or whatever."

"Are you sure?" I was almost floating.

"Of course." I could tell she was smiling.

When I asked my mom if I could go, she answered with an immediate, "yes." I think she was happy to see me doing things I used to do, which included being excited about something, probably thinking that if I got out of the house, I'd feel better, like getting fresh air when you're sick. My mom drove me over to Emma's, even though it was a Thursday. I wasn't normally allowed to go out on weekdays.

Emma and I began the night by watching *Pitch Perfect* while wearing our pajamas. Before long, I was laughing through the scenes like it was the first time I'd seen the movie, and every laugh made me feel better. Laughing with someone, with Emma, was the best feeling ever. After the movie, we sat cross-legged on her mattress gossiping through the current high school drama and chatting about boys. It got to the point where I felt so good, so safe, I didn't want to bring the woman up at all. But after a while, Emma gave a light slap to my thigh. "So, do you, like, want to talk about *her* at all?" She didn't know how to bring it up, like I'd gotten pregnant or something. But being a good friend, she knew she had to.

I didn't know how to begin. I started with a sort of interlude, "I was thinking about Curtis the other day."

Emma stopped me with a shake of her head, which tossed around the seasonal streak in her hair, now colored red and green for Christmas. "Wait, what about that woman?"

"I'm getting to it."

"Oh, okay. So who's this Curtis or whatever? You mean that Junior who drives that old rusted green car? It's like the ugliest thing ever."

"No, no. A different Curtis, back from middle school. He used to wear a yellow wolverine shirt like three days a week and his jeans were always too short."

Emma thought a second, smirking. "You mean that boy with the bowl cut?"

"Yeah, but don't be mean," I scolded, even as I chuckled with her.

"I'm not being mean. He had a bowl cut, and you know, he owned a total of like two t-shirts."

"Stop laughing, Emma. It's mean."

"Then you stop laughing."

But I couldn't stop. "You're making me laugh by laughing."

"Okay, I'll stop."

"You're not doing a very good job."

"Neither are you! This is your fault anyway."

I threw up a hand. "Okay, let's both try and stop."

We held our breath, cheeks puffed out. But Emma chuckled, then I chuckled, then Emma snorted, and I laughed harder, pointing at the angry expression on her face as she told me I better not tell anyone that she snorted.

After the laughter fizzled, Emma said, "Okay, well, why'd you want to talk about Curtis anyway? You want to ask him to prom or something?"

"Curtis? Not at all."

"Okay, so what about him?"

I was regretting my interlude. "Remember our eighth-grade camping trip? It was in the woods for whatever reason and we had to do team building obstacles and we slept in those horrible cabins?"

"Those cabins were *disgusting.* My mattress was all soggy. Anyway, sure, I remember. It rained the whole time. I got poison ivy and Jared broke his arm trying to jump some obstacle but was stoked anyway because he won some stupid award or medal or whatever."

"Remember the campfire that first night? There was a big group of us telling ghost stories?"

"Sure. It was the only night it didn't rain. What about it?"

"Do you remember Curtis?"

"We're still talking about Curtis?"

"Yeah, it's why I brought him up."

"Okay. What about him?"

"Do you remember what he did when we started telling ghost stories?"

"I'm not the one who had a crush on him."

"Oh my gosh! I didn't have a crush on him!"

"You seem pretty obsessed." Emma laughed at how angry I was getting.

"I'll tell everyone you snorted."

Her eyes went wide. "Don't you dare. Okay, okay, so Curtis and whatever. What did he do?"

"He went to sit near the trees by himself. Then he pressed his hands over his ears to keep from hearing the stories."

"Yeah, yeah. I remember now. We kept yelling at him to come back and join us."

"No, we didn't. Remember. That's when we all laughed at him because he started crying."

"You feel bad about laughing at him?"

"I guess. Yeah. I mean, he was scared. But we just kept teasing him and telling the ghost stories anyway."

"That was Jeremy's idea."

"Yeah, and he told the ghost stories even louder."

"And this has to do with that woman?"

"Yes. Curtis was scared and I didn't understand back then what that would feel like. But now, I'm the one who's scared. I was thinking about how we treated him. It makes me feel *bad*."

"We were in middle school," Emma offered, seeing how guilty I felt. "Why are you crying?" she asked, touching my hand.

I laughed between the tears. "Well, if you haven't noticed, I've become a complete mess. I'm *seventeen*. I'm not supposed to be afraid of the dark anymore. And if people find out about the woman, they'll think I'm crazy."

"So what if they do? I won't think those things."

It felt good to hear that. "I know."

"What's happening? Tell me about her."

Even though I'd told her everything on the phone, I told her again, partly to get it off my chest, partly to try and find some clue that was hidden between the dreams, the visits.

When I finished, Emma stretched over the mattress to pull me into a hug. "I'm sorry," she said.

"It's okay. I just hope it ends soon. And thanks. For letting me come over."

"Are you kidding me? We should do this more often, like, all the time. Like we used to. And I used to go to your house too, remember?"

"I miss that," I admitted.

"What happened anyway?"

"I don't know. Maybe it's because of what happened to our parents. Our houses got pretty serious for a while."

"Way serious," she agreed. "I hope we're not like that when we get old."

"Me too. This makes me so happy. Being here."

"Well, now that you're here, hopefully you can sleep. You look ready to crash out right now, you can barely keep your eyes open."

"I know. Guess I'm not much fun anymore."

"You will be," she promised. "Go to sleep. I don't mind at all. You'll get through this and then we can have late nights talking about boys and gossip like we used to."

"We did that tonight," I said.

"Yeah, but you were only pretending."

"Only a little. I still liked it though. Maybe next time, we can even talk bad about Ben."

"That we can definitely do! He's so stupid. I love that Destiny flat out rejected him to his stupid face. Did you know she's going with Adam?" Emma burst out laughing.

"Yeah," I said.

"Ben is such an idiot."

"You're being mean again."

"Yeah, well, Ben made a mistake. And he always thinks he's so smart."

"Has he always been like that?" I asked, wanting to know. "I feel like I just noticed or something."

She rolled her eyes. "Absolutely. But he's so much worse lately. Now he puts too much gel in his hair and sprays on about a gallon of cologne."

I laughed. "I know. I think he was trying to impress Destiny."

"He's trying to impress everyone or whatever. Like, he thinks his brain is twice the size of everyone else's. When I found out he asked Destiny, I was glad he didn't ask you."

"Then why did you sing that song or whatever with Valeska and the other girls?"

"You've liked him for years and I knew you wanted to go with him. Besides, forget Ben, there were a few other boys who were talking about asking you, boys *way* cuter than Ben."

"Then why didn't you tell me?"

Emma shrugged. "I don't know. You were so happy about going with Ben or whatever." Emma prodded my shoulder, edging me towards the mattress. "Go to bed. No more talking."

"Thanks."

"Don't even." She reached for the light. The room went dark. "Goodnight."

"Goodnight."

I couldn't have kept my eyes open if I wanted to. The softness of the bed helped me towards sweeter thoughts. In that feeling of safety, I wondered dreamily if I could just move in with Emma. I fell asleep.

A scream split the night. I sprang up in terror. Emma jumped out of bed and flicked the light on, almost knocking the bedside table over. Then she shuffled to the wall, looking over the corners of her room as she fidgeted in panic, her eyes wide with fear, her arms crossed over her chest, legs tucked together. I knew that pose.

Uncurling a finger from her chest, Emma pointed to the end of the bed. "She was here. She was there. A woman. *That* woman. The window was open. Even though it's closed now. But it was open. It was cold. I wanted to close it because the wind was so loud. The blankets were blowing from the bed. And it was freezing. You were in bed, sleeping. But I was sleeping too. Even though I was standing – standing here. There were two of me. I wanted the light on. It wouldn't work. That's when I saw her standing at the end of the bed. She was tall. So tall. Her black hair was blowing in the wind, hiding her face. She was staring down at our bodies. She just kept staring. Then she reached down to grab my feet and pulled my body out of the bed. But you kept sleeping. I wanted to scream at you from the corner to wake up, but I couldn't, I was too scared she would see me, the real me. The other me kept sleeping, even as she lifted me into her arms. She carried my body to the window. That's when she turned to look at me. She smiled. At me. It was horrible. She left through the window with my body. I didn't want her to take me. I started screaming." Emma's eyes finally turned to me. "Sarah," she said. So many emotions and unsaid things could be heard in my name.

"I'm sorry," I said. "I'll go home." I got up and began grabbing my things.

Emma was still shaking, glancing around the room with her back to the wall, making sure nothing could ever get behind her again. Emma said almost distractedly, "No. You can't go. It's still night."

"It's okay. I'll go downstairs."

Emma said, "Wait. I mean. It was just a nightmare, right?"

I answered honestly, "I don't know."

"But. But it was her. That woman. Right?"

My bag was in my hand, filled with my things. "Yes."

I was at her door. "Wait," Emma called. "I'll go down with you."

I didn't know if she wanted to be a good friend or if she didn't want to be by herself. Maybe it was a mixture of both. We sat side by side on the couch, waiting out the night, saying nothing to each other. When the sun finally rose, we ate breakfast in silence. Then we went back to her room to brush our teeth and do our hair, masking our fear in silent routine.

Emma's mother met us in the kitchen in a rush after we came back downstairs. "We're behind schedule! Good morning, Sarah!"

"Good morning."

"Get in the car, girls."

She scooped up her keys and drove us to school. As I watched Emma's neighborhood pass by, I knew there'd be no invitation to her house again, not until the woman in the window was gone. And maybe for the first time, I doubted whether that would ever happen.

"Are you two ready for the competition?" Emma's mother asked, sounding excited for us.

"Yeah, Mom," Emma said.

"Sarah, how about you? You've got the lead part. Are you ready? We're so proud of you, you know."

I tilted my face from the window to meet her eyes in the

rearview mirror. "I'm ready."

Emma flipped around in the front seat to look at me. "Sarah is going to kill it!" I could tell she was already trying to forget what happened in her room. The sun helped.

"We all are," I corrected with a conjured up smile. But I felt sick, like my stomach could only take so much of all the faking.

"Have you been practicing?" her mother asked.

"Of course."

"I can't believe it's in two days!" Emma said, throwing her hands onto the dashboard in front of her. Coincidence is easy to trust – so I'm sure Emma passed it off as a nightmare she'd had simply because she'd heard about mine. A part of me wondered if the woman in the window would go after Emma now. But I didn't think so. She'd gone after Emma to isolate me, to punish me for thinking I could get away. I was getting to know the woman.

"Sarah?"

"Yeah?"

"It's only in two days," Emma said.

I looked at her, letting her know I was still thinking about other things.

Emma turned back around to avoid my sobered expression.

Emma's Mom tried to bring up the competition again, but Emma said, "Mom, we're like so done talking about it. Quit stressing us."

"Oh, sorry," her mother said, then, "Sorry, Sarah."

"It's okay."

When we got to school, there was this momentary pause between Emma and I, as the students bustled around us. Emma gave me a hug. She said, "Just focus on the competition. It'll help."

Pretending to be comforted, I said, "You're right, I will."

"And, you know, if I can help at all, with *that,* I will, okay?"

"Okay."

"I promise."

"Okay."

Emma went to her class. I went to mine.

# 12

Frightened children are provided a measure of sympathy when scared by nightmares in the middle of the night. But as children age, adults expect the child's imagination to shrivel up, just as theirs once did. Childish whims – both nightmares and wishful dreams – are to dry out like parched scarecrows, fit to be burned and forgotten so that *real* worries and *real* hopes can take their place. There is only homework and grades, graduation and college. Marriage, bills, and divorce. So, kill your imagination, sweet child, and when you kill it, kill it with your own hands. There is no place for such a thing in the adult world. Kill your imagination, sweet child, for it has no use; there is nothing to believe outside of what we see. So, grow up. Grow up, as we have done, and let your imagination stay behind to die away right along with the child you used to be.

# 13

I stood center stage.

The spotlights were blinding. My hands trembled, tucked together at my waist. My heart was beating fast, sped along by a rush of performance adrenaline I could never quite get used to. My lips felt dry. In the periphery of my vision I could make out the outline of the coliseum seats. The auditorium was filled with people. Attendees had come to witness the competition and cheer their school, their own acapella group. They were quiet, waiting for me. My feet shuffled beneath me. I cleared my throat. A note of music from the piano signaled for me to begin, heard beneath the discreet clamor of controlled anticipation that was coming from the packed audience.

I looked up. My lips parted. My voice began, small and timid, but rose with courage. My song soon carried itself to the ceiling and to the far walls, displaying my gift as I sang for those gathered, for my team, and for me:

*Ave Maria, maiden mild*
*Oh, listen to a maiden's prayer*
*For thou canst hear amid the wild*
*'Tis thou, 'tis thou canst save amid, despair*
*We slumber safely till the morrow*
*Though we've by man outcast reviled*
*Oh maiden, see a maiden's sorrow*
*Oh mother, hear a suppliant child.*

There was silence when I finished. I remained where I was. Then the cheers and clapping resounded. I felt suddenly whole. I bowed in the lights.

Making my way to the back of the stage, I was unable to hold down my smile, expecting to be immediately enveloped by the enthusiastic greeting of my acapella group. I had done it. Emma, Valeska, Tonya, Courtney, and William would be ecstatic.

When I stepped from the bottom step, I was met by no one. It was dark. A child dashed past me, running ahead, disappearing at a corner which led to the changing rooms where the teams all prepared and went to after the show. A young girl then bumped into my hip. She looked up at me with a smile of apology, then bounded away in the same direction as the boy. I turned at the corner. The hallway was dark like a cavern. The exit sign at the end of the hall provided the only light, a soft glowing red. The two children stood in that red light, looking back at me.

I stepped into a changing room to keep from getting any closer to them, not caring if it was the room designated for our team. I found myself in a vast open room, shaped perfectly square, like an enormous plain box. I couldn't see where the walls met the ceiling because of the thick darkness, and looking up, I felt as though I were at the bottom of a hole.

As though they had been hiding or lying on the ground all around me, children came alive, springing up from the floor. Giggling, they began dashing around, crisscrossing among the shadows so that they disappeared in spots. I could barely count how many children there were because of the darkness and could only catch glimpses of their shoulders and feet, their hair tossing, but never their giggling faces. The children appeared unbothered by the darkness, a darkness that easily unnerved me, and so I knew these children were not the right kind. I wanted to go back out the way I came, but there were far too many children near the door, as though they knew I wanted to go there.

I pretended not to be bothered at all, that I was in fact pleased to see children enjoying themselves so much, that their joy gave me joy. I forced a smile onto my face, but it was a poorly made disguise, and I knew the children knew because of the way they began to cluck.

The children sucked me into their play, running closer to where I stood, like hornets drawn to something sweet and sticky. I began to work my way towards the exit sign, at the other end, which now seemed so terribly far away. Children pressed on me, then would dash away again, only to be replaced by other children who circled me. I had to struggle forward, my arms moving against them and I was trying not to cry. I placed my hand on the head of a boy who began pulling at my arm. When I touched him, I could feel his childlike curiosity at how my fingers might taste in his mouth. How they might snap off. More children came, encouraged by the eager tastes of the boy. A tiny tongue licked my hand. I pulled away, laboring against the tide of children, terribly afraid because my fingers had always been mine and I wanted to keep them.

Then the children took up a melody. The song they sang was:

*She loves us for who we are,*
*And wants us in her belly.*
*Even as she eats our parts*
*She tells us, "Call me, 'Mummy.'"*

*Come a little closer,*
*We have a secret to tell.*
*After she's through with eating you,*
*You're going straight to hell.*

I might have clapped at their gift for music just to maintain my forged and placid pose, but I made my way closer to the exit sign and pressed through the door beneath, shoving them behind me to escape the children who continued singing and licking at the air like blind lizards. I locked the door. It was a bedroom and there was no other door.

I wanted to go home.

"Go to sleep," one of the children encouraged through the door. The children had gathered at there and I hated myself for how afraid I was of them. They sang their next verse:

*She's here, she's here*
*Our Mummy dear!*
*Open the door and let her in!*
*Not to do so would be a sin.*

*It won't take long!*
*Only the length of a song.*
*When she's through eating you,*
*We can eat you too!*

The doorknob rattled and I threw myself into the corner. The deadbolt unlocked. The knob turned. The door opened. Children flooded through the entrance and I collapsed beneath them as they smothered me, grasping at my parts, yanking at my clothes and hair. I could hardly see through their small fervent faces. I tried to scream, but a hand filled my mouth and I gagged and cried as they weight of them pressed me downward. They parted suddenly, kneeling beside my body as if they meant to pray over me while they continued to hold me flat to the floor with their tiny hands. In the doorway stood a tall woman, watching. Her face was expressionless, but for an excitement in her eyes that spoke of other things.

I began to struggle, but only in futility, and I felt like a child myself, more of a child than they. I fretted fearfully, tearfully, shaking helplessly and crying.

The woman came to my feet and stood there. She then bent to me, as though she wanted to listen to a secret I might tell her. Then she reached for my hand and drew it up as three children released it for her. Prying a finger loose from the fist I had made, the woman placed my pinky finger in her mouth. Her teeth bit down slowly. Then harder. The children began to lick at my skin and face, tempting themselves with a taste.

I screamed until my lungs burned. I screamed and screamed and screamed. The children mimicked me with their terrified, pathetic, helpless little petrified screams of mockery, and I screamed even more.

# 14

I woke. In my bed. Released. Free. Like the sensation of a thousand shackles dropping from my body after an unjust captivity. I wanted a shower. The lingering touch of fingers and tongues caused me to feel filthy. I wanted to scrape thin layers from my flesh until I was raw so that my nerves would then grow in new. But in the crescendo of my waking, I was interrupted by a sudden surge of pain. I raised my hand to my eyes. Indentations circled my pinky finger. Teeth marks. Pulsating and particular. I began to sob, holding my hand to my chest. Overcome with despair, I dropped to the floor, curled up on my side, where I sobbed and sobbed.

# 15

The bite marks were red and obvious, the final proof I needed to show my mother. The woman in the window was not a figment of my imagination. My mother was sitting at the kitchen table with her computer out in front of her. "What is it, Sarah?" she asked.

I held out my finger.

She refused to look. "Use your words," she said, as if I was two.

"Mom. Look. Please." I refused to cry or look weak in that vulnerable moment.

"Look at what?" She was intent on something, sipping at her coffee, focused on everything but me.

"Please. My finger. Please, look."

She finally turned. "What about it?"

I extended my hand again.

"I don't see anything." But she was too busy scrutinizing my demoralized expression. My shaky mind was being exposed through the rampant blinking of my eyes and the trembling of my limbs, which made her less concerned for my finger and more interested in what was going on inside my head. I felt as though I could not be trusted.

"Right there." I pointed with my other hand. "The bite marks."

"I see them. Sarah."

"Mom. Please." I started to cry, though I told myself not to and though I hated myself for doing it, but the unspoken accusation was there between us, and she had placed it there, and it hurt. I said, begging, "I didn't bite my own finger, Mom. Please. You know I wouldn't."

"I thought we were done with this. That's what you said."

I hung my head. "I know. But it hasn't changed. I stopped talking about the woman because you wouldn't believe me."

"Don't put this on me, Sarah."

"I'm not."

"But the finger."

Her lips twisted into an expression of disappointment. "Sarah."

"She hasn't left, Mom."

"Who hasn't left?" This wasn't like her. The harshness. I could feel the presence of the woman in the window in my mother's lack of sympathy and my mother's hair had never before appeared to take on that dark of a shade.

"Her. The woman."

"Sarah." She shook her head, as though the girl before her was someone she didn't know anymore and the real me had disappeared, leaving behind a husk that only resembled her daughter in basic features. "Can we be done with this?"

"She was there. In the dream. But it wasn't a dream. Because she bit my finger. I have bite marks. What does that tell you?"

"I'm not convinced you didn't do it yourself." My mother turned back to the computer. "I've been doing some research," she began in an abrupt conclusion.

"Please don't, Mom." I felt smaller and smaller before her.

As though I'd said nothing, she continued, "I'm starting to think this may be mental illness, especially with this *finger incident*."

"Please, Mom, don't."

"Don't what?"

"Don't talk like that. Don't talk like I'm crazy. Please, just believe. That's all I want."

"I'm not saying you're crazy. I'm just saying, with these

hallucinations and your paranoia. What I'm saying is, I'm starting to believe that *you* believe this woman is real. They say schizophrenia can manifest around your age. I refuse to believe this woman is real. But I am willing to believe that you need help."

I brought my finger to my chest like some wounded delicate thing cupped within my hand, too sensitive to let out again. "I'm not crazy," I said quietly.

"Don't look like that, Sarah. You don't need to look so sad."

# 16

"Sarah. Sarah. Sarah."

I looked up to see Ms. Bradstreet, my art teacher, going from table to table gathering up used paintbrushes into a wooden crate she was carrying like a picnic basket.

"Yes, sorry, Ms. Bradstreet. What was that?" I had been staring at a corner, making sure the coat hanging there was only a coat.

"Sarah, class is over," she stated.

There were no other students in the room.

"Oh, yeah, right." I gathered up my own things and accidentally knocked some paint to the floor. When I reached down to begin cleaning it up, Ms. Bradstreet touched my arm. I flinched away. "Sarah, don't worry, I'll get it." Her eyes had sympathy for me, and she wouldn't look away. "Are you okay, Sarah?"

"Yeah. I'm just tired."

"You don't look well," she agreed.

"I've been sick," I explained.

My explanation seemed to make her feel better. "I'm sorry to hear that. But you've been like this for weeks now. Has your mother taken you to see anyone?"

"Yeah," I lied. "The doctor said it's just a long case of the flu."

"You should get rest then. Stay home a few days to sleep."

"Yeah," I said. Sleep was the last thing I wanted, even though it was the only thing I absolutely craved. "But you know, classes."

She smiled. "Yes, classes." Then she said, "I heard you missed the acapella competition."

"Yeah." My head sunk.

"I know how much that meant to you."

I had missed the competition because I couldn't bear to stand on stage, fearful that when my song was done, children would be waiting for me, a long hallway, a red exit sign. I had locked myself away, ignoring my mother's pleas to open the door and go to the competition and she only left me alone after I screamed at her. I said to Ms. Bradstreet, "I know, but I was too sick. It was probably better that way. If I had tried to sing, I probably would have messed it up. I had no voice." I was skating along the truth. Nothing was a lie, but nothing was honest either.

"Well, you can't help it if you're sick," she said, collecting the last of the paint supplies. "It sounds like you did what was best."

"But I'm sure I disappointed everyone," I admitted, hoping everyone didn't hate me.

"Well, high school isn't forever," Ms. Bradstreet stated.

"Yeah." I didn't know what else to say. Exhaustion made every effort hurt. Even small conversations drained me of the little energy I had.

The bell rang.

"If you need to talk to someone, let me know," Ms. Bradstreet offered.

"Thanks, I will."

I stumbled my way to lunch. Before I knew what I was doing, I had flopped down next to Ben out of habit, like my body was running on an out-of-date auto-pilot setting. I wanted to fold my arms over the filthy table and lay my head down to sleep. I was so tired. It was all I could think of. My bloodshot eyes blinked constantly. My legs tingled. That morning, tests had been returned in Calculus. I had gotten a D. I couldn't remember ever getting a D before in my life. I thought about that. Then I realized I didn't really care. There was a droning sound. Ben was talking to me. He was still talking. Did he always talk so much? Did he not see how detached I was from anything he was saying?

"What?" I asked. I would have gotten up and gone somewhere else, but I didn't feel like moving. I laid my head back down.

"Are you hung over?" he asked with a smirk, like he already knew the answer.

"What? No."

"Are you sure?" he asked, still smirking.

"No – I mean, yes – yes, I'm sure. I've never even gotten drunk." I burrowed my head between my arms.

"Then why are you acting so weird?"

When I wouldn't respond to any of his ongoing attempts to lure me out of my own self-made cave, Ben stated with disapproval, "I can't believe you didn't even go to the acapella competition."

"I don't want to talk about it."

"You didn't even go to watch them."

"I said, I don't want to talk about it."

"They did great, just so you know."

"I don't want to talk about it!" I yelled against my forearm.

"Look at me," Ben said.

I did. Ben began circling his face in front of mine for inspection, as though counting my freckles. The fluorescent lights stung my eyes. "You really are sick, aren't you?"

"Yeah. Super sick."

"Are you upset about not going to the competition?"

"Of course I am."

"Well, you can't let it get you down, right?" he said, trying to cheer me up or something.

"Sure. Couldn't do a thing like that."

"And you can't let being sick ruin senior year. You're sick all the time now."

"Couldn't do a thing like that either."

"I mean, YOLO."

"What?" I shook my head miserably. "Did you just say 'YOLO'?"

"Yeah, so what if I did?"

"No one even says YOLO anymore."

"I know that. I was saying it to be funny. You know, like retro."

I corrected his recollection, "You used to say it all the time. Like, all the time," I said again.

"Yeah, when it was cool."

"It was never cool."

"Yeah it was."

"Whatever." I shook my head.

"You used to laugh when I'd say it."

"Just so you wouldn't feel bad about yourself."

"Feel bad about what?"

"Your life." I chuckled darkly. This wasn't like me, but it felt kind of good.

"Whatever. More like *your* life." He rolled his eyes.

"Good one."

"I know it was."

"Whatever."

"What's your deal anyway? Like for real? You're not yourself anymore."

"I'm just tired."

After taking a bite off the corner of his rectangular pizza, he offered, "Then you should probably try and get some sleep."

"Wow. Thanks. I wasn't sure what the answer was until now."

He ignored my sarcasm, then went on to instruct further, "At our age, we need close to 12 hours of sleep each night."

"Yeah, thanks."

"I'm just trying to help."

"You're really helping, thank you so much."

Then Ben did something I hadn't seen him do in a long time – he leaned closer to me, and in his eyes, I saw subtle hints of concern and care, maybe even affection. His cologne, which he was still applying in heavy doses, wrapped the two of us into a potent cloud. He asked, "What's wrong, Sarah? You keep saying you're sick, but it's something else."

I wanted to tell him. I wanted to tell anyone. Being exhausted meant I had very little will left to stay composed and controlled, and before I knew it, I said, "There's a woman."

"What? You're talking too quiet. I can barely hear you."

"There's a woman. In my window."

Ben touched my shoulder unexpectedly. I flinched away so hard, I almost fell out of my chair. Ben chuckled, fist to his mouth like he didn't want to laugh but couldn't help himself, and I sat up and shouted, "When did you become such a jerk?"

The cafeteria fell silent.

Wanting a few laughs from everyone watching, Ben turned the volume up and asked like a jerk, "There's a woman in your window?"

It felt like everything inside of me was trying to find a place to hide. My face flushed with embarrassment. Whispered comments and sniggers rose all around. I wanted to disappear.

"Where are you going?" Ben asked.

"Somewhere else."

I scurried between the tables to get away and left the cafeteria behind me. I went to my next class, sat in the empty room and wished there was some other place to go.

Twirling into the classroom, Emma called out, "There you are!"

I couldn't help but smile. "Here I am."

"Why are you sitting alone?"

"Just because." I didn't want to ruin her happiness by bringing up what had just happened. Ben was Emma's worst enemy – even if Ben didn't know it – and I didn't want to spoil her joy.

Emma spun a chair around to face me. With her arms on my desk, she leaned in and asked, "Did you hear?"

"I did." I smiled a little. "You won."

"No! We won!" She was positively beaming.

"And you sang my part," I said. I was happier for her than she knew, and a part of me was glad she got to sing the part and not me.

"I sang it, sure. But you would have sung it like way better."

"I doubt that."

"Oh, stop it! You would have! But it wasn't just me, Sarah! Everyone did *great*!" Emma then asked, "Do you mind at all that it was me who sang your part, or nah?"

"Definitely *nah*." I smiled again. "You're the one I would have wanted to sing it."

Emma said, almost whispering, "Your mom called my mom and told her you were sick and that's why you couldn't go."

"Yeah." It was all I could say.

"Is that what it was? Or was it *that?*" she asked, making reference to the woman in the window in her own way.

"No, no," I assured her. "I was just sick."

Emma took a deep breath. "I'm so glad. I didn't want to ask, but I knew I should, wanted to, that sort of thing, you know or whatever."

"I know."

"So, *that* is like, gone, or whatever?"

"Yep." There was no way I was going to steal Emma's excitement.

"How?" she asked in amazement.

"I don't know. She just stopped," I said as convincingly as I could by sprinkling in a little false relief.

"That's is *so* good. I'm happy for *you!*"

"Yeah. I would have been there to cheer you on but I was super sick all weekend. I'm so happy you won."

Emma touched my face with both of her hands. "Not me. And not us. *We* won, Sarah. You're a part of that too."

"I wasn't there."

"But you're still a part of the group. Everyone thinks so."

"They weren't too upset?"

She rolled her eyes. "Of course they were *disappointed*! But they weren't upset. We would have wanted you there with us, but we understood."

"Okay, good. That means a lot." And it did.

A few students began drifting in. One boy pointed at me and chuckled. Emma snapped at him, "Don't know why you're laughing! You're the one who peed all over himself after getting drunk this weekend!"

Everyone started laughing at him and he turned away.

"Thanks," I said.

Emma winked. "Well, got to scoot. The bell is about to ring."

"See you later," I said.

"Later, Sarah gator!" Emma offered as she waved and twirled her way back out into the hall. I was glad to have smiled with her, share in her happiness.

Ben was at the door. Emma didn't notice him at first and she bumped right into him during mid-spin. She didn't even apologize, just gave Ben a push, declared, "You're in the way!" and resumed her twirling.

Ben came in. He didn't sit, just walked closer to stand nearby.

77

"I can't stay long because class is going to start, but I just wanted to say, you know, I'm sorry, for how I talked to you in the cafeteria."

"It's okay," I said. "I'm sorry, too."

"What's with what you said though? About a woman or something?"

The bell rang. More students came in.

"Nothing. It's nothing."

Ben looked again like he cared. I missed that look. It was endearing, comforting. His eyes weren't looking around for who he might impress. "What is it?" he asked. "What's wrong?"

I wanted to tell him. I wanted to spend time with him like we used to. "There's a woman. She's been in my dreams."

"Like a recurring nightmare?"

"Yeah, well, sort of. Only, I think she's real."

Mark came in and yelled, "Ben, what are you doing in here? This isn't your class." He sauntered over with a cocky smile. "Hey, Sarah." Then he coughed. Hard. Like he had a hairball in his throat, and he elbowed Ben to join in on the joke.

Ben said, "Dude, don't."

"I was just coughing," Mark said.

"Sarah," Ben tried.

"It's okay," I said. "You should go to class."

"Nightmares. They'll go away eventually. See you later. Get some rest."

"See you later," I said.

Mark gave Ben a slap on the shoulder and bellowed, "Later, homie!" which caused Ben to regain the newer version of himself and he strutted away.

# 17

It didn't take long before the outburst in the cafeteria between Ben and I – along with his loud mention of the woman in the window – led to another rumor, causing my rumor collection to pile up even higher. The hair ball. My daily attire (gray sweatpants and gray sweatshirt each day). My hygiene (which had gotten pretty bad). And the woman in the window. None of the surrounding comments were ever quite right, of course. It was more like a game of telephone, where the guesses get worse and worse the longer the game goes on. The popular ones went something like this and had a thread of evolution to them:

A woman had fallen out of my window.

A woman had broken through my window.

I had drawn a woman in my window because I was obsessed with her.

I had seen the ghost of a woman in my window.

And then, there was a woman who came through my window each night to molest me.

Nice, right?

Kids are jerks. Especially teenage boys. They're the worst.

But strangely, the last rumor might have been closest to the truth. Molesting me sexually? No. Molesting my life with her unwanted touch upon my life? Every night, yes.

During those days, I *wished* more than anything. I wished. And I wished. And my wishes were played out in daydreams before a faceless timeless being, a genie of some sort, maybe something greater.

*"What is your wish, Sarah?"*

*I wish the woman in the window would leave me alone.*

*"But Sarah, she has to haunt someone."*

*Then I want her to haunt someone else.*

*"Who do you want her to haunt?"*

*Anyone but me.*

*"But what if she haunts a small child?"*

*Please, don't say that.*

*"Or someone you love?"*

*Stop.*

*"Maybe your mother, or your father, or Emma? Is that what you want?"*

*No, but please, just make her go away. I just want one night without her. Just a little sleep. Just a little. Please, just leave me alone. Please.*

# 18

"Dreams." The word had been said.

I straightened in my chair before I even really knew why. I saw Mr. Travinski, which meant I was in psychology class. He was leaning back against his desk as he talked about dreams. He asked if any students ever had dreams of significance, dreams of impact.

Almost every student raised their hand.

Students were called upon. Dreams were told – significant dreams, dreams of impact. Mr. Travinski did his best to navigate that delicate balance between remaining patient with each invested telling, yet moving the class along as he permitted each student a measure of time that didn't suck up the minutes for everyone else as I listened intently. But as the dreams came and went, they began to sound like paper plates and plastic utensils – real, but lacking. Dreams were significant, but only to the person telling them. Dead relatives returned. Dreams about the future. Then others that were construed in their retelling to sound spectacular or even bizarre, but couldn't really be categorized as significant.

Mr. Travinski eventually called my name, "Sarah."

"Yes?"

He smiled. "Is there any dream that has impacted you that you would like to share?"

"No. Not really."

"Are you sure?" he offered almost kindly.

"Yes."

There were a few sniggers and a good amount of head shaking at my expense. My response made me out to be as bland as a lima bean, which didn't surprise anyone with how I had become and they found that amusing. I was the outcast with a personality as gray as her sweatshirt. But I didn't dare tell them. I knew the looks I would get. The laughs. The disgust. The woman in the window was mine – in some horrible demented way – mine alone, not to be shared.

"That is enough!" Mr. Travinski bellowed, silencing the chuckles and I was grateful for that. Then he stated, "Now, I am quite aware that Christmas break begins" – he checked his watch – "in thirty minutes. But, I have a fun homework assignment for you over break." There was some grumbling. "Now, now, I said fun. This is why we are discussing dreams: there is the possibility of influencing dreams through the use of word repetition prior to falling asleep, which is something I have personally had success with. When I first tried doing so, I used it as an opportunity to see a friend of mine who I hadn't seen in years. So, before bed one night, I repeated the name of my friend until falling asleep. Then, in my dream, my friend popped out from behind a bush and yelled, 'Hey, Dave!'" Mr. Travinski chuckled.

One of the boys yelled, "I know who's visiting me tonight! Scarlett Johansson!" That unleashed a barrage of other women all the boys planned on conjuring up.

Mr. Travinski rolled his eyes. "Wonderful. I give you an opportunity to take command of your dreams, and you boys, with your hormones, can only think of women. I should have known."

One of the boys said, "Don't tell me you weren't thinking the same, Mr. Travinksi!"

Mr. Travinksi pointed at his ring. "I'm quite happily married."

"It's not like imagining hurts," the boy challenged,

"Considering I am the one who has been married twenty-three

years, I would say it does. Of course, given that you are about seventeen years of age, I am sure you know far more about life and marriage than I do."

"Whatever."

"Ah, yes. The intelligent quip of your generation." Pulling up the sleeve of his corduroy jacket, Mr. Travinksi glanced at his watch again. "Where was I before the lovely Ms. Johansson entered my classroom?"

I answered, wanting more, "You were telling us to try and influence our dreams."

"Why, yes. Thank you. That is the basic idea, and I want you all to try it and to come back with reports on your experiences, all rated PG." He then asked me, "And what are you hoping to discover in your dreams tonight, Sarah?"

"I'm going to try and get rid of my fears."

Some of the boys laughed again and somebody called out, "What a whack job!"

Mr. Travinski ignored them, then said to me, "Then I hope it works."

The class bell rang. Students stampeded for the door. I remained at my desk, gathering my things.

Mr. Travinksi said, "Don't worry about those boys, Sarah."

"It's okay. I'm not."

"They're jerks, sure. But they don't know it yet. Someday they'll look back and be embarrassed by how immature they were."

Out in the hall, someone yelled, "Scarlett Johansson! I'll see you tonight!"

Mr. Travinksi corrected himself, "Or perhaps not."

I smirked brokenly.

"Have a wonderful break, Sarah. I hope you find an opportunity to relax and come back in the new year ready to regain some traction on your grades. I've graded your makeup work, and you did quite well."

"Thanks," I said.

"And Sarah?"

"Yes?"

"I truly hope it works for you, influencing your dreams. I hope it doesn't work for the boys. In fact, I hope it all goes terribly wrong for them and doesn't turn out like they hoped it would."

"Like in real life," I said.

He laughed a moment, then considered. "Yes. Like in real life."

"Merry Christmas," I said flatly.

"Merry Christmas," he said.

On my walk home, I considered what I would say to myself that night before falling asleep. It felt as though I was preparing for a camping trip, skimming through my list of things I couldn't forget, afraid I'd forget that one most important thing.

What would help me? A weapon? I didn't know if anything would ever hurt her. A hiding place? She always found me. Supernatural powers? I couldn't comprehend anything being more powerful than her.

At home, I dropped my bag in the corner and stood in the kitchen staring out of the window like an invalid. My daily routine.

My mom came home and I was still standing there. I pretended to be busy with something. She asked if I was excited for Christmas break. Turning towards her with a big smile that hid my despair, I said, "Of course!"

That night, I went ahead and changed. Showered for the first time in days. Put on clean pajamas. Slid into bed and pulled the covers up, staring at the window. The deeper tingling of my body told me sleep was coming soon, whether I wanted it to or not. Before drifting away, I repeated my tiny whispers of courage:

*She's only a dream. She's only a dream. She's only a dream.*

# 19

"She's only a dream," I whispered.

I couldn't remember why I was saying those words and I didn't know why they sounded so important in my ears.

The room I was in was silent. I took in the new surroundings, unsure of where I was and was immediately overcome by the thick smell of plastic. It was all around me, heavy on my skin like a sheet, sinking into my lungs and almost uncomfortable to breathe. Beyond the smell of plastic were white walls, which surrounded me on four sides and a high white ceiling above. In front of me was a dining area. A kitchen area was far off to the right, with plastic counters and plastic appliances, beside which was a fireplace and white plastic furniture. Everything was a plastic recreation of what would be real, every detail and edge within the home made colored white, like I was standing in a dollhouse not yet painted.

I held my arms out before me to look at my own skin, concerned they'd be plastic as well. I was glad to find my flesh was as it had always been, and from what I could see, I was the only color in the entire home. It made me feel like a pop up in a pop-up book.

I called out into the thick plastic air for my mother, hoping she was there. I wanted to see her and I wanted someone to talk to, to shake the feeling that I didn't belong. But when I opened my mouth, the plastic air absorbed my words almost as soon as they left my mouth, like the words were trapped in a bubble that sank to the floor. I didn't like the sound of my own voice or the way it seemed to die at the walls, so I didn't call out again, but I still wanted to find her. I decided to explore the home and try to find my mother that way, keeping my voice to myself.

I came upon a mirror on a wall nearby. My cloudy replica was there waiting for me, and she gazed back at me as I gazed at her. She was a plastic version of myself. Her skin and clothes were completely white. Her hair too. She had plastic eyes. I lifted my hands to inspect them once again, and the girl in the mirror did the same. I looked back, and when my plastic reflection blinked, there was disappointment or jealously in her eyes. I couldn't tell if I had blinked or not, and I didn't want to know the answer, so I turned away.

I became intent upon finding the front door, thinking I would wait for my mother outside just in case she was on her way home from work. But when I turned towards the front wall, there was no door to be seen, nothing but white. I went to the great white wall and began inspecting it in hopes of discovering a hidden door. I traced my fingers along the wall, walking the length of it, but I found nothing. No groove, no edge. Yet, I found words scribbled in red about midway down that read: *There was a hole here.* I refused to touch the colored writing because there was something about it I didn't like and so I continued past, bringing my fingers with me.

The strangeness of the home was unsettling me further, no matter how much I tried not to be bothered, no matter how much I straightened my spine as I walked. I didn't want to explore any further but I didn't want to stay there either. I walked back the way I had come, making my way through center of the vast open room, past the chandelier and mirror, and discovered a spiral staircase far at the other end where the shadows were thick, being so far from the muddled plastic chandelier light of the dining room. At the top of the staircase I saw nothing but darkness. But a light switch was there. I climbed the stairs, circling as I rose. Darkness stopped me when I reached the highest step. The darkness was thick in the hallway ahead of me. I flicked at the light switch, expecting it not to work, but was happy when the light fixtures poured light from the ceiling.

I walked towards the first door to my left. I pressed it open slowly. Inside the room I saw stacked boxes, as though someone had recently moved in. Some boxes had been opened. Some were still closed. SARAH was written in red on the largest box and I didn't like that. I guessed this was a new home for my mother and I, my mother's way of taking us from our troubles. My troubles. A part of me was thankful that she finally believed me.

I returned to the hallway to search the other rooms, hoping to find my mother's bedroom and expecting her to be there unloading her own boxes, maybe putting her clothes away. I continued along the hall, checking doors on both sides. Each was locked, leading me further down. Further down the hall, I came upon a music box set neatly upon the floor. It was a curious place for a music box, and it was the first thing in the home made of something real, made of wood. I pulled the lid open. Beneath the lid were brass pins and silver gears. A tune struck up. The antique melody tinkered along, and I suddenly heard my own voice within the music. My voice began to sing: *She's only a dream, she's only a dream.*

I whispered, "She's only a dream."

The music box stopped. And then, with a *click,* it struck up again. The same song began and continued. But when it was time to hear me sing, the music box played my screams, shrill and unbearable, my screams ushered out with the sounds of a tortured and ruined soul. I covered my ears, but the sound of the screams pried their way through my fingers, and so I kicked the music box away. It tumbled down the hall.

Everything was quiet. I shuffled backwards, watching the doors and listening intently in case any of them began to open, feeling as though I was being watched by the doors and the walls. In the silence, I heard something, like the sound of a button dropping. Someone was downstairs. I took a step towards the room with the boxes, thinking I should hide as I padded along as quietly as I could. The person below me on the floor below began tiptoeing faster, closing in on the spiral staircase. I fled. A shadow neared the top of the stairs and slunk low to hide from me as I watched. The sound of long fingernails could be heard going *tatatatatat* up the remaining steps. I scurried into the bedroom and into the bedroom closet where I balled myself up in the corner, shutting the door with my foot. I didn't know what to do. My heart was beating wildly.

I could hear the woman enter the room. She was slinking along on her fingernails and toes, *tatatatatat*. She began sniffing the air for me and was searching for me among the boxes. Then her shadow darkened the bottom of the closet door where I was hiding. Strands of her hair skimmed along the floor as she sniffed left then right. A fingernail traced a path beneath the door. I whimpered, and her shadow jumped with excitement. The door opened.

I wrapped my head in my arms and closed my eyes to hide, huddled in the corner and refusing to meet her eyes. *Tatatatatat* the woman scurried feverishly to me and began touching at me all over, as though too eager to know where to start. I tucked myself away at each touch. Annoyed by my efforts to shield myself, the woman ripped my plastic arms and plastic legs from my body and tossed them behind her. My limbless torso slid flat to the floor and the woman climbed on top of me. She interlaced her fingers behind my plastic head, and I closed my eyes, unable to watch, unable to look at her. She began to lick my face hungrily, pausing only to mock me with a single raspy whisper, "She's only a dream, she's only a dream."

I could do nothing but scream. When I heard them, I knew they were the same screams the music box had played, and I screamed and screamed.

*Sarah! Wake up!*

*Sarah! Wake up!*

"Sarah! Wake up!"

I woke to my mother shaking me. But in the blackness of my room, my mother's dark hair was all I could see, and I clawed at her face in a frenzy, screaming at her to get away.

My mother snatched my wrists in both hands to stop me and she yelled back, "Sarah! Sarah! Sarah!" startling me to my senses.

I froze. I was gasping, swallowing air. My body drenched in

sweat. My sheets thrown around. In crazed hysterics, I was barely able to make words. "The music box screaming it was me my voice screaming I tried to find you needed you the house was plastic I thought we had moved there she was there right after I shut the music box I was hoping it was you even though I knew it wasn't but you were all I could think of her shadow on the stairs crawling like a spider or something horrible not human I tried to hide tried to say the words she's only a dream she's only a dream but she ripped my arms away she was licking me licking me all I could do was scream I promise Mom she's real I promise please please please she was there it was real you have to believe me. I can't do this anymore. I can't do this. I can't pretend it's not happening. I can't. You have to believe me."

"I know. I know," she said, consoling me.

I was startled. "You – you believe me?" I leaned away to see if it was true. That's when I saw what I had done to her. Her face was bleeding from red claw marks down her skin. I said, "I'm sorry, I didn't mean to hurt you." I started crying again, ashamed for what I had done.

"I know you didn't mean to hurt me."

"I'm so sorry," I apologized over and over. With the terror gone, my voice became overwhelmed and tired, as though I might fall asleep right there in her arms. It was all I wanted. Safety and rest. "I'm so sorry, Mom."

My mother whispered, "I know you are." Brushing my face with her fingers to calm me even more, my mother asked, "The woman is real?"

"Yes, Mom. She's real."

"You're sure?"

"Yes."

"Sarah."

"Yes?"

"I want you to go ahead and pack up a few of your things, okay? Maybe enough for a few days."

I didn't ask why. I simply got up and obeyed. In my bathroom, I washed my face. Then I packed a small bag. When we got into the car at three in the morning, I didn't ask why, and when we drove into the night, I didn't ask where we were going. My mother eventually parked in a lot that was mostly destitute and empty. We passed a glowing sign that announced our location, the place my mother had taken me. It was a crisis center, a place for people who were a threat to their own safety or to the safety of others. It was a place for people like me.

# 20

Following a four hour assessment process, my mother left me to stay at the crisis center after giving me a kiss I did not return. What she told the staff (the people with clipboards and analyzing eyes) was validated by the scratch marks on her face which seemed to glow red beneath the stretch of fluorescent lights. I was soon transported to a local mental hospital where I was to be further assessed by more people who wanted to shine a light on my brain and poke at it. Depending on what I said while I was there, I could be there for just a few days or a lot longer than that. The hospital was tucked away right in the city, which was strange, because I'd never noticed it.

While there, I was allowed to wear my own clothes, except for my shoes. They gave me slipper socks. Maybe because you can't be too dangerous when you're slipping along a waxed floor. The bed I slept in had springs that jabbed into me, but I actually slept okay while I was there and I napped anytime I was allowed to.

I didn't say much about the woman in the window to anyone,

only enough to be accommodating. I stayed away from saying the things I knew I shouldn't say – like the woman in the window was real – that was easy enough to figure out. I kept my story simple and mostly kept my mouth shut. I explained that I had been sick for a few days and sleep-deprived, and as a result a fevered dream had caused me to lose a momentary grasp on reality, which is why I had attacked my mother. And I was all better now because I had found reality again. It was so silly of me to have misplaced it. I promised never to do so again.

Sometimes my therapist lady, Courtney, she'd ask more specific questions about the woman in the window, especially about the times I had actually seen her in my home (my mother hold told them about the police visit and the bite on the finger). But it felt like a trap. So I explained, "The woman in the window is in the dream but some of the dreams just feel so real that it feels real like a dream that's real but not but it's so real that it feels real but isn't because it's a dream you know those dreams where it's super real but they're really not." Yeah, it confused her, which is what I was going for. Courtney would say, "uh-huh," and jot down a few notes. Then she'd ask me about my childhood, like there was something else to figure out about me. When she asked about my dad, I refused to say anything at all.

On the first day there, I participated in a group session, surrounded by other girls. They were close to my age and each of them had a reason to be there. One girl had driven her mom's car into her boyfriend's house. Another had tried to kill herself with pills. One girl had more than twenty make-believe friends, some that tried to get her to hurt herself, and some that hurt each other. Some girls hallucinated. Some heard things. Voices. When it was my turn to introduce myself, which mostly meant talking about the reason I was there, most of the girls were sympathetic even to the little I told them. I liked that. I was in a place for crazy people, so I wasn't crazy anymore.

After the group session, it was recreation time. A girl named Katrina introduced herself and asked if I wanted to play a game. We sat at a table, the legs of which were screwed into the floor, and played *Connect Four.* We plopped the plastic disks down randomly, not caring about the actual game. While we played, Katrina told me about Billy Bob.

Billy Bob had been haunting her for years. He lived in the corner of her room, standing next to her Hannah Montana poster. Billy Bob wore a suit and tie. He had a pale face and a smile that never changed, and he always stared straight ahead, never moving his eyes. Never blinking.

Katrina told me that the woman in the window reminded her of Billy Bob because he just came out of nowhere, and while everyone in her life said that Billy Bob was a figment of her imagination, he wasn't. Billy Bob brought nightmares, except he wasn't in the nightmares himself. The nightmares got worse and worse. She explained, "One night, I dreamt I killed my family. When I woke from the dream, I was covered in blood and my brother's head was between my legs. Then I woke up again, because that had been a dream too. Billy Bob was in the corner, staring ahead like always. I never talked to him before, but when I asked if the dream would come true, he turned his eyes towards me and nodded. So, I tried to kill myself. Didn't work though. My mom saved me. And so, here I am."

"How long have you been in here?" I asked.

"Almost six months."

I couldn't believe it. "Really? Why so long?"

She laughed. "Guess I'm *that* crazy."

Katrina showed me her arms. She had thick scars on both wrists, pale and fresh, standing out from her dark skin. She had tried quite a few different times.

"I'm sorry." It was all I could say.

"I'm sorry for you, too."

"That's such a goofy name for someone who's so creepy. Billy Bob, I mean."

Katrina laughed a little. "I named him."

"You named him?" I laughed a little myself.

"I was a lot younger when he first showed up. My mother asked me what I had seen. While I tried to explain what he was like, that name popped right out of my mouth."

"It's all so weird," I said. "Our little worlds."

"I know that's right."

Katrina and I spent the rest of recreation talking about things that had nothing to do with Billy Bob or the woman in the window, and during those seven days I spent there, Katrina and I hung out as much as we could. But by day four, there were sounds at my window at night. And on day six, I saw the woman in the window walking down the hall.

On the seventh day, it was time for me to be discharged. The hospital didn't have enough reason to keep me, and when I was about to leave, Katrina asked me to think about her from time to time. I promised I would. We hugged. I was sad to leave her and she was sad to see me go.

My mom was there in the lobby, smiling uncomfortably, like she wasn't sure how I'd react to seeing her. When she tried to hug me, I walked past and went to the car. On the drive home, the world passed by at a distance, like everything was being viewed through binoculars. By the time we were pulling into the driveway, I was resigned to my fate, knowing that the woman in the window would probably return that night, more excited to see me than my own mother had been.

Out of nowhere, I blurted out, "I love you, Mom."

The barrier of awkwardness between us crumbled. My mom filled the car with promises that she loved me, that she didn't want to do what she had done by having my hospitalized, and we were going to get through this together. Her and I.

I said, "I know." But I knew that wasn't true.

Despite getting some rest at the hospital, exhaustion ruined me as I stepped into the kitchen as though I'd never gotten any rest at all. I walked aimlessly around the counter, scheming a way to avoid going upstairs, even though I had to put away my things and my mother would ask. Near the fridge, I noticed on the calendar: *Treatment Place 4:00pm.* I asked "What's the *Treatment Place?*"

"Oh, that's for your follow-up appointment the hospital scheduled it for us."

"Follow up appointment?"

"You know, for your assessment."

"No, I don't know," I said. "What assessment?"

"They didn't tell you?" I couldn't tell if her surprise was genuine.

"No. And if they did, I must not have been listening."

"Well, you should listen more carefully, Sarah. You're seventeen years old."

"You're right, I should listen more carefully when I spend time at the mental hospital, because you know, I'll probably end up there a few times every year. I made a friend there, Katrina, and she's been there four times and she's *only* sixteen."

"Please, don't talk like that."

"What? That's what you're thinking."

"I didn't say that, Sarah."

"You didn't have to, Mom."

"Well, your therapist, Courtney, she said it would be good for you to get checked by a local mental health provider, and maybe enroll you for services."

"Enroll me for services? You mean, like a therapist or whatever. Like a regular one." I could imagine all the latest rumors at school.

"Yes, Sarah, we have to start somewhere."

I thought about it. "Okay."

"Okay?" she asked.

"Okay." I nodded. Maybe it would help somehow. "So, who are we meeting? I mean, who's my appointment with, my therapist, or whatever?"

"Well, from what I understand, we meet with an intake clinician first to sign off on paperwork. After that, we have a meeting with the psychiatrist."

"And who's that?"

She plucked a card from her purse and read, "Dr. Daniel Tariq."

# 21

My name was called. My mom and I stood, and were met by a round little lady with a soft face and a bright smile as she looked up at me from behind glasses. She introduced herself as the intake clinician, and did so cheerily. With a stack of papers in her hand, she escorted us out of the waiting room and into a large room nearby where she shut the door behind us. My mother and I sat at the long conference table like we were the first people at an important board meeting. The intake clinician sat beside my mother. Beginning with the top page, the intake clinician moved us through the stack with brief explanations of each form. My mom signed page after page. I signed as well, my signature wilting flat as I gave my half-hearted consent to whatever was put in front of me.

Deeper in, the real questions began. Most were directed to my mom, as if I wasn't an expert on my own life. My mom expressed her own concerns and described the ways in which I had changed, and with a hushed voice, she described my encounters with the woman in the window and what led up to my recent hospitalization, my mental breakdown.

Questions and answers continued back and forth.

The clinician asked, "Are there hallucinations?"

"Yes. I think so."

"Are they ongoing?"

"Yes."

"Anything else of concern?"

"Sarah bit her own finger."

"She bit herself? Explain."

"Sarah bit her own finger and told me the woman had done it."

"Did she do it to get attention, or did she actually believe the woman did it?"

"She believed the woman did it."

That's when she asked me, "Sarah, did the woman in the window bite your finger?"

She wasn't going to believe me, but I answered anyway, "Yes. I wouldn't bite my own finger."

The lady nodded to herself and checked a box.

When we were almost done, my mom asked, "Can you tell me if there's a diagnosis?"

"It's hard to say. There is evidence of possible schizophrenia, but because your daughter has only been experiencing these symptoms for two months, I can't jump to any conclusions."

"But it *might* be schizophrenia?" My mother asked.

"Again, I'm not about to make such a conclusive diagnosis just yet."

"But it could be. Eventually."

"If the symptoms continue, yes."

"Okay," my mother said, satisfied.

Schizophrenia. Because how else could everything be explained? With the things I saw. My paranoia. My depression. My declining hygiene. My lack of appetite. My loss of friends. My messy room. My outbursts and the ways in which I had begun failing at life. Not to mention, the woman in the window. The woman in the window. The woman in the window. The woman in the window. The woman in the window. The woman in the window, the woman in the window, the woman in the window. The woman in the window. The woman in the window. The woman in the window. The woman in the window. The woman in the window. The woman in the window. The woman in the window. The woman in the window.

When we finished, the clinician walked us back out to the waiting area where we sat and waited again, this time to meet with the psychiatrist, Dr. Daniel Tariq.

# 22

Dr. Tariq's greeting was both friendly and welcoming. He treated my mother and I as though we had been invited to dine with him at his house and not in the stale lobby of a therapy building. He shook my mother's hand, spoke kindly to her. Then he introduced himself to me. He smiled, and when he did, I was unable to escape those amber eyes. He asked if I would prefer to talk with him alone or if I wanted my mother to join us. I liked that he gave me a choice. I admitted, "I'd like to talk alone."

Dr. Tariq turned to my mother. "We will be back."

"Oh," my mother said. "Okay." And she sat back down.

Dr. Tariq led me down a long hall where sound machines were spaced intermittently along the floor to conceal the confessions being told behind closed doors. I was surprised by how many doors and sound machines there were. Was the world so full of broken people?

Dr. Tariq escorted me inside his office, holding the door open for me. I sat down in a chair off to the side, comfortable enough to be well suited for long conversations. Dr. Tariq sat across from me, rolling his own chair to the side of his desk so that we could see each other fully. His cologne filled the room – subtle hints of honey and spices. He was dressed in a crisp gray suit. A silver watch on his wrist. He had a slender, yet masculine face, clean shaven and smooth, with dark, almost golden skin. His features were handsome, yet he didn't seem vain, and there was an elegance about him that made me think of a prince.

Dr. Tariq began with cordial questions about who I was. My family and my friends and the things I enjoyed. When I told him I enjoyed singing, he sat up straighter, as though he was captivated by such a gift. He smiled often, easily. Led my answers with other questions, gaining a better understanding of who I was. The more we talked, the more I came to realize that to Dr. Tariq, I was not an oddity, I was a person.

At the time when Dr. Tariq diverted the conversation to questions about the woman in the window, his demeanor changed. He became serious and intent. I explained in detail everything I had been going through, beginning with the first night and ending with the music box.

"What does your mother think?" he asked.

I wiped my eyes. "She thinks I'm crazy."

"Are you?"

"No. But no one believes me."

"I believe you."

I turned my eyes to him, hopeful and suspicious. "You do?"

"Does it help if I say such a thing?"

"It helps. To talk to someone and to think they believe you. Yes."

"Does it change anything?"

"No, not really, I guess."

"Tell me, why not?"

At that point, I knew treatment had begun. "It doesn't change that there is a woman who comes through my bedroom window to torment me. Whether it's in my dreams or in reality."

He considered me in silence, touching his fingers together at his chin. "This is true. It changes no such details. And so, I will ask, will talking through your ordeal in therapy or being prescribed medications change any of these facts?"

I pulled in a feeble breath of despair. The last thing I wanted was medications, or even therapy. They would be the final proof that it was all in my head. Proof to everyone but me. "My mom thinks they'll help."

He smirked, a slight upturn at the left corner of his lips. "I did not ask what your *mother* would think. I would like to know what you think." He raised his prescription pad. "Will writing you a prescription change anything pertaining to the woman in the window?"

"No."

"Do you want medications?"

"No."

"And why not?"

"They wouldn't help." I was fidgeting in my seat, biting my nails.

"Sarah," he said.

"Yeah? What?"

"You are safe with me." His voice soothed my nerves enough to continue, and he asked again, "Why won't they help?"

"Because I'm not crazy. Because the woman in the window is real."

"You must be aware, Sarah, that I have numerous patients who are truly mentally ill, plagued by a mind that haunts them. It is heartbreaking. These individuals are truly helped by the medications I prescribe for them. So, how do you know you are different from them?"

"I don't know." I tried to figure out how to explain but couldn't.

"Try."

"Like, I have no idea." I felt like such a teenager.

"Try."

"I just know it's different."

"That is a child's answer."

"Because, like you said, it's in their mind. So, medication can help them, right? But the woman in the window. She's actually done things to me. Like when she bit me. Or when her hair was in my throat."

"Yes. These are your proofs. Both proof of your sanity and of your insanity."

"What do you mean?"

He shook his head, his face resolved, yet gentle. He would give me no more answers. "You tell me what I mean."

My brain felt like it was in gym class doing pushups. "It's proof of my sanity because the woman in the window has actually done those things. But other people would never believe that, so they think I did it to myself, which only makes me look super crazy."

He paused with a grin. "Super-crazy. Yes, I assume that in the eyes of some, such a term might accurately describe you." He winked. "What is it you want, Sarah?"

"Honestly?"

"Always."

"I want the woman in the window to leave me alone. And I don't want to be afraid anymore."

"Yes. Very good. We are finally presented with a choice. You want the witch in the window to leave you alone. And you don't want to be afraid anymore. Which one of these is your choice?"

"Woman," I corrected.

"What?"

"You said *witch*."

"My apologies. The *woman* in the window." He asked again, "Where is your choice?"

I considered the two. "My fear is the choice." Saying those words provided a sudden sensation, as though someone had handed me a key, but I still didn't' know which door it would open.

"Yes. Precisely. Your fear is the choice. You cannot choose away the woman in the window. But you can make a choice with regards to your fear. Despite the horror of this woman, your fear is not necessary, nor does it help." Seeing my obvious reluctance, Dr. Tariq offered, "Yet, choosing to not be afraid can be the most difficult task of all. Sometimes, and for many, it is impossible."

"Easier said than done," I said, even though it wasn't something I ever said.

"Yes. Easier said than done."

"Can you help me?" I asked. "So that I won't be afraid."

"Possibly. First, I have another question. When you are rid of your fear, Sarah, what will you do? The woman will remain in your window and she will remain in your life. So, what action will you take if and when you are able to rid yourself of your fear?"

I looked to his office window where the lush red curtains were drawn open. The far off buildings of the city and the clouds which touched them were doused in the rich colors of the dying sun. Dr. Tariq said, bringing my attention back to him, "Yes. The sun sets. Night will come. Sarah, what will you do when you are rid of your fear?"

"Does it matter?" I asked with sudden resentment.

He remained calm. "More than anything."

"Why?"

"Because the woman remains in your window, and from the way you have described her, she intends to rip you apart whether you are afraid of her or not. Yet fear will inspire the victim in you, stealing away the choice that is yours. But it is not the only choice to make." Dr. Tariq cupped his hands together as though holding something precious before him. My choice. "To remain afraid is to flee away to small rooms and closets where she will eventually find you each time. What you do with the fear, that is your choice."

"It's not that easy."

"I never said it was." Dr. Tariq pinned me with his gaze, seeming to know my thoughts before I did. "Do you believe in God, Sarah?"

It was the oddest question he could have possibly asked. "No. Not really. Do you?"

"More than I believe in my own existence."

"I didn't think psychiatrists were supposed to believe in God."

Dr. Tariq smirked at that. Smirked at me. "Ah, Sarah, do not be fooled by the seat I occupy as a psychiatrist. It is true, this profession entices intelligence, small faith, and even smaller imagination. I am a psychiatrist, yes. Yet, each of us is quite different from one to the next, for we are only human after all. But do not permit the title to fool you. This labor, this practice, is one of subjectivity masked by objectivity, and while we may pretend to have the answers, we are simply men and women ourselves, and at times, we are no better than blind leaders of the blind, as one once said. So, Sarah, I ask again, do you believe in God?"

"I never thought about it much."

"Well then. Whether you do or whether you do not, does not matter. God is neither hindered nor manifested based upon what you believe of him. And so, I will ask another question: What do most men do when Death reaches for them in that moment of reclaiming?"

"I don't know." His questions had become so abstract, I was struggling to follow along.

"Come, now, Sarah, you are very intelligent. I want you to think. Think of the stories where men are before that unhearing and unfeeling keeper of mortality. What do men do when they are on their knees, watching helplessly as their very lives unravel?"

"Beg, I guess."

"They beg," Dr. Tariq confirmed with a smirk, as though he found it amusing. "And *who* do they call out to?"

"God, I guess."

"You guess?"

"Well, I don't know."

"Well then, you don't know. I shall tell you. They call out to God. The same God they never believed in. What is my point? I want you to try something when you find the window rising again. Possibly tonight. I want you to pray. It cannot hurt. If God is not there, then he will not hear you. But if he is. Well, maybe he will answer."

"Are you allowed to talk to me about God?" I asked.

Dr. Tariq chuckled amusedly. "Did I offend you with my beliefs?"

"No. I was just curious."

"Well then, you were curious. Let us say that I prefer to talk of those things I believe in the most. It provokes my sincerity, without which, I am of no help to anyone. Am I allowed? I am not a child. Therefore, I shall talk of whatever I want, so long as I remain sincere in my conviction to help you and others."

"Okay."

"Okay, you guess?"

I smiled. "Okay, I guess."

"I cannot save you with trifle words." Dr. Tariq paused to scribble something. Then he walked to me and handed me a prescription. "I do this for your mother. But it is your choice to take the medication. If you choose not to, I advise you not to tell her. It will only make her nervous, and it would be best for you to assure her of your willingness to listen, especially your willingness to listen to me. By doing so, you will enable your mother to believe that you are returning to the daughter she has always known and raised. That is what she desires the most."

It made me sad to remember. "I know."

"But before you leave, Sarah, remember, your fear is the choice. You are not some senseless creature who must fly off to a nest or burrow beneath the earth when the hunters come. Now, if you do not want to take the medications, but you want to keep your mother appeased –" he opened his mouth and touched the inside of his lip with his tongue, showing me how I might hide my medication.

"Oh," I said. "What's the medication?"

"Trazadone."

"What does it do?"

"It will help you sleep."

It felt as though I were in a deep hole, and Dr. Tariq, instead of reaching his hand down to me, had given me a shovel to dig myself deeper.

He saw my anxiety. "I provide this to you for two reasons. First, sleep can be good for anyone, and it is a start. That is what I will tell your mother."

"The second?"

"It has to do with the choice you have." Dr. Tariq stood beside me and ushered me up from my seat. Our session was done.

Before I stepped out of his office, I asked again, "Do you really believe me?"

"Do I believe your story about the woman in the window?"

"Yes."

"Does it matter?"

Embarrassed, I dropped my eyes to the carpet and our feet. "Yes."

"Sarah, look at me."

I did.

"Do I believe you? Such a vast question. I believe all things, if I might put it so simply. But more than anything, I believe in the darkness. I believe in the darkness and the ways in which it inspires men to obey the perverse cravings that fill their being. I believe in the darkness and the way it births the monsters around us, even men who smile easily, and even your woman in the window. And so, yes, Sarah, in a world as dark as the one we live in, I believe you."

# 23

My mother spent the evening sifting through dusty books filled with collections of family photos, most of which had been stowed away in her bedroom closet. As she flipped through the plastic pages, she removed particular photos, which were then strewn out over the kitchen table like a scattered craft project she was masterminding. By ten o'clock, they were all organized, and my mother called me over, ready to reveal a mystery she had solved.

With me at her side, my mother began by explaining that, according to what she had read, schizophrenia had likely been passed down to me through genetics. She plucked up various photos, rehashing old stories, going back through the generations. Some stories she knew personally, while others had been told to her by other family members. My mother took time pointing out distant relatives who were the possible perpetrators, the ones who may have passed down the same disorder which had hatched inside of me.

There was a great-grandfather who believed the government

had poisoned his well and had isolated himself away from anyone who might turn him, becoming a recluse.

There was a great-aunt who hoarded old namesakes and memorabilia, filling every room in her house with an abundance of useless collections. Her husband, my great-uncle, had left her because of it.

There was a cousin who had committed suicide, hanging himself in the woods. Numerous rumors had spread throughout the town, and most people were convinced that he was a devil worshiper.

Then there was another relative, maybe a distant cousin, who raised five children in a trailer and lived off of food stamps. Her trailer was filthy. Nothing was ever clean. Everyone agreed she was bipolar.

My mother exposed these ghastly tales to me (none of which were very ghastly at all), and as she did, a new family picture was created, one of those dreary sepia ones taken at a circus. There I was, standing between lobster boy and the bearded lady. Because the family tree, it turned out, had a branch colored puke green. And I was its newest shoot.

# 24

We were done by midnight. When I was ready for bed, my mother came into my room after a quiet knock on the door. A small pill was in her palm. She looked nervous. Maybe embarrassed by the new routine. She offered me a fragile smile as though she was sorry for me and sorry for what she had to do because this was as new for her as it was for me, and she wanted me to know she was trying her best.

The pill, which could have been confused for an Aspirin, was popped into my mouth. I drank some water, gave my mother a hug and told her, "Thank you." I loved her still, even if I felt that she was somehow drifting further from me, or I from her.

My mother whispered, "We'll get through this, Sarah. We'll get through this together." She had tears in her eyes.

"I know."

"Goodnight. Sleep well."

"I will. Goodnight."

My mother walked down the hall, and I felt as though she had left me behind in the woods, bundled up in a cap and mittens and forgotten. I glanced at my bedroom window, vacant and ordinary. Then I went into my bathroom and spit the pill into the toilet.

The woman visited that night. A return to normalcy. There was never a choice to be found.

# 25

It was the last night before everything would change. I had resorted to my old ways, holding off sleep for as long as I could. But it had been five days. I was sitting in bed. Blinking. Mind and body tingling. Drifting further away. Losing myself. Losing my will. Sleep swallowed me, even as I told it, "No."

I dreamt of a cat.

Nuzzled to my chest, she purred contentedly. Her fur was soft. Warm. She stood and circled to get more comfortable, and I smiled and shied away as her fur tickled my chin. She finally laid down, making a bed of my body. I began petting her. By then, she no longer purred. She hummed.

The cat began padding at my shirt with her claws. At first, I didn't mind. I even enjoyed it. A cat. Having her with me was such a wonderful change. But she continued to scratch until it hurt. I pressed her to the side, letting her know it was too much, but instead of touching fur, it was human hair.

I looked down. The woman in the window was knelt beside my

bed, her head resting on my chest. She was faced away from me, her wild hair tickling my chin and her finger scratching at my bare belly.

I was about to scream, but the woman said, "Don't."

*It's a dream*, I told myself. *It's a dream! It's a dream!*

But I couldn't wake up. Because it wasn't a dream at all.

The woman turned toward me slowly. She had never been so close. I could feel her breaths on my skin, my lips, my nose. In her eyes was a bizarre appearance of affection, affection for me. It made me sick.

I uttered in dumb horror, "uhuhuhuhuh."

"Shhhhh," she said. She put a finger to my lips. "Shhhhh."

I fell silent.

Content with my obedience, she returned her attention to my belly. I laid there, tears streaming down my face. The ridge of her jaw moved against my bare flesh as she commanded in a single word, "Sing."

My mind went blank, as though I had never heard a song before in my life.

She said again, "Sing."

The only song that came to mind was the song meant for me at the acapella competition. The dryness in my throat ruined my voice so that the words and melody scraped out. I was trembling. But I sang. The woman hummed with me, continuing at my belly.

I spent my thoughts on unspoken prayers, begging and begging throughout the night. A great part of me died during those hours, the last part of me that hoped at all, and I became numb, but for the feeling of her.

The sun began to rise, even though I had been convinced it never would. When it did, the woman stood. She was so tall. Her head was almost to the ceiling as she looked down at me. I looked away, but she turned my face back to her with a finger on my cheek. "Tomorrow," she said.

Then the woman walked to the window, opened it, and left. I stayed in bed, my pillow soaked with the tears I had spilled throughout the night. Scratch marks disfigured the skin of my belly, deep enough to leave ridges that bled in small trickles. A constant throbbing pain. It was the only part of me that had any feeling.

111

*Tomorrow.*

I did not get up that day. I ignored my mother's calls for me to get ready for my first day back at school now that Christmas break was over. I didn't feel like pretending. I was catatonic. When she came home that night, I ignored her then, too. When she told me she would have to make a call to the crisis center and have me assessed, I turned my head away in answer. Only when my mother went to her room for the night did I finally get up. I wanted a shower. I wanted to feel clean.

*Tomorrow.*

The heat burned against my belly. The soap stung. But I wanted it to hurt more, and more, and I soon reopened the parts that had begun to heal. I dried off only after the water became cold. My arms felt so weak, the towel was almost too much to lift.

I swiped away a streak of steam from the mirror. I stared at myself. My eyes were dark and sunken. My cheekbones were bony, hollowed shadows beneath them. My hair had thinned, I noticed, like I was suddenly someone who was elderly. Fear had robbed me of any beauty I'd ever once owned, replacing it with a riddled recreation of meager similarities that barely resembled the girl I had ever been.

*Tomorrow.*

I thought of ways to postpone the dread countdown. But maybe it didn't matter what I did. Maybe nothing mattered. I returned to bed and permitted myself to be swept away by sleep, like an animal dying out in the cold.

Tomorrow had come.

# – Part 2 –

## *Stitch Mouth and Balloon Girl*

# 26

"Hello."

I woke to the tiny call.

My bedroom was quiet and dark. But someone was there. I could feel myself being watched, observed. I permitted my eyes to barely open while pretending to remain asleep, even as I quivered beneath my covers.

"Hello," the greeting came again, gentle in the night.

I hid my breaths as best I could, opening my eyes just enough to glimpse the outline of the corner of my room and whatever or whoever was there. I saw balloons. They were rustling in a bundle near the vent in the ceiling. There were faces on each balloon, I saw. But I didn't want to look at them any longer. I followed the strings, and they me led down to a pinched skeletal fist and bone fingers. My eyes continued up the arm, then to what was there. A skeleton girl stood in the corner, a skeleton wearing a pink dress. The two dark hollow holes she had for eyes appeared to be looking directly at me. I looked away, my heartbeat rising. Beside the skeleton girl stood a second girl. Her skin was purple as a plum, like the color of a deep bruise. Her dress was a lighter shade of purple, with a bordered hem that caught the moonbeams in a white outline glow. Her eyes were red as Christmas bulbs, and they were staring at me as well, wide and round and shiny. The two girls were eerie, yet barely as tall as my dresser, standing side by side as though presenting themselves for some spelling bee for awful ghouls.

Were these two girls the children of the woman in the window, sent to unlock further fears I hadn't even thought possible? Would they drag me away? Would they tie me down here?

I was not prepared for this at all. I wanted to shoo the girls away, scream at them to leave me alone.

The welcome came again. "Hello."

It was the plum colored girl. She was smiling at me. She tilted her head, putting her eyes in line with mine and waved. "We know you're awake, Silly."

Caught in my ploy, I opened my eyes, sat up, and shuffled back, bringing my knees to my chest in a ball of self-protection as I banged against the headboard. I clenched my fists, wrinkling the sheet into clumps. There I sat, staring at them while they stared back at me. In horrified agitation, I asked, "What do you want?"

"To help," she said with a nod.

"Are you going to hurt me? Are you going to take me to the woman in the window?" I was becoming more brazen, like an unruly prisoner in a dark dungeon cell, too tired of the abuse to care.

She looked almost hurt. "Not at all. And never." Her words were muffled, and when I looked, I saw that she had stitches through her lips.

I thought maybe she was going to do the same thing to me, sew my lips together, a peculiar torture the woman in the window sent her to do, and I asked like an accusation, "Why is your mouth sewn shut?" Horrid expectations flew through my mind, and in them all, I could hear my music box screams as I imagined the two girls climbing on top of me, working at my flesh with their tortures. First, my mouth would be sewn shut. The skeleton girl, maybe she was going to flay me alive.

The plum colored girl took a step closer and I screamed. "Don't come near me!"

She bowed her head. "I'm sorry. I was only going to show you the binding of my mouth. And no, I would never do such a thing to you. Or to anyone, I don't think. Well, maybe the witch."

The skeleton girl nodded.

"Then why is it like that?" My voice was shrill with fear.

She plucked at a single thread. "The witch did this to me."

"The witch?"

"Yes. The very same witch who has been haunting you."

"Witch? She's a witch?"

She giggled a little. "What else would she be?"

"I – I don't know."

"Well, she's definitely a witch," she assured.

The skeleton girl nodded along again. She still hadn't said a word.

I pointed a feeble finger at the both of them as if the gesture would keep them there. "You're taking me to her, aren't you? That's why you're here."

"No. We're here to help you, Sarah."

More confused than ever, I asked, "Help me?" I glanced to my bedroom door, ready to dash away. They couldn't possibly be as fast as me with how small they were. And they definitely couldn't be as fast as the woman in the window. My feet twitched. I leaned towards the other side of the bed for a head start.

Raising her hand, the plum colored girl made a request, "Please, don't run. We're not very fast." Then she smiled at the skeleton girl, like there was a joke between them I didn't know.

"Maybe that's what I should do then."

She giggled. "Well, that would look quite silly, of course. You running away. The two of us running after you. And the witch chasing all three of us." She sounded almost cheery, amused. She said, "We're here to help you, so please don't go. That would make everything quite difficult. Stay, just a little longer, please."

I made my terms. "If you stay where you are, I won't run."

"Agreed." She curtsied.

"You said you're here to help me?"

"Yes."

"The two of you?"

She placed her hands on her hips. "Who else, Silly?"

Though she had been speaking with me, I suddenly heard the sound of her small voice, like a musical note, soft and sweet as honeysuckle. But I shook off the gentleness of her voice, thinking maybe it was some kind of hypnotism, part of a trap, and I asked "Why are you standing *there*? That's where the woman always stands."

She looked around the room as though contemplating a hide-and-seek spot. "Well, we knew that if we stood by your bed and woke you, we'd give you quite a fright. But we also knew that if we stood in a place where you couldn't see us, then that probably would scare you, too. And we definitely didn't want to climb into your bed because that would be the scariest option of them all." She tapped her heel to the floor. "So, we stood here, in this corner. Does that make sense?"

It did. Strangely so. And her voice remained sweet with sincerity. "Yes. It does."

"Sarah," she said.

"What?" I pulled the sheets to my chin.

She glanced at the window. "We must begin."

"Begin what?" I asked, looking at the window as well.

"To protect you from the witch. But we must begin soon. Very soon."

I was almost in tears with confusion. "How – how do I know you won't hurt me?"

Her nose scrunched up as she pondered an answer for me. "Sarah, I'm not really sure how to prove it right this moment." She looked to the skeleton girl for an answer and turned back to me. "Yep. We just know we're not going to." They nodded at each other, content with their own answer.

In an act of rude fear, I asked, "Does that skeleton *thing* ever talk?" I was afraid that she could, and was certain that her voice would be that of a demon. She was far more unnerving than the purple girl, silent and staring. I looked at the balloons again, the faces of which seemed alive with thought, blinking at times, and shifting their expressions like a horrid circus trick. But when I asked that question, the faces on the balloons each looked embarrassed, their faces turned downward and eyes closed.

The plum girl corrected sternly, "She's not a *thing*. She's my *friend*. And no, she can't talk."

"Why not?"

"Because she was burned alive, so she doesn't have any lungs, Silly." Despite her horrid comment, the plum girl giggled as though she'd told a joke, while the skeleton girl seemed to blush, tucking her skull chin to her bone chest.

"Burned alive," I said as though it made sense. "Was it the woman in the window who burned her?" It felt as though I had a thousand puzzle pieces, and I had possibly connected the first two.

"Yes. Of course." She fiddled at her stitched lips. "The very same witch who did this to me."

"I don't understand. And you're here to protect me? Protect me from the woman in the window?"

"Yes."

"But you're just little girls."

She nodded her agreement. "We are. And we are not what you would desire. We are both –" she paused, looking over the both of them "– not what we used to be. Really, we're quite scary looking." She laughed a little. "But this is not what we asked for. Just as you never asked for the witch to haunt you either."

"The woman. She made you that way?"

"Yes."

"And you're here to protect me?" I had such little faith in anything good, but a part of me wanted to believe.

"Yes. I promise, Sarah. With all my heart." She pointed to her chest, then said gently, "Sarah?"

"What?"

"We must be quick, but may I ask *you* a few questions now?

That startled me. "Um. Sure. I guess."

She smiled, those red eyes bright and gleaming with some strange affection for me. "Sarah, if the witch has entered your life, bringing her world to your own, is it so hard to believe that there might be two girls like us who want to protect you?"

"No. I guess not."

"And if the witch wants to get you, then the two of us can't really make things that much worse, can we?"

"No."

"And when you first saw the witch, did you have any doubt that she was terrible and awful and gross?"

That was an easy one. "No. Not at all."

118

"Sarah, if we did want to hurt you, which we definitely don't, well, something bad was going to happen to you anyway, right? So, again, we can't really make things that much worse."

I thought about it. "That does make sense in a weird way."

She bobbed to her toes. "Well, we're kind of weird, so maybe it's perfect."

"I guess," I said, though I sort of liked everything about what she'd said.

She then commented in a very serious tone, "Sarah, the witch wants you. She wants to eat you. Sorry, I know that's terrible, but it's the truth. But we're here because we are going to protect you. And it's what we want to do more than anything."

I wiped my eyes with my sleeves. "But *why?*"

"Why do we want to help you?"

"Yes." I took a deep breath to keep composed, stifling my desire to give up and fall away.

"Well. The witch killed us years ago, and quite simply, we want to stop her from hurting you. We don't like her very much."

She glanced at the window again, as though she'd heard something. Subtle clues of anxiety tightened her purple face. The balloon faces turned towards the window as well.

"She's coming, isn't she?"

"Sarah," the plum colored girl said, "Look at me."

I tried, but couldn't.

Her voice remained kind. She snapped her fingers. "Sarah. Look at me. Sarah. Sarah."

I turned.

"Thank you." She smiled. "Yes. She is coming. But that's okay. It is time for us to begin the first step in proving our promise to you. But Sarah. Sarah, look at me again. In order for us to help you, you must give us names."

"What?"

"Our names were removed from us when we died. So, you must give us new names, for in naming us, you give us the ability to stand."

"But you're standing already."

She smiled. "Yes, I am quite aware. I was speaking symbolically. You must name us, because it will provide us our gifts." Before I could utter any other thoughtless questions, she said, "Sarah, you need to name us and you need to name us right now."

The skeleton girl pointed at the window with a bone finger.

"What, what should I name you?"

"Whatever you please." Approaching steps could be heard along the leaves outside my window. "Sarah, soon."

Fear gave words to my lips as I blurted out, "Stitch Mouth. And Balloon Girl."

"Stitch Mouth and Balloon Girl!" Stitch Mouth was almost giddy, and she clapped her hands twice. "Perfect names! Because that's what we are, of course!" She curtsied and Balloon Girl did too. "I love our new names, Sarah. Thank you."

"Um. You're welcome."

Opening a small purse, Stitch Mouth declared, "And now for our tricks."

I didn't know what to expect. A gun seemed unlikely. A knife, maybe. Maybe some ancient relic decorated with hieroglyphics which would glow with mystical power. Instead, she pulled out a black piece of chalk.

Stitch Mouth turned to the window and waved mockingly at the unseen witch, instantly becoming the bravest person I'd ever known. I could hear twigs snapping and crunching steps and a shriek of rage. Stitch Mouth stretched to her toes, reaching the chalk high. Then she colored the window in wide strokes until it was covered black from top to bottom. She crushed the chalk against the wall, startling me, and my bedroom window simply disappeared, as if becoming part of the darkness itself. Stitch Mouth gave the blackened window an approving nod and proclaimed, "Done!" while brushing her hands free of the dust.

"What'd you do?" I asked.

"I hid us from the witch. She won't be able to find us now."

"But she was just there."

"She was."

I continued to stare at the window, ready for it to open or shatter to pieces. "How do you know it worked? All you did was scribble over the window."

"It's what I do, Silly."

Any encouragement that may have been mine to enjoy disappeared, just like the window. "I don't understand."

Stitch Mouth shook her purse, causing things to toss around inside. Then she tilted the opening towards me to display different colored chalk inside. "These are my tricks. My gifts. Each colored chalk lets me do something a little different." She looked at the window again. "The witch won't be able to find the window, so she won't be able to find us. She's going to be *so* mad."

"But she was just there." I shied away to the opposite side of my bed, just in case the witch did find the window.

"Yep, which will only make her angrier." She giggled and Balloon Girl appeared to giggle with her, a bone fist to her mouth.

"She won't find us?" I asked.

"No. She can't. The window is gone. She's probably looking all over the place right now. I bet she's even clawing at the air." She mimicked a haggard expression that may have been on the witch's face, swatting around blindly before she couldn't hold it together anymore and burst into a fit of giggles. Balloon Girl touched Stitch Mouth's arm and seemed to say something, and then the both of them laughed.

"What?" I asked, not sharing their amusement.

"Balloon Girl said she hopes the witch trips over a root and breaks her head."

"Oh."

Balloon Girl then mimed this, holding her skull as though she'd cracked it, but stopped when I wasn't entertained. The balloon faces seemed strangely embarrassed.

Stitch Mouth then said, "Sarah, I know we're not pretty anymore. I know we're even a little scary. But that's okay. The witch is the one who's actually scary. Also, I am sure you have many more questions and are in need of many more assurances. Those will come with time. Tonight, you need rest."

"Not a chance," I stated.

"You need to."

"I'm not tired," I lied.

"You must."

There was no way I was falling asleep with two creepy girls standing sentry nearby. My window may have been colored over. Stitch Mouth may have promised the woman couldn't find the window. But maybe they were only pretending to help. Maybe they were actually helping the woman in the window by building false trust, like the soft mouth of a Venus flytrap. Or maybe they wanted me for themselves. Maybe I was some prize to capture in a world of darkened misfits I had only barely begun to glimpse.

Stitch Mouth seemed to hear my every thought. "It's okay, Sarah. You are safe with us. I promise. With all my heart."

"But how do I know?" I asked desperately.

Stitch Mouth seemed upset that she wasn't able to convey what she wanted to. "I'm really not sure. For now, all I have is our promise and the proof I have provided in hiding you this night. You need sleep, Sarah. You will want the best of you from now on."

"Why?"

Balloon Girl seemed to say something to Stitch Mouth. Stitch Mouth then said, "Very true, my friend. Let's not talk of such things just yet."

"Why not?"

"It is not the time. Now is the time for sleep."

"I don't want to sleep."

"I know." She seemed sorry for me.

With nothing else said, Stitch Mouth took hold of Balloon Girl's hand. Then she began to sing a hushed song. The melody was innocent, like a lullaby sung from a rocking chair, sweet and tender. I blinked heavily. The song continued. I laid down. Still blinking.

The last thing I heard was a whisper, "Goodnight, Sarah. You don't have to be alone anymore." And in that night of moonbeams and promises, I fell asleep.

# 27

I slept as though I had never slept before. My night had gone unmolested. The witch never came as she promised. A different promise had been kept.

I woke, blinking against the vibrant sun which was beaming like an overly eager visitor I wasn't quite ready for. My body felt like it had sunk two feet into the mattress. My limbs were heavy with the tingling remnants of hibernation. Instead of tears, my pillow was soaked with drool. I checked the bedside clock. It was 2:30 in the afternoon.

I flopped my legs over the side of the bed, peeling myself up from the mattress. I stretched my arms. Stretched my legs. My loud yawn was like some proclamation of victory. I shook my head in disbelief. When had I ever slept so well?

I stood on wobbling legs, stumbling towards the window, teetering side to side. I had to catch myself at my dresser to take a moment and regain control of my body as bubbles popped in my vision. I stopped at the window. There wasn't the faintest trace of black chalk. The surface was clear. Through it, I saw the vibrant crystalline colors of winter. Our neighbor was scraping his windshield. His son shivering beside him. Frozen bushes and frozen grass. A bird cut across my vision, and I followed it as long as I could.

I met my mother downstairs in the kitchen. She was sitting at the table with a cup of coffee and a book. She smiled at me. "Sleep well?" she asked. It was always the first question of the day, her first test to gain an idea of my mental and emotional state.

"I did," I answered, and for once, it wasn't a lie.

"Well, you're lucky it's Saturday or I would have had to wake you for school," she scolded in a harmless, motherly way.

I closed my eyes and grinned. "Saturday."

"Yes, Sarah. Saturday."

"I love Saturdays."

My mother smiled. "What's gotten into you?"

"Nothing's gotten into me. I just slept well." I stretched, then rubbed my eyes once more before plopping myself down into the chair beside my mother. I said, "Last night felt like the first night's sleep in months."

"No woman?" she asked, another test.

"No woman." I couldn't tell if she believed me.

"Well, I'm glad to hear you slept well. Dr. Tariq said sleep is healthy for you. That's why I let you sleep in so late. My goodness, though, it's almost 3:00." She continued to inspect me, maybe searching for any sign that my curved horns and leathery wings had fallen off, or hadn't.

"Yep," I acknowledged with a grin.

My stomach growled. My mother slid a corner section of homemade coffee cake to me on a thin paper plate. It looked like the tastiest thing I'd ever seen, and I ate it gladly and closed my eyes at how delicious it was. My mother smiled and offered me another section, a piece with even more brown sugar crumble topping. I ate that, too. "My goodness, someone's hungry," she said.

"I kind of wish we had cinnamon rolls. The kind Dad used to make. That would be perfect."

"Well, you'll have to tell him next time you talk to him."

"That won't be anytime too soon."

My mother didn't say anything, simply accepted his absence as a fact of life.

Coffee cake crumbles scattered to my lap as I said, "I feel like I haven't eaten in weeks. I was looking at myself in the mirror the other day. I looked terrible!"

"You're still beautiful, Sarah."

"You don't have to say that."

"You're right, I don't. But it's true. Anyway, you should eat more often. I feel terrible for all the food I throw away lately, all of the leftovers that go bad because I still make meals for the both of us, but then I'm the only one who eats."

"Yep." The sugar soon made me jittery, almost giddy. I wanted to go outside. Maybe run around or something. I wanted to smile. I wanted to laugh. And sing.

"I was reading something yesterday about treatment –"

I raised my hand as though I was in the middle of something super important. "I'm still hungry."

She laughed a little. "Okay, sure. There's some fresh grapefruit in the bottom drawer of the fridge, oh, and some baby carrots and hummus on the top shelf. I know you like those."

"Yes, I do," I said comically.

"Though that's certainly quite the breakfast."

"Yep, but I'm making up for all the meals I've missed," I said from the fridge.

"Enjoy, then."

"I will."

I scanned through the refrigerator, bending down to take in the full view. Everything looked amazing. I returned to the table, carrying in my curled arms a bowl and a spoon, a grapefruit, a bag of cherries, carrots, hummus, Greek yogurt, and a plastic container of blueberries that was just below half-full. I began with the grapefruit, ripe and perfect. It made my hands sticky. When I finished, I licked at the tart juice at my lips while peeling open the yogurt.

After I set aside the empty yogurt and blueberry package, my mother asked, "Done?"

"Not quite."

"You don't mind if I begin, do you?" My mother had her

computer on the kitchen table with websites opened up to show me the research she had read.

I pointed the yogurt-tipped spoon at her. "Go ahead."

After a smile I hadn't seen in a long time, my mother filled the next hour with summaries of research articles she'd been reading regarding the most up to date findings on schizophrenia, all of them giving her hope – so I should have hope, too. I nodded a lot, sometimes offering agreement or a shared contemplation. She continued to highlight the research conclusions and advice from psychologists, like new constellations in space, intended to guide me. I wanted to remind her *you know, mom, no one said I actually had schizophrenia.* Instead, I just munched on carrots dipped in hummus, getting very full.

When she finished, my mother said, "I just want you to know that I'm here, and I'll do everything I can for you."

I loved the way she said those words. "I know, Mom."

She closed the computer. "Well, I'll leave you to your good mood and your food."

I held her arm. "Don't go. Hang out with me for a little bit."

"While you eat everything in the kitchen? I may need to go to the store so we have something to eat for tonight."

"Yep, you should go now," I teased. But then I said, "No, just kidding. I want you to stay. With me. You can keep looking up articles or whatever."

"Sure. Okay. I'd like that. But let's talk about something else."

"That'd be wonderful."

"Well, guess what?"

"What?"

"I applied for a new job."

"Really?" I was excited for her.

"Yes. It's for a paralegal position at a new law firm. Well, actually, they've been around for a while, but one of the lawyers recently left the firm and has started his own and is hiring immediately. It would provide benefits and would pay enough so I wouldn't have to work two jobs anymore. Oh, and I'd get two weeks of vacation and two weeks of sick leave per year."

"I love it already," I said.

"Really?"

"Of course."

"I could be here for you more, you know, for when your symptoms get worse." She quickly apologized, "Oh, I'm sorry. I'm just saying. Schizophrenia doesn't get better usually and I'm just saying I'm committed to being here for you."

I lifted my eyes again, trying not to sulk. "I know, Mom. Anyway, tell me more about the job. I'm sure you've researched every last detail about it already."

She smiled. "You know me too well." Then she went on to talk about all the details of the position, as well as everything she'd found out about her potential boss by stalking him on social media. His name. *Galen.* His family. *Wife and children.* His background. *Farmer,* which surprised her and me. As she talked, I began to gaze out of through the kitchen window to where the sun had begun its downward arch. Remnant fears returned. But not in the same potent way in which they had commanded every nerve in my body each and every second of the past months. That is not to say the fear was gone. Not at all. But I was less afraid. Just a little. Like being buried up to your mouth in mud, but then someone does something nice by shoveling some away so you can breathe easier. It felt good.

Through every following second of that day, I thought of those two girls. My macabre protectors. Stitch Mouth and Balloon Girl, in their eerie dresses, their bodies showing the obvious evidence of their deaths, and I had named them. But how could I possibly put my hope in them?

Yet, I did. At least, had begun to. And that hope was growing, increased by how good I felt from sleeping, and the realization, the sensation, of someone actually helping me.

"What are you thinking about?" my mother asked, interrupting those thoughts.

"Oh. Nothing. Just stuff."

"Are you thinking about that woman?"

"No. Not at all," I said.

"Oh, okay. Good." Then she said, "You're so enjoyable today."

"That's good, isn't it?"

"Yes, but *why?*"

I didn't know how to answer. "I don't really know."

"Tell me," she said.

I patted her hand. "Mom, is it so hard to believe that I'm simply enjoying spending time with you?"

My touch and my words seemed to assure her. "No, I guess not," she said. "It's just, strange, is all."

Could I tell her? Could I give my mother a tiny hint? Not a chance.

*"Funny you should ask, Mom. I know I'm acting different. It's totally obvious. And I know my answer of a good night's rest is feeble as all get out. So, are you ready? I'll tell you. The reason I feel better is because, yeah, sure, I slept great and all last night. And it definitely helped. But do you know why I slept better? I bet you think it's because the woman in the window didn't come? Good guess, and you're right. And I'm SO glad you finally believe me by saying that. But I slept great because there were two young girls standing in the corner of my room. Oh, yes, I was definitely freaked out at first. I still am a little. Anyway, listen. I think they probably came through the window, just like the woman did. I agree, it seems likely. So, anyway, one of them was a skeleton. She was wearing a pink dress and holding balloons. Yep, the balloons had faces on them. How'd you know? I guess it does make perfect sense. And the other girl, she had purple skin, so dark it was almost black, and her mouth was sewn shut. Yeah, the woman in the window did it to her. And the skeleton girl was burned alive by the woman. I don't know. Maybe I'll ask them. But wait! They called her a 'witch.' Weird, right? A witch. Agreed, weird. Well, we talked for a while and it turns out they were sent to protect me. I know, super cool. And then, of course, the girl with the purple skin, I named her Stitch Mouth, she colored my window black so the woman in the window couldn't find me. Did it work? Yeah! The woman never came just like Stitch Mouth promised. What color was the chalk? Black. From her purse. Yeah, she has lots of other chalk. No, you don't have to worry, the window isn't stained. I checked when I woke up this morning. I'm positive, it's clear now. You can check if you want, Mom. Yep. But then, I still didn't trust them, I mean, they're kind of ugly, but cute at the same time, but the woman in the window has taught me not to trust anything. But then, Stitch Mouth, she sang this beautiful song that calmed me and before I knew it, I woke up this afternoon. They'd kept me safe, just like they promised. And so, they were sent to protect me. Isn't that, like, the greatest? So, anything new with you?"*

No. My mom could never know.

I may have rested well that night, sure, and felt better because of it. And both Stitch Mouth and Balloon Girl could have made a thousand promises each and it wouldn't have gained an ounce of my trust. But one promise had been kept, kept as told. Not only that, it was the song of Stitch Mouth that truly lifted me that day, and I hummed it like new medicine. It was beautiful. It was innocent. And it gave me assurance that they meant what they said, a promise upon a promise that had not been broken. Humming the song, I let myself believe in the possibility that everything was over, simple as that. The chalk had been used. The song had been sung. The woman in the window would never return.

I believed those things.

# 28

"Sarah."

I woke to the small whispering of my name. My clock blinked at me in glowing red numbers *11:59*, the eternal time of my dream-like world. The two girls stood in the corner of my room. Stitch Mouth had her hands clasped together near her waist and was rocking slightly, as though anxious about giving a presentation. Balloon girl, well, she was just being Balloon Girl, but the faces on the balloons were avoiding me, looking up at me just a moment before looking down again.

"You're back," I said. I had forgotten just how scary the girls truly looked. But I was also thankful for a second night in a row that began with them and not the woman in the window.

Stitch Mouth asked guardedly, "Do we look so terrible? When you first sat up and saw us, I could tell we frightened you."

I released the sheets from my hands. I had been clutching them. "Yeah, but no. I mean, you're definitely – I mean – I don't know how to say it." I didn't want to hurt their feelings.

"Go ahead," Stitch Mouth offered.

"Well, you're definitely freaky."

She smirked sadly. "We are. Even if we don't want to be."

"But that's okay," I assured.

"Is it?"

"Yeah. I mean. It's just something I can't quite explain, I guess. I mean, you may look like you do, but I'm still glad you're here."

"Are you sure?"

"Compared to waking up to the woman in the window, I'd have to say having you in my room is a million times better. But it's not just that – there's something else too."

"What else is it?" The bob of Stitch Mouth's hair tilted with her head.

"Your song. The one from last night. It was as if – as if nothing evil could have a voice like yours or sing such a song. I sang it all day."

"You liked it?" She was happy.

"Very much. It may be the most beautiful thing I've ever heard."

"Oh, I doubt that."

"No, really. It was beautiful."

"So, you don't mind if we help?"

"No." I shook my head in absolute confirmation. "Not at all."

Stitch Mouth thought about something. "But Sarah, you say you enjoyed my song, that nothing evil could have sung it, but what of the Sirens?" she asked.

"Those Greek things?"

"Yes. How do you know we are not like them, enticing you towards death with angelic voices?"

"Oh. Well. I guess you could be. But I don't think so."

"Why not?"

My words touched along. "Well, the Sirens never did anything to help anyone, but you helped me last night. And according to the myth, they were beautiful, right? And, well, you know."

"Yes. We are certainly not that." Stitch Mouth winked, and Balloon Girl nodded. The faces on the balloons were looking at me again, curious about who I was, as though trying to figure out if *I* could be trusted.

I continued my logic, validating my growing belief. "The song you sang last night, it was different than anything I've ever heard. And even though you colored the window to hide me, it was your voice that made me believe you were here to help me. I slept the best I ever had. It felt like I was safe."

Stitch Mouth bowed, then asked, "Are you ready?"

"For what?"

"For the night to begin."

"Oh, like, for you to hide the window again?"

"No. I can't. Not until I must. Are you ready to begin? Are you ready to change everything?"

I didn't budge. If anything, I stiffened. "Wait, but what about the window? I thought the woman couldn't find us. Remember, you colored it black with your magic chalk." Despite the window being right there for everyone to see, I still wanted to believe that the woman's entrance into my life had been closed off forever.

"It's not *magic*, Silly, and it only works for one night. That's the rule. It's only a trick."

"A trick?"

"Yep."

"Then do it again."

Stitch Mouth paused. Considered me. "As much as I would like to, I cannot."

"Why not?"

"I only have a limited amount of chalk. And you are not ready."

"Ready for what?"

"You are not ready," she said again. Balloon Girl shook her head, validating Stitch Mouth's claim.

I assured, "I'm ready," having no idea what she was even talking about, but hoping my response would make her do something else with her magic chalk.

"I don't want to say this, Sarah, but you are not ready. Not yet."

"Well, if you're here to help me, why can't you just make the woman go away with your bag of chalk or something so that she never finds me again?" I sat up higher. "I thought you were going to keep her away. I thought she wasn't coming back."

"I'm sorry, Sarah, I am. But she's far too powerful to be defeated by simple chalk, no matter how powerful my gifts, our gifts, might be."

I took a deep breath, accepting what she said. "I know," I

acknowledged. "I just, I guess, I was just hoping it was done. I thought maybe you hid me and it would all be over. But I guess I really knew this wouldn't be over so easily."

"It never is," Stitch Mouth said. "But the witch is coming. Her time has begun. Tonight, we run." Stitch Mouth turned and focused her gaze through the window, pinching her red eyes together, as though peering through a telescope. "Yes. She's getting closer. We must go."

"But —"

"There will be time for questions, Sarah." She waved, beckoning me over. "Come. We must go."

I climbed out of bed. "I've never been through anything like this before," I admitted.

"Neither have we," Stitch Mouth stated lightheartedly.

The three of us went to my bedroom door. Balloon Girl remained a step behind, oriented towards the window, like a final guard, with her balloons drifting at the ceiling.

"Where are we going?" I asked. I thought maybe we'd be running downstairs and out through the front door.

Stitch Mouth answered while sifting through her purse, "Somewhere else." Her purse matched the red bow in her hair, as if being color coordinated mattered even if you were dead or undead or whatever she was. As I watched her, something changed in an instant. Stitch Mouth suddenly appeared to be a little girl, as though a layer of her morbid appearance had disappeared and beneath was a sincere and thoughtful young girl I could see. It disappeared again.

Balloon Girl backed into me. Reflexively, I edged away from her, not wanting to touch her scrawny bones. I said to Stitch Mouth, "But the woman always finds me when I run."

Stitch Mouth smiled and held my hand, and while I expected her touch to be cold as a corpse, it was surprisingly warm. She said, "That's why we're not going to *her* places." Then she colored the knob of my bedroom door green. "No more questions for now, Sarah. We must go." And with that, I heard my window slam open. There was a grunt. An irritable huff. The woman was coming through, and she was not happy.

Stitch Mouth pulled the door open and we all went through, entering a place that was no longer my home.

# 29

We were in a black hall. More like a rectangular box. The walls were tight. Stitch Mouth quickly sketched doors on the three walls ahead of us, and we went through one, entering into another box that was very similar, maybe exactly the same. She did the same thing again, three more doors. We went through a different door than the last time and entered a box again. Stitch Mouth did so again. Another box. Three more doors. Again. In the last box, Stitch Mouth colored four doors, all of them purple except for the last, which she created with a different chalk altogether, still purple, but a darker shade than the others, all of which had glowed like neon signs, while this one was dull. This last door was so dark it was almost invisible. That was the door she opened.

We were bathed in cold. My breaths came and went in quick bursts that told my growing fear as Balloon Girl shut the door silently behind us. Then the door changed. It was no longer a black door with purple edges, it was wooden and weather worn. I touched it, as if testing whether or not it was real at all, and felt splinters. Then I peered through a split in the door that was just wide enough to see through and on the other side was a path and a forest, and I had no idea where we were. We were in a house with a low wooden ceiling. There were windows with wooden shudders. Cobwebs were in every crevice. There was a cobblestone fireplace. Four chairs were set in a semi-circle around it. A stack of books was nearby, the top book covered in dust.

Stitch Mouth waved from a door inside the home. "This way."

"Where does this door take us?" I asked, wondering what magical place we'd travel to next.

She smirked. "My bedroom."

Balloon Girl shut the door behind us again. I was still gasping, unable to control my lungs or nerves. As we stood there, I began to realize the dismal simplicity of what we were doing. We were running. Running through doors and rooms to escape. I had been doing that on my own for months. And now, here I was, running again, only this time with two girls with legs far shorter than mine. Despite the magical chalk and the multi-colored neon doors, the woman in the window was still somewhere behind us. A spasm of fear shook me. I wanted to keep running, to get further ahead. Run away from this house. Away from the woman. Away from the girls.

A small hand touched me, luring me out of my thoughts. Stitch Mouth said with quiet assurance, "You'll be okay. I promise."

"But she's coming."

"I know."

"But we stopped."

"I know."

Bending over a rug in the center of the small room, Stitch Mouth called Balloon Girl to her. "Come help me."

Balloon Girl pinched at the edge of the rug. The balloons strung from her other hand looked down in focused concentration. Balloon Girl raised the rug as high as she could, giving Stitch Mouth enough space to sketch a yellow door onto the floor. When the door was finished, Stitch Mouth touched the center of it with the tip of the chalk, and the outline transformed into carved edges. It looked as though a real door had been there the entire time.

Someone could be heard in the house. The woman had found us. The cold was eating at me, making me more vulnerable to my growing fear, and I clasped my arms around my body. I could hear the woman getting closer as she searched through other rooms, clanging and clanking. But the house was small. She would find us soon.

Stitch Mouth yanked the door up and palmed the air, waving for me to go first. I clambered down, lowering myself into something like a cellar. Stitch Mouth followed, her hand at the bend of my back as we hunched our way into darkness. Balloon Girl came last. Down a few steps, she turned to reset the rug over the door as best she could, sliding her hand through the tiny gap just before shutting it completely. Balloon Girl remained near the stairs, her skull head upturned and waiting. The balloons curved back behind her, tossing silently along the ceiling.

I shuffled as far from the steps as I could. Stitch Mouth came to my side.

"What now?" I asked.

"We wait."

"Why?"

"Because," Stitch Mouth whispered.

"Because what?"

Stitch Mouth slid her hand into mine and squeezed. "It's okay."

With a slow creak, the bedroom door above us opened. The woman in the window went slowly, tiptoeing across the length of the room. She could sense how close we were. The boards of the floor bent and groaned with the weight of her quiet steps. My gaze remained focused on the tiny gaps between each plank of wood, following the woman's shadow. It passed over us, darkening the meager light that had been ours. The woman came to a stop on the rug. She began sniffing the air, just as she had in my dream. I almost let out a whimper, but Stitch Mouth squeezed my hand.

The woman took another step, moving towards the closet. She hissed in irritation as a board squealed beneath her. When she opened the closet door, the hinges let out a rusted creak, giving her away again, and the woman shrieked in rage. Giving up her attempts to remain silent, the woman erupted into a furious tantrum, destroying everything in the room. Clothes were shredded. Furniture flipped. The drawers of the dressers flung throughout the room.

Beneath the racket, I asked, "Are you going to kill her now?"

I was hoping for, *Yes, Sarah, of course. Balloon Girl and I are going to march up those stairs and get rid of that icky woman in the window for good. Be back in a jiffy.*

Instead, Stitch Mouth asked, horribly confused, "The witch?"

I bent to her ear. "Yeah, are you?"

"No, Silly."

"Why not?"

"We are not permitted to. We only have our tricks." She patted her purse as a reminder. "Now, shush."

Then there was silence. The minutes passed. The silence throbbed.

I couldn't take it anymore. "What's she doing?"

Stitch Mouth winced. Balloon Girl shivered at the stairs.

Slim paths of light burst through the cracks of the door as the woman flung the rug aside. The door was ripped open. There, the woman stood.

Stitch Mouth rummaged through her purse for another chalk. Pulling one out, she scratched out a door onto the wall directly behind us while I simply stared at the woman in terror, knowing there wasn't enough time for another door. I had been caught. We had all been caught.

Balloon Girl's ghostly bones stood bravely between the woman and me, even as the shadow of the witch stretched out over her. Balloon Girl touched the tip of a single string to the step behind her, releasing a balloon. In a swirl of pink glitter, the balloon spun and spun until transforming into a real-life girl. She was wearing a pink dress. She faced me a moment. Her blue eyes sparkled. Balloon Girl pointed the girl towards the steps. Nodding, the girl raced up. The woman was crouching her way down to us when the new girl lunged upward, tackling the woman back out of the hole. The woman cried out in fury, and as she struggled to get back up, the girl grabbed one of the woman's legs, heaving it further out. But the woman grabbed the girl by the arm and stood to her feet, lifting the girl into the air. But the girl didn't care. She swatted at the woman with small fists, and when the woman buckled over after getting kicked in the stomach, the girl kicked the woman in the face and laughed. The woman grunted and spit blood, then began choking the girl in the air, and I looked away.

Balloon Girl came near and pushed me through the newest door.

I could hear the dying sounds of the girl as she was murdered by the witch, and despite wanting to go back and help her, I didn't. We scurried to the end of a narrow hallway where Stitch Mouth sketched four more doors and we repeated again our earlier retreat.

# 30

We scuttled along dark passageways of Stitch Mouth's making, door after door after door. I thought we would spend the night doing so until we suddenly returned to the small bedroom where we had been earlier. I was shocked to be there.

I said, "What? Why?"

Shredded clothes had been flung in all directions. A wooden shutter dangled from the single window of the room at a broken angle. The four drawers of the flipped over dresser had been scattered to different parts of the room. The bed had been flipped over as well.

Balloon Girl remained near the door. The knobs of her knees were knocking and her arms were shaking. I thought she had been hurt or that her own fear had finally caught up to her. But when I looked towards the balloon faces, they were all smiling. Some even laughing.

Plucking sweaty strands of hair from my face, I asked, "What's so funny?"

Stitch Mouth answered, "Balloon Girl is laughing because we came back here."

"Why is that so funny?"

Stitch Mouth remained as composed as she could, trying not to lose herself in her own fit of laughter. "Balloon Girl thinks it's funny –" but she couldn't finish. The sound of her laughter was almost better than her song.

"Okay." I chuckled a little too, unable to resist. "And why does *she* think it's funny?"

Stitch Mouth stood upright in an attempt to stiffen away the humor. "No, Sarah."

"'No,' what?" I asked.

"I want you to tell me why Balloon Girl finds it funny."

Balloon Girl pointed at Stitch Mouth.

"Yes, yes," Stitch Mouth corrected, "I thought it was funny, too."

I answered, "I don't know she thinks it's funny. I'm not a mind reader."

"You don't have to be a mind reader, Silly. You just have to use your brain."

Stitch Mouth led me over to her toppled bedframe where she sat on the wooden edge. I sat beside her, still thinking over her question. After giving it some thought and considering the giggle fit I had witnessed, I answered, "Balloon Girl was laughing because you tricked the woman."

"Yes," Stitch Mouth said, sounding quite happy with me. "The witch didn't think we'd come back here. So, that is precisely what we did."

I finished the punchline, "And all the other doors have been leading the woman in other directions."

"Yes."

"That was smart."

"Thank you," she said graciously.

And it was. Yet it was so simple. "But how'd she find us, back when we first came here?"

"Well, my doors are only possibilities, so, if she chooses correctly, then she finds us."

"Oh."

Stitch Mouth patted my shoulder. "It might be a little

disappointing, but it is the limitation of my tricks. And the witch is no fool, even if we want her to be."

"So, why don't we just keep doing that?"

"What? Creating doors?"

"Yes."

"Good thinking, Sarah, maybe the witch would just give up." But when Stitch Mouth realized I was being serious, she said, "Oh, you weren't joking."

"Nope."

"The witch wouldn't just stop, Sarah."

"Why not?"

"It's just not what she does."

"That's what I figured. I guess, I was just hoping, you know."

"There's nothing wrong with that. Balloon Girl and I used to hope and wish many things."

"Do you know what I would have done if I had magic chalk like you?" I asked as I sketched out imaginary doors in the air with an invisible chalk. "If I had chalk like you, I would have drawn a single door to run through. Then drawn another door to run through. Then another."

Stitch Mouth stretched her hand through my invisible doors. "Leaving an easy path for the witch to follow."

"A very easy path," I said. I was even more thankful for the two girls than before. "I'm sorry, you know, for whispering down there." I pointed at the rug.

"Don't be," Stitch Mouth assured. "You were afraid, and that's okay. We all do dumb things when we're afraid."

Balloon Girl nodded.

"Yeah, but that's the problem. I'm always afraid."

"That is untrue, Sarah. You weren't afraid earlier today, were you, when you awoke for the day?"

"No, I wasn't as afraid. And the first thing I thought of was you and Balloon Girl – not the woman."

"And you weren't afraid tonight when Balloon Girl and I returned to the corner of your room. Not like the previous night."

"Sure, but that doesn't make me Super-Woman."

"*Super Woman?*"

"Yeah, sorry. Never mind. I don't know why I even said that, it's not like I even read comic books or anything."

*"Comic books?"*

"They're sort of like books with pictures."

"I love books with pictures!" Stitch Mouth exclaimed and Balloon Girl clapped, which sounded like dry twigs snapping. Balloon Girl must have said something, because Stitch Mouth said to her, "I miss them as well."

"I could probably find some for you to read," I offered.

"Oh, I would love that very much! Comic books?"

"Yep."

"Wonder Woman?"

"Yep. She's a woman with super powers who fights bad guys or super-villains or whatever. She has a lasso, I think."

"Oh, I like her already. But enough of that for now." Stitch Mouth then asked, "Sarah, what did you learn tonight?"

"You mean about the woman in the window?"

"Of course. Or anything else that comes to mind."

I was being quizzed, and I could tell how much it mattered to Stitch Mouth that I have an answer. "Okay. What did I learn? Well, I used to think the woman in the window could always see me. But tonight, she couldn't see us when we were down there."

Stitch Mouth gave a purple smile. "Yes. The witch can only see what her eyes show her, and in that way, she is no different than you or I or Balloon Girl. Except Balloon Girl doesn't have eyes like us, of course." Balloon Girl nodded, pointing at a single empty socket. I turned away again.

"What else?" Stitch Mouth asked.

I was still in awe of the bravery of the balloon girl who had fought against the witch. Thinking back to her, I answered, "The woman can be hurt."

"Yes. Good," Stitch Mouth said, like it was the most important point of all. "And if the witch can be hurt, what else do we know?"

"If she can be hurt –" I hesitated before saying "– she can be killed."

"Yes."

I didn't want to talk about that, so I hurried along, "The woman can get angry."

Stitch Mouth rolled her eyes. "Yes. But we all knew that."

"I'm not sure I did," I said. "With me, she was almost emotionless."

Stitch Mouth nodded. "Yes. I understand. There was no reason for the witch to be angry, because all you did was run, which she enjoyed. But I promise you, Balloon Girl and I have witnessed the witch's anger, and she can become super angry."

"You said, '*super.*' Like I say."

"I hope you don't mind. I like it."

"Of course I don't mind."

"Okay, good. Is there anything else you learned?"

I lowered my head, unable to look at them in that moment. "I learned that you really are here to help me. And your tricks are pretty great."

"They're super great. And, yes we are here for you. Do you believe me?"

"Yes."

Red tears suddenly came to the eyes of Stitch Mouth. I couldn't tell if they were red themselves, or clear, pulling from the color of her eyes. "Good," she said.

"Why are you crying?" I asked.

"I don't know." She smirked. "I just know that it makes me happy to hear you say that." Stitch Mouth then turned her attention to Balloon Girl. "I'm sorry. About the balloon you used. She was beautiful. Beautiful as you."

Balloon Girl pointed at her skeletal face where the nose holes and gum-less teeth remained gruesome, then she shook her head and said words which Stitch Mouth alone was able to hear.

Stitch Mouth corrected, "No. That is not what I said. I did not mean beautiful as you *used* to be. I meant beautiful as you are."

Girl pointed at her bone chest to where her heart might have been.

"I know," Stitch Mouth offered.

I said to Balloon Girl, forcing myself to look at her, "Thank you for using your balloon. I know you had to because I messed up."

Balloon Girl nodded.

"You said earlier that this was your room."

"It is."

"Who built it? This house?"

"My father."

"Your father?" I asked. "Like. You have a dad?"

She smiled. "Of course. I *had* a dad. I even had a mother, if

143

you'll believe it. As well as a brother." She stopped to look at something.

"Will you tell me about them?"

"I don't think so." She could see my disappointment. "Not tonight."

I changed the subject for her, kicking at some clutter. "The woman destroyed your room tonight."

"Yes. But call her a witch, Sarah."

"Why?"

"It is important for you to remember what she is."

"Okay. Well, the *witch* destroyed your room."

"That is quite obvious."

I chuckled, then yawned.

Stitch Mouth stood from the bed and began settling out the room. She asked me to stand, then she and Balloon Girl managed to return the bed to its four legs. "Sarah, I would like you to rest."

"That's very tempting," I admitted.

"Good." Stitch Mouth shook a sheet out a few times before letting it glide flat to the mattress.

"In here? In your room?"

"We are safe here tonight, so it is the best place."

I climbed in, tucking my body tight within the tiny bed. A blanket was laid over me by Balloon Girl. "Thank you," I said.

The room darkened. Only the outline of Balloon Girl's ghostly bones and the red eyes of Stitch Mouth could be seen. Stitch Mouth sang delicately, and the song was as sweet as before.

I soon fell asleep, crying softly. I didn't cry for sadness or despair. I cried because I had hope, and when I woke in the morning, I was in my own bed. I woke, feeling better than before, and lived my day.

# 31

I was sitting on my bed. Stitch Mouth sat beside me. Balloon Girl stood near the door. A single motion passing across the surface of the window caught my attention at the corner of my eye. "She's watching us," I said, doing my best not to burst up from the bed.

"I know. Pretend we're talking about something."

"Like what?" My heart jumped. "I just saw her again."

"It's okay. Just talk about something. And don't look directly at the window, Silly."

"I can't help it."

"Balloon Girl is watching for us and she is more than capable. We are okay. Talk about something, Sarah."

"Can I talk about how crazy it is what we're doing?"

"Sure," Stitch Mouth said, giggling.

"Okay, well, here we are. Sitting in my room. With the witch watching us from the window. When we should be miles ahead of her. I'm very scared. And it feels like I'm on a roller coaster."

"Ooooh, what's that?"

I tried to think of how to relay the idea of a roller coaster. I still wasn't quite sure what time they were from, and they weren't quite sure either. "Well, it would be like sitting in a horse carriage – you had those, right?"

"Of course. And I know what cars are, if that would be better."

"Okay, perfect. So, a roller coaster is like being in a car that's on a train track, but the train track is on super high hills. You sit in the car, strapped in, while the roller coaster clicks its way up. The first hill is always the biggest. You sit there, going higher and higher. A part of you wants to get off. But you can't. You watch as the peak gets closer and closer. *Click, clack, click, clack.* You get to the very top –" I raised my hand steadily above my head, then launched it towards the floor "– then the car flies down the hill."

Stitch Mouth clapped as she bobbed up and down beside me. "That sounds like so much fun!"

I laughed, feeling miserable inside. The witch could be heard working as quietly as she could at the window, thinking we were oblivious to her being at our backs.

Stitch Mouth asked, "So, if this is like a roller coaster, what part of the ride are we on?"

"Close to the top, I think. Why are we doing this again?"

"To show the witch we are not afraid."

"But we are afraid."

"The witch doesn't have to know."

"I'm sweating."

"Me too!" Stitch Mouth bounced a single time with excitement.

"She's still trying to open the window."

"I know that, Silly."

"I don't think I can do this."

Stitch Mouth patted my hand, the she held it. "Of course you can. We're afraid. But we're doing it too."

"But you're crazy," I said, smiling.

"Crazier than you know." She winked. "And you're crazy too!"

"Everyone at school thinks so."

"See?"

"Why is she taking so long?" I wanted more than anything to glance back at the window, but Stitch Mouth widened her red eyes at me in warning.

"Who cares why she's taking so long? She's a witch."

"I love when you talk about her like that."

"Why?"

"I just do."

"Let's start laughing," Stitch Mouth said.

"Why?"

"Because it will make the witch angry."

"That's the last thing I want to do."

As if on cue, Balloon girl presented herself before us. Her jaw sagged and she brought her fingers down in front of her face to symbolize hair – like charades – she was acting like the witch. She took the longest strides she could, passing back and forth like an angry drill sergeant. Balloon Girl then acted out the witch dying in a bunch of ways. She used hanging motions, stabbing motions, choking motions, and falling motions.

We laughed. It wasn't that funny, but it was funny enough.

The window was opening.

"She's opening the window," I said through my teeth.

Stitch Mouth said through her own, "I know,"

Cool air came in.

"Wait for it. 1-2-3. Go!"

Balloon Girl flicked the lights off. We dashed through the darkened room, running to our own assigned doors. In the light, the doors Stitch Mouth had drawn couldn't be seen. But in the darkness, the room was decorated in sketched doors every which way, like dizzying neon colored wall paper from a fun house at the fair. Stitch Mouth had given each of us a color to follow, and as long as we followed that color, we would all meet up together at the end. I went through my doors, colored yellow canary. I went through one after the other through the black boxes where doors of different glowed on four walls. Stitch Mouth had created such an intricate path of varied possibilities for me to follow, there were times I had to stop to make sure I was choosing the right shade of yellow. I pressed on, flying along. My lungs burned. In the scurrying, I became aware of how alone I was, hoping, hoping, my path would end as it was supposed to in reunification with Stitch Mouth and Balloon Girl. Yellow doors. Left, left, left, right, down, down, right, left, right, left, down, down, left, down, right, left –

then – suddenly, I stepped out into a vast open room and skidded to a halt.

I looked around. They weren't there, not yet. I felt vulnerable. I began to pace, keeping my eyes on the single yellow door we were all supposed to come through. In my growing panic, I wondered if something had happened to one of them, maybe both of them. The seconds ticked by, feeling like heavy hopeless minutes. I imagined the witch stepping through the yellow door, bending down and rising again with a smile of wicked victory. I began biting my nails. I couldn't take it anymore. I went to open the door again but it burst open. Balloon Girl dashed through. She turned, closed the door, and a second later, Stitch Mouth was next.

My hands dropped to my knees in relief. All the nerves hit me in sudden exhaustion. I felt like I was going to be sick.

"Are you okay?" Stitch Mouth asked with concern.

"Yeah, just a little overwhelmed, I think."

"Pretty fun, right?"

"Not at all."

"Maybe a little."

"Nope."

When the floor stopped spinning around my feet, I looked up. The yellow door was gone. There was only a white wall. A high white wall. It seemed strangely familiar.

"Where are we?" I asked.

Stitch Mouth stretched her arms out wide in presentation. "We have come to the home of Balloon Girl!"

"Really?" I asked with subtle thrill.

"Yes!"

Balloon Girl was saying something to Stitch Mouth. Stitch Mouth shook her head. "Yes, yes. We are *finally* here. *Finally*! I'm so sorry it took me *sooooo* long."

Balloon Girl nodded in acceptance of Stitch Mouth's apology.

"You can be quite intolerable, you know," Stitch Mouth said.

Balloon Girl nodded again. Then she stepped away from us in small measured steps, as though unsure of what to think of the floor at her bone feet. She walked out a little further. Stopping in the center of the vast open room, the ceiling high above us in white rafters, Balloon Girl gazed around in awe. She straightened to the tips of her toes and began to twirl, circling the room like a ballerina. Her motions were surprisingly graceful, trained and precise, and as she danced, the balloon strings intertwined from her fist like a braid. Balloon Girl then turned and pinched the tips of her dress to offer a curtsy to Stitch Mouth who smiled and curtsied in return. Then she was off again, skipping and dancing, waving her skeletal arms up and down in sync with the pitter patter of her feet.

Looking around, it didn't take long to realize how Balloon Girl's house was a stark contrast to Stitch Mouth's in every way. Rich versus poor. The house was made of long beams and large windows which sparkled with crystal moon glow. White-cushioned chairs stationed in a large sitting area. Couches looked just as comfortable, with tassels at the bottom. Furniture with golden knobs. A dining table with a golden chandelier hanging above. There was a mirror in which I could see the three of us in our varied proportions. A bizarre group. Such peculiar friends.

A realization struck me. I turned towards the opposite end of the home and saw a spiral staircase. "I've been here!"

# 32

Balloon Girl froze in mid-pose.

Stitch Mouth asked, "What?"

"I've been here," I said again. "The table. The chandelier. The spiral stair case. Only, when I was here, it was different. Everything was plastic. The entire house was made of white painted plastic. And there was no front door." I turned and pointed to the same exact spot we had come through, now just a white wall. "Right there, right in that spot on the wall, something was written. It said *there was a hole here.*" I walked beyond the girls as they watched and listened. "And the home. It was just like this. Almost exactly the same. But again, it wasn't the same at all." I stopped at the spiral staircase, frightened to take a step, as though doing so would resurrect my nightmare.

Stitch Mouth came over to me. "That home was only the representation of how the witch remembered this place."

"But why was it all plastic?"

Stitch Mouth guessed with a pleasant chuckle, "Because the

witch has a super bad imagination."

"So, this is Balloon Girl's house, as Balloon Girl remembers it, but not the witch?"

"Yes. We have changed her world with our return."

Balloon Girl placed a hand on Stitch Mouth's shoulder and asked a question. Stitch Mouth responded, "Of course." She interlaced her fingers with Balloon Girl's and helped her climb the spiral stairs. Balloon Girl's stiff bone legs permitted little bend. I followed behind the two of them with my hand on Balloon Girl's back to support her.

Standing at the opening to the hallway, even more details were different than they had been in my dream. A long carpet stretched the length of the hallway, patterned with golden swirls. Intricate lanterns hung from the ceiling. There were numerous doors on either side of the hall, but not half as many as had been in my dream where the doors were countless and the hall was endless. I was grateful to see there was no music box.

Balloon Girl guided us to the other end of the hall and pressed the last door wide. In the center of the room, against the wall, was a king-sized bed covered over by a white silken canopy, and at each side of the bed were tables. A large dresser six drawers wide and six high was positioned at the wall opposite the bed, and Balloon Girl went to it. Reaching over the tall edge, Balloon Girl grabbed for a picture, though it took her a few attempts to secure a grip at the frame. She held the picture for a while, gazing at it. Then she returned to us and handed the picture to me.

The image was faded. Black and white. Three people stood together in front of two front doors of a home – this home. A tall, dark haired man, with a cane in one hand, smiled beneath a thick mustache. Wrapped in his arm was a woman in a white dress. Stunning. Fair. Her eyes were piercing, warm, with deep affection for the man beside her and the girl who stood between them. The girl. Her beauty and blond hair had been passed down to her by her mother, a hint of mischief in her smile. With one hand, she touched the wrist of her mother, and with the other she pinched at the coat of her father. She looked ready to skip away.

I said, "That's you."

Balloon Girl nodded.

"Those are your parents."

Balloon Girl touched the faces of her parents in the picture.

"I'm sorry." I could already sense the tragic story that would be told and I suppressed the coming sadness by handing the picture back. Balloon Girl pinned it to her chest, swaying back and forth. Then she went to the dresser and returned the picture to where it had been.

Back in the hallway, I closed the door behind us, preserving the memories inside. We went into Balloon Girl's bedroom, which in my dream had been the room full of boxes. I glanced towards the stairs before entering, expecting *tatatatatat.* We went inside and Balloon Girl went to her closet, sifting through countless dresses with her back to us. I felt she wanted to be alone.

Stitch Mouth and I slid to the floor, sitting side by side. "What happened to Balloon Girl and her family?"

Stitch Mouth's red eyes revealed Balloon Girl in a curved reflection as Balloon Girl remained at the closet, and for a second, Stitch Mouth didn't answer. Content to watch her friend. She said, "Before being abducted by the witch, Balloon Girl and I had known each other, just barely. Our families were very different, as I'm sure you've already been able to tell. My family was poor. Balloon Girl and her family were wealthy. My father and mother had warned me about playing with the naughty, frolicking, golden-haired girl who was so often in trouble in town." Stitch Mouth laughed a moment. "The witch was a nanny here."

"What? Where?"

"In this home."

"Here?" I pointed at the floor.

"In the original home, yes."

"But how?" I couldn't imagine it. "She's so awful."

"She's awful now because she's allowed to be. Back then, she was beautiful and kind, smart and charming. What better way to make people think you care about children than to care for them?"

My expression soured even further. "That's disgusting."

"How did she become a nanny?"

"You see, the witch was always *motherly.* She could cook and sew. She could teach lessons. She could sing and play piano. However, it didn't take long before the witch began to show her true nature. One day, Balloon Girl caught the witch stealing letters from her parent's bedroom, letters her father had written to her mother. When Balloon Girl told her father, and he found the hidden letters, he sent the witch away."

"They didn't go after her?"

"There was no reason to."

"What happened next?"

"After a year or so, she began taking children. I was the first."

"Why you?"

"My family and I lived in the woods, so it was easy for the witch to watch and wait. She stole me from the edge of the forest and took me to her home." Stitch Mouth continued before I could ask more. "And other children were brought as well. She had a large bedroom for us to share, with eight beds, but I was alone for weeks before she brought another child. Back when it was only me in the house, I had no idea how to be or what the witch wanted. I learned quickly though. If I cried for my family or said I wanted to go home, I was beaten. If I refused to do something, I was beaten. If I was caught sneaking towards the door – or if the witch even thought I was thinking about sneaking towards the door – well, you get the idea."

"How long was it before another child was brought in?"

"I'm not sure. But the witch had a very specific child she was intent upon having."

"Balloon Girl," I said.

"Yes. I was in the room, locked away as usual while she was gone, when I heard scuffling. When the witch finally opened the door, she was covered in sweat and her hair was all over the place, having been wrenched and pulled at. That's when I saw the naughty golden-haired girl from town. Balloon Girl was dragged inside, kicking and biting, until the witch flung her to a corner." Stitch Mouth smiled, watching her friend. "The witch left us in the darkness of the room, locking the door. Balloon Girl and I introduced ourselves, then whispered together for a while. Then Balloon Girl stood, *I'm bored, I want to do something,* she said. *Like what?* I asked. *I want to dance.* I couldn't fathom such an idea. *You want to dance? Here?* I asked. *Of course. And you'll sing for me while I dance,* she said. *But what if the witch hears us?* I asked. *I want her to hear,* Balloon Girl said. I was more shocked than ever. *Why?* I asked. *I want her to know we're not scared,* she said. *But we were just crying a second ago about how scared we were,* I reminded. *So? She doesn't have to know that.* And so, that's just what we did. I sang and clapped for Balloon Girl as she danced and twirled. The witch came in. *What are you doing?* she screamed. Balloon Girl kept spinning between the beds and she simply stated, *I'm dancing and she's singing.* The witch beat us and sent us to bed. Lying there, Balloon Girl laughed in pain. *Why are you laughing?* I asked. *She was going to beat us anyway, but at least we got to forget where we were for a little bit,* she said. I was in awe of her. It was the first night I didn't cry myself to sleep."

"Did you do that a lot? Sing and dance?" I asked, unable to imagine ever being so bold.

"No." Stitch Mouth chuckled. "We could only take so much. But the witch would sometimes leave for days to hunt for children. Then we would sing and dance."

"When she brought more children, did the other children ever sing and dance with you?"

"No. Some didn't like that we did it at all. If it wasn't for Balloon Girl, I would have been just like them." Stitch Mouth then said, "Enough of old stories. You should rest." I wanted to know more, but knew she was done.

I placed a kiss on her cheek.

She turned to me, smiled, then had to look away for reasons I didn't understand.

# 33

It was the following night. Stitch Mouth kept us moving through a world of doors. A couple of times, I thought I had a sense of our next door, but picked wrong. Stitch Mouth would smile and pull me back. "This way, Silly." And once, she used a yellow and orange swirl patterned chalk, and the in-between room did just that – swirled – so that we had to shuffle on our hands and knees to stay on the ground.

We stepped suddenly into Stitch Mouth's bedroom. I looked around. Everything was perfectly restored. "What happened?" I asked.

Stitch Mouth had three chalk pinned between her fingers. She returned them to her purse. "What do you mean?"

"Your room is back to normal. But the witch destroyed it."

"Look closer. My room is back to normal because I cleaned it." She looked at Balloon Girl, listening to her. "Yes, yes, you helped, too."

"Oh," I said. "I just thought –"

Stitch Mouth smiled, brushing her hands of chalk. "There were no elves or magical forest creatures who came to help us."

I smiled. "Do you think we lost her?"

"Let's just say that I gave the witch enough doors to confuse her for the rest of the night."

Balloon Girl made a twirling motion with her finger.

Stitch Mouth seemed to agree. "That chalk is my favorite!"

Looking over the room again, I no longer had the same dire dread of the witch appearing in the door like I normally did. I said, "I like your room."

Stitch Mouth came up beside me. "Thank you. It is small."

"Perfect for you."

"Yep!"

I sat beside her on the bed while Balloon Girl remained near the door, prepared to block the witch.

"Will you tell me about your father and your family?" Stitch Mouth had been telling me more and more. But I was insatiable, eager to know everything she'd tell me, both about herself and about Balloon Girl.

"I would love to." Stitch Mouth's body relaxed, her eyes fixed themselves onto the far corner. Stitch Mouth opened her imprisoned mouth and her voice softened. "My father was large. He had broad shoulders. I loved to sit on them and bounce with his steps. His hands were strong – calloused and rough." Stitch Mouth observed her own hands, as though imagining them in comparison to her father's.

"You don't have to tell me if you don't want to."

"I'm okay." Stitch Mouth closed her eyes as a small smile rose between her stitches. Her eyes stayed closed. "This house is the only one my father ever built, though he could have built many more. When I asked him why, he told me it was only in him to build one. I told him *we wouldn't have to be so poor if you built houses*, but my father said *some things are worth more than riches*. I was in his arms when told tell me that. I could smell the woods on him. Soil and sawdust and sweat. I loved those smells." Stitch Mouth reached down for her doll, unconcerned with how mangled it was. "This doll was my mother's, though it became mine when I was born. I carried it everywhere. Often, in the evenings, after a day of chores and gardening, my mother would bathe me, scrubbing me from head to toe while talking about all things that were on her mind. While I lay in bed at night, she would run her fingers through my hair and sing to me until I fell asleep."

"Is that where you got your voice? From your mother?"

"Yes. If I had my father's voice, well, you may not like to hear me sing at all." She smiled. "My brother couldn't sing either. He had such a terrible voice, croaking along like a bullfrog. I told him once *your voice is so ugly.* My mother corrected me and said *his voice is just fine. I love listening to him sing.* I made sure to tell him later that mother was lying to him, but he said *you're just jealous because I sing better than you.* He was so annoying. Every morning, he would wake me up, tugging my arm. By afternoon, his curly hair would be matted to his forehead and dirt streaks would be up and down his face thick enough to make you think he'd painted them on. Once – I was very upset with him – he had taken my doll, this doll, and buried her in the garden. I couldn't find her for days. And when I did find my doll, it took forever to clean her of all the smears and the grit in her hair. I was so angry with him. I told my mother and father *I wish I had a sister.* I'd never seen my father so stern, and he said, *go to your room until you're ready to come out and act like someone who loves her brother.* I said *that's what it'll be – acting!* They were very upset with me. And that night, when my brother woke with nightmares and came to my bed, I pushed him away and told him to go back to his own room." Stitch Mouth's voice broke. "My brother –" Stitch Mouth stood. She wiped her eyes.

I watched as Stitch Mouth walked across the room. "Wait – where are you going?"

"Please don't follow me." She blew Balloon Girl a kiss, then shut the door as she left.

I remained on the bed, stuck in shock. I could hear Stitch Mouth open another door in the house and shut it again.

"Why did she leave?" I asked Balloon Girl.

Balloon Girl mouthed silent words, then simply shook her head.

"Did I upset her? Should we go make sure she's okay?"

I could easily recognize the simple unspoken word. *No.*

I fidgeted on the bed, hoping more than anything that I hadn't somehow ruined anything between Stitch Mouth and me.

"Is she going to be okay?" I asked.

Balloon Girl nodded.

The room remained cold in sadness and silence. After a while, I said, "I'm sorry. I'm sure it hurts. Coming back."

Balloon Girl looked at me, then nodded one last time.

# 34

I woke in my own bed. I wanted to see Stitch Mouth, just to make sure she was okay. I had school that day. Despite wanting to stay home, I had to go because going to school was my way of proving to my mother that I was making an active and concerted effort to control my schizophrenia, which I didn't even have.

When I walked through the front doors of the school and into a huddle of other students, I instantly transformed into my typical invalid self, uninterested in schoolwork or class participation or the drama buzzing throughout the hall. I spent most of the day doodling in my notebook. Pages filled with sketches. A forest and a small house. A garden and a pile of split wood. I couldn't draw very well, or at least, not the best, but I drew various interactions between Stitch Mouth and her family. Her dad cutting wood. Her mom gardening or singing. Her brother running around or sneaking off with her doll. Stitch Mouth nearby.

"Sarah. Sarah."

I looked up. I wasn't quite sure which class I was in. By the tone of the teachers' voice, I wondered if I had accidentally gone to the wrong class, which wouldn't have been the first time. I asked, "Yes?"

With a hint of sarcasm, Mr. Cahoon asked, "Is everything okay back there, Sarah?"

"Yep." I didn't like Mr. Cahoon very much. He was one of the few teachers who never seemed to notice how I had changed, probably because he was too busy helping the girls between classes. The prettier the girl, the more motivated he was to help them. Weird, right?

"You seem quite absorbed in your notes. Is there anything you need clarification on based on the information I've been providing?" He was leaning back casually against his desk, staring at me through his fancy Armani glasses.

"Nope. I'm fine." I slid my arms over my notebook.

"You don't have any questions?"

"Nope."

"So, the things I have been saying have been helpful to you?"

"Yep."

"Are you sure?"

I was missing something, but I didn't know what. The class was muffling their chuckles throughout the awkward banter between myself and Mr. Cahoon. I was used to the sniggers. They followed me everywhere I went anyway – I was like a hippo carrying around those little birds, birds that were always laughing.

I wanted to be left alone, but I didn't want to talk back and upset Mr. Cahoon. If I did, he'd probably do the teacher thing and take the notebook from me. I didn't want that. I didn't want him or anyone in class to know anything about Stitch Mouth, even if they would have no idea about the little girl in the sketches. But they didn't have that right. They didn't have the right to know about Stitch Mouth or her family at all.

Mr. Cahoon probed, "So, why are you so focused upon your notebook? I don't think I've seen you *this* interested in class since the semester began. Well, Sarah, for your information, I have been explaining to the class why I am wearing the same exact outfit I was wearing yesterday. Some of the students were quite attentive to the fact that my pants and tie were the same."

"Oh. Why is that?" I hoped my question would return Mr.

Cahooon to his favorite topic – himself.

It worked. "Well, as I already explained, I was locked out of my house last night. But being that I live off a teacher's salary, I was unwilling to pay for a locksmith at 2:00am. So, I slept in my car. When I woke up, I found that my phone had died. With nowhere else to go and being unable to call anyone, I simply came to school in order to call a locksmith from here. And since I was already in the building, I decided to stay and teach."

"Why were you coming home at 2?" I asked.

Mr. Cahoon's face went suddenly red. "That is my business, Sarah. And not yours."

"Sorry."

My question sparked others. Students began to ask Mr. Cahoon why he was out so late, filling the room with predictions, which included bars and strip clubs and midgets and drugs. Mr. Cahoon got so upset, he sent two of the boys to the principal's office and warned the rest of the class that anyone bold enough to make any more accusations would face a similar fate. After that, Mr. Cahoon actually started teaching.

I returned to doodling.

I drew the inside of the house. Stitch Mouth's father and brother sat near the fireplace. Her mother stood near, singing, and at her side was a small girl with no stitches and no purple skin. A girl with her family.

As I drew, I wished more and more that the witch had never taken Stitch Mouth. That she would have been content to leave them alone. But then I realized something. Something that revealed an uglier part of me. If my wish came true, Stitch Mouth never would have returned to help me. I didn't know how to feel about the selfish and desperate desires that rose up so quickly inside of me. It was a battle between two wants, and I couldn't exactly say which one I wanted to win out. I wanted Stitch Mouth to have never been taken. But I wanted her with me, needed her with me. I placed the pencil down and closed the notebook for the day.

# 35

With a piece of black chalk, Stitch Mouth outlined a broad circle on the white marble floor. "This circle represents the real world." She tapped the center. "In it, you have your house and your school and all the real things in your life." She drew another circle, separate from the first. "There is also a dream world, which is represented by this second circle. But it does not consist only of dreams. You see, regular dreams, the common ones you dream most nights, happen in the real world, the first circle. And they're just, you know, dreams." Stitch Mouth scratched her head with the chalk. "This is kind of hard to explain."

"No, you're doing good," I said. "This is helping. So, that second circle is only a dream world?" I asked, encouraging her along.

"Yes." She tapped the two circles separately. "Real world. Dream world." She continued to point the chalk at the second circle. "Dream world. This is where everything in your dream feels real. Your home feels like your home. Your body feels like your body. This is where the witch does most of her haunting before coming into your real world, the first circle. It is where she prepares children before taking them by making them afraid, so afraid they go crazy or want to give up."

"I know the feeling. I did both."

"They all do." She continued, "The dream world is where you dreamt of the witch in the most vivid of ways. But here, in the dream world, she does not have power to actually hurt you. Just to haunt. Does that make sense?"

"So far, I think. So, when the witch was eating my bedding, that was in the dream world." During the past few nights, Stitch Mouth had forced me to tell them everything I could remember about every single time the witch had made an appearance in my life.

"Yes. Exactly."

"So the witch can go to both worlds?"

"Yes."

"And right now, we're in the dream world?"

"No," she answered, smirking at my instant frustration. "If we were in the dream world, it would more than likely mean that only one of us were dreaming. For three of us to gather together in the dream world would take a lot of luck. It is a confusing place."

Balloon Girl interrupted by pointing at Stitch Mouth and then at me.

Stitch Mouth laughed. "That's true! If one of us is dreaming, that means we have dreamt Balloon Girl into a ghastly skeleton girl."

There was a pause. Balloon Girl was saying something else.

Stitch Mouth responded, "Yes, we know you would never dream *yourself* into a skeleton girl. You would *never* do such a thing. I'm sure you would dream yourself into the *fairest* girl in *all* the *land*!" Stitch Mouth said dramatically as she teased, then said to Balloon Girl, "We're very afraid."

"What did she say?" I asked.

"She threatened me and then said, *you're darn right I'd be the fairest girl in the land.*"

Stitch Mouth giggled. She then drew a third circle, which connected the first two, forming an interlacing sliver of space between. "This is the third world. It is where we are now. It is the world of the witch. It is very real, yet can feel very much like a dream. The witch lives here, and it permits her to travel between the other two worlds. It is how she comes into your deepest dreams. It is how she comes through your bedroom window, bringing her world to yours and your world to hers."

"Weird." It was the smartest thing I could think of to say.

She smirked. "Yes. Weird." She tapped the third circle. "We have been permitted to be in her world, and to manipulate it with our tricks. We have also changed some of this place, this third circle, with our memories of how things once were. *Weird*, right?"

I smiled. "Very weird. Super weird. Okay, so why can't we just stay in the real world and not let the witch take me into her creepy gross world?"

Stitch Mouth looked disappointed.

"That was pretty stupid, wasn't it?"

"Maybe a little. But tell me why it wouldn't work."

"Well, we know the witch isn't going to just give up. Plus, she has the ability to go between all three worlds. So, she'd have a lot of ways of getting to me."

"Yes. Her ability to inhabit all three worlds is *her* trick."

"So, what is this place?" I asked. "Like, what is this third world or whatever?" I felt like every science and every history book had been lying to me.

"Some of that remains a mystery to me. It began as a small place. But it has grown over time."

"How?"

"With each child taken, this world expands to include the world of that child. It is built from their reality, their first circle."

"That's terrible! So, the witch can find other kids easier each time because she can go further out into the first circle."

"Yes." In the center of the middle circle, Stitch Mouth sketched out a house and thin trees, and I knew it was a place we hadn't been to, and by the crooked look of it, I knew it was the home of the witch. Finished, Stitch Mouth put the chalk away and zipped her purse.

I looked over the three circles again, going over the new details in my mind. After a moment of attempting to sort everything out, I said, "Everything is more confusing than ever. How'd she get to be able to do any of this anyway?"

"You mean travel between the three circles?"

"Yeah."

"Well, answering that would only make it all much more confusing."

"Tell me."

"Not long before the witch killed us, a man with golden eyes visited her at the home. He made a deal with her. He said this world, the one you and I are in now, was his. He was willing to let her make her home here, where she could never be found."

"What do you mean a man with golden eyes?"

"Eyes pure gold. He was very scary."

"You were right. This is getting more and more confusing."

Stitch Mouth chuckled. "You'll understand soon enough."

"I don't think I want to. I just want it to be over."

"Yes." Stitch Mouth looked to Balloon Girl. "We have wanted that for a long time."

"Why can't we just trap the witch somewhere?"

"I'm sorry, Sarah, but that answer remains the same – the witch always finds a way."

"I wish you didn't always say that."

"Me too."

We stood from the floor and began walking towards the couches to sit. Seeing Balloon Girl remain by herself at the door, Stitch Mouth called out, "Come with us, you silly stubborn girl!"

Balloon Girl barely glanced back.

Stitch Mouth said, "Yes, I'm sure it's safer with you standing there, but I don't want to be in the same room with you, yet feel like you're so far away. Oh, stop that nonsense and come here. Oh, you stubborn girl!" Stitch Mouth rolled her eyes in aggravation. "Balloon Girl thinks we don't want her to spend time with us."

"Of course we do," I said.

"See!" Stitch Mouth said to Balloon Girl. "Now, stop being you and come over here. What does that mean? Well, you are certainly the most stubborn girl I've ever met in all my life. Yes, I am very aware that I grew up in the woods and didn't know many people. Come here!"

It was my fault. For all the ways I had shown my apprehension toward Balloon Girl – all of which had disappeared – I had made her think I preferred her at a distance. I asked, "Will you come sit with us?"

"See, she wants you to."

"Please?" I asked again.

Balloon Girl waddled over. We sat together.

"When you left the room last night, after talking about your family, I was worried you were upset with me," I said.

Stitch Mouth shook her head. "I wasn't upset with you, Sarah. It was just too much for me. It hurts to remember. That's all."

"You wouldn't be back here if it wasn't for me," I said.

The thought had never crossed her mind, I realized. "Nonsense, Sarah. We are here because we want to be."

Balloon girl slapped her hardened palms together, gaining our attention with the loud noise. Then Balloon Girl dragged her index finger across her throat.

"No," Stitch Mouth said to her.

"What?" I asked.

"It's nothing:"

"You can tell me."

Balloon Girl slapped her hands again, almost angrily, mouthing words.

"What did Balloon Girl say?"

"She said I *cannot sugar coat everything all the time*. That I have to remind you about the true reason we are here."

There was no confusion. "I have to kill the witch," I said.

"Yes."

"And if I don't."

Lifting her chin to expose her bone spine, Balloon Girl traced her finger across her throat one last time. I didn't know if she was referring to the witch, or to us.

# 36

Our greetings were becoming shorter each night.

"We have to go. She is close."

Nails scraped frantically at my window. I glanced behind. The witch was there. Her eyes widened at the sight of me. We escaped through the door, even as the breeze from the opened window brushed our heels.

But while we had spent a few nights in relative peace, something changed. The witch picked the correct door twice in a row. Then she picked the correct door again. Stitch Mouth barely had opportunity to sketch a new escape for us before the witch could be heard opening the door we'd just come through. We dashed along, racing through single countless doors thrown against the black walls until two full pieces of chalk eventually crumbled to nothing, and still, the witch remained just a couple of doors behind. A pink door opened to light. Stitch Mouth and I darted through. Balloon Girl remained behind in the in-between room to ensure the door stayed closed on the witch. *Bang!* Balloon Girl ricocheted against the door, her bone heels dug in, holding the witch back as best as she could. The witch shrieked, banging again and again.

We spent the night running.

# 37

Dr. Tariq's gaze was as stunning as I remembered. I was in his office, divulging everything I could about Stitch Mouth and Balloon Girl, rambling along in a convoluted mixture of stories which included things the three of us had done together, along with stories of their pasts.

"Sarah," he interrupted.

"Yes?"

"Will you look up, please?"

I did.

"There. Now we may speak together." He was smiling, with no hint of amusement or condescension. "I want you to continue. In fact, I shall say very little. But I wanted to make an observation."

"What's that?"

"At our first introduction, you were someone who appeared to be hopeless. I may have even described you as someone who was *doomed*, or at least as someone who considered herself to be." He waved a hand over me. "There is stark evidence of change."

"That's good, right?"

He smirked. "It is wonderful. Now, continue with the story of your friends, your beloved Stitch Mouth and Balloon Girl. I want to hear the rest. But I want to hear about the time your friends spent in the house of the witch, long before they ever came to you."

"Why do you want to know about that?"

His countenance dissolved into something severe. "Because you have focused on all the wonder of your two friends. But you have purposefully left out the parts that are necessary for me to know."

"Um, yeah, sure. Okay." My gaze lowered again to a spot in the carpet. The room seemed to darken. Shadows at my shoulders. "Stitch Mouth was taken first. She was walking near the forest, kicking pine cones after an argument with her brother and her mother. The witch called to her from a tree, promised her a basket filled with food for her family, then grabbed and took her when Stitch Mouth got too close. Balloon Girl was taken next. The witch brought more children. She was trying to create a family. Every night before bed, one child was chosen to brush her long hair while all the children were forced to sing."

"The witch chose those children for the same reason she chose you. For your voice."

It was a puzzle piece I had added weeks ago. "Yes. At first, the witch just wanted the children to *love* her and to pretend that they were a family." I looked up to see how Dr. Tariq would respond to this, but he appeared neither intrigued nor surprised. "But one night, there was a boy. He wouldn't stop crying because he wanted his *real* mom. The witch shushed him, but he wouldn't stop, so she led the boy downstairs after telling everyone to go to sleep. Stitch Mouth could still hear the boy crying. Then the crying stopped. He never came back. Stitch Mouth told me that's when the witch really changed. That's when other children went missing."

"The children with the most gifted voices lived the longest."

"Yes. That's why Stitch Mouth and Balloon Girl lived as long as they did. Stitch Mouth still has the most beautiful voice I've ever heard."

"And Balloon Girl?"

"I don't know. She can't speak or sing."

"She has no lungs," he concluded, almost disappointed with himself for not having immediately guessing that fact.

"Yes."

"What happened next?"

"Well, one night, when it was time for everyone to sing, Stitch Mouth and Balloon Girl sang a different song. It was a song that made fun of the witch, and she hated it. The witch slapped Balloon Girl. Some of the children ran to their beds. Some hid in the corners. The witch turned on Stitch Mouth and began beating her next. Stitch Mouth just kept singing with her mouth full of blood and Balloon Girl jumped onto the witch, but she was too little. They were both too little. The witch dragged Balloon Girl out of the room. The door was shut and locked. Stitch Mouth could hear the rushing of the furnace."

"Continue," Dr. Tariq said.

"I don't think I can."

"You must."

"Why?"

"Because. What happened next, Sarah? Tell me."

I hurried my words. "Stitch Mouth listened to Balloon Girl's screams until they finally stopped. Then the witch returned to the bedroom. Stitch Mouth began to sing again. The witch strapped Stitch Mouth to her bed, took a needle and thread, and sewed Stitch Mouth's lips together. But when Stitch Mouth sang anyway, the witch choked Stitch Mouth to death."

"Why are you crying?"

"How can't I?" I asked, angry at him. "It's all so sad. The way they died. Living in that horrible house. Losing their families like they did. Having to relive it all."

"Yet they do not wallow in their own sadness."

"I know."

"They have returned for you, Sarah, to help you do what they were never able to."

"That's what scares me the most." It was the first time I had admitted it, even to myself.

"What is it that scares you?"

"That I won't be able to."

"Able to do what?"

"You know."

"Then say it, Sarah. Say it before you lose the nerve. What is it, Sarah, what is it that scares you the most? Say it. Say it!"

"That I won't be able to kill the witch!" I screamed at him. I turned away.

"Good. Back when you first entered my office a few month ago, you were afraid that the witch would hurt *you*. What scares you the most now?"

"That Stitch Mouth and Balloon Girl will get hurt because of me."

"Sarah, may I provide you with a word of encouragement?"

I turned back to him. "Of course. Please."

"If you do nothing, your friends are going to die."

It felt as though he had stabbed me.

Dr. Tariq continued, "You cannot live like this forever. Running and playing each night. Even if you want to."

"But that's all I want. To spend time with them."

"I understand." Dr. Tariq nodded. "Sarah, you have been witness to the choice that is yours."

"I have?"

"Yes. Your two friends made a choice years ago. And they have made a choice in returning for you. It is a choice that comes by caring and love. A choice found in a song. Do nothing, Sarah, and that song ends." Dr. Tariq raised a silent hand before me, his palm towards the ceiling, as though cupping water. Then he raised the other, displaying two possible outcomes. Staring at me, Dr. Tariq shook his head.

# 38

"Hey, Stranger," Ben attempted as I walked past him in the opposite direction. He twisted back around to catch up to me. "Didn't you hear me?" he asked.

"Hey," I said.

"Did you get fitted yet?" he asked.

"What?"

"Did you get fitted yet?"

"For the cap and gown?"

"Yeah. What else?"

"Yeah, I just finished. Did you?"

"You know it, you know it."

I just kept walking.

Ben chuckled away the awkwardness. "What's with you?"

"Nothing."

"In your own little world?" he asked.

"I kind of always am."

We climbed the slope of the hallway. Walking past the

auditorium door, I heard the booming voice of Logan Frazier as he called out theatrical judgments against Mephistopheles. Logan had won the role of Faust and seemed to be enjoying himself.

"Yeah, you are," Ben said. "Full time resident of Sarah-ville."

"That was pretty witty."

"Can't take a joke anymore?" Ben said, punching me playfully on the shoulder. But when I glared at him, his playfulness tripped over itself. I didn't want him touching me. I didn't really want him talking to me. "Easy, easy," Ben said, throwing up hands like I'd pulled a gun on him. He was trying to pretend nothing had ever changed between us all of a sudden. It was super annoying.

"What do you want?" I asked.

"Can't I talk to my friend?"

"Is that what I am? Your friend?"

"Yeah. Of course."

"Why are you being all weird?"

"Me?" He leaned his head closer to mine to make sure I didn't miss his look of astonishment. "You're the one who's been making things weird for weeks now."

"Me?"

"Yeah, you. But I wanted to be the bigger person about it when I realized you weren't going to be the one to try."

"That's very mature of you."

"Whatever. Really though, you don't talk to me anymore, what gives?"

"I talk to you."

"Only when you have to. Like a couple of weeks ago when we were paired up for that project in chemistry, which you barely helped me with."

"Sorry."

"No big, no big."

I wondered when Ben started the habit of repeating himself. Would the old Sarah have even noticed, because the new Sarah found it annoying as well.

"At least I got us an A," he said.

"We got an A?"

He laughed like anything below an A was unthinkable. "Of course I got us an A."

"Did I help?" I asked, curious.

"You helped enough."

"Thanks for doing most of it."

"For sure, for sure."

"Oh, jeez." I rolled my eyes.

"What?"

"Nothing." I wanted to change the subject. "I heard you're graduating Valedictorian."

"You heard about that, huh?"

"Yeah."

"And I got into Duke," he disclosed.

I was happy for him. "Duke? That's great. I know that probably means a lot to your dad."

"Not just him."

"And you," I said. "Sorry for not giving you immediate credit. I'm really happy for you though. Valedictorian *and* Duke. I'm not surprised. Are they going to expand the walls in the gymnasium for the graduation ceremony though?"

"Why?"

"To accommodate the size of your big fat head. They'll probably need to sew about fifty caps together to make one special one just for you."

"Very funny." He laughed dismissively. "It's not like I'm telling everyone about it."

"I know. You're being super humble. I just hope you don't topple off the stage when Principal Jackson congratulates you with a slap on the back. I'm just concerned for your safety, that's all."

"I get it. You got jokes."

"All of them." I smirked from my shell.

We split apart for a moment in order to fight our way against a slew of backpacks and swinging arms before regaining our path at the top.

"You do that all the time now," Ben suddenly accused.

"What am I doing?"

"You barely talk to me. And when you do, you hardly even look at me."

"I've been like this for months, Ben. Besides, why are you asking now? Is it because you want to be my friend again? Or because you don't want to feel bad about how terrible of a friend you are?"

"Me?" he asked loudly. "I'm the terrible friend?"

He was upset. His cheeks were red. I kind of liked it. He finally sounded normal, like the Ben I had always known with real feelings and real mannerisms. But we had both changed so much. To the outside world, Ben was on his way up in life, accumulating successes and accomplishing goals, while I had taken a nose dive in the opposite direction, straight down. Could the people we had become ever be friends? I wasn't sure. I didn't think so.

I said, "Yes, you. You're a terrible friend."

He took a sudden hop in frustration. "You've got to be kidding me! You're the one who got all weird and immature about – you know – what happened!"

"What happened, Ben?"

"You know – with like – prom and stuff."

Now I was the one getting upset. "You think this is about prom?"

"Yeah, prom." He made an expression like it was more than obvious, like I was a dunderhead. "Things happened between us. But you can't blame me for it, it's not like I knew."

"Knew what?"

"That you wanted me to ask you to prom. I guess I broke your heart or whatever."

"I can't believe." I trembled a moment in anger and disbelief. "I can't believe." I couldn't believe it. "After all these months, you think it's been that. Get over *yourself*, Ben."

"Then why have you been treating me like this?"

I pulled Ben aside from the flow of students. "The reason I stopped talking to you was because you told people I went to the mental hospital. That was the *last* thing I wanted anyone to know. Do you know how that feels? To have your name whispered when you walk by? To be the school freak? Do you know how lonely that makes you?"

"That was months ago. And I was only joking."

"What part of that was joking? You want to talk about friendship? That's not what friends do. You didn't ask what happened to me. You didn't ask how I was doing. You just went along trying to be cool while hanging out with your cool friend, Mark, who's a jerk, by the way. That hurt, Ben." I refused to cry in front of him, but I was getting close. I jabbed a finger into his chest, which helped me feel better. "So don't blame me for how our friendship turned out."

"I'm sorry. I just thought you were upset about Destiny. And, I don't know, I guess I was embarrassed by it all because I knew I should have asked you to prom. And that's when you started acting all weird and dressing different and not caring about classes or whatever. What else was I supposed to think?"

"It's fine," I said. "Besides, I've made two friends who actually care about me."

Ben became instantly curious and doubtful. "Who?"

I started walking away. "You –uh – you don't know them."

"C'mon, Sarah. I know just about everyone in school. You don't have to say you've made friends if you haven't. It's okay."

"You don't know them."

Ben held his arms out, showing me just how many people there were in my life that he didn't personally know. "What friends, Sarah?"

I screamed, "What do you care?"

My outburst was a slap across his face. He worked to hush me. "Okay, okay, you've made friends. That's cool. Who are they, I mean, if they're your friends, maybe we could get together and hang out or something."

"You wouldn't like them."

"Why not?"

"They're even crazier than I am." I smiled, and walked away faster. He fought to keep up, talking to my back.

Our conversation ended abruptly as we walked into class. I skimmed my way between filled desks until finding an open one at the back corner of the room. I slid my book bag to my feet and sat. Spring had erupted in warmth and flowers outside and excitement inside. Graduation was in a month. A part me wanted to feel what everyone else felt. To be who I once was. But in another way – a very real way – I didn't want to have anything in common with any of them at all. I spent a moment watching Mike and Ben talk together, slapping along in their own made up handshake. Mike sat down where I used to sit, directly beside Ben in the front row. A part of me missed that. But as I watched them joke, their animated interactions only added to the mounting evidence of how much the old Sarah was so different from the Sarah I had become, with no interest in that world or that life.

I turned away. The sounds of the room hummed further and further into the distance as I drifted off into my own thoughts. I thought of my new friends. An easy smile touched my face. I whispered to the window, "They're even crazier than me."

# 39

Balloon Girl lay perched atop the canopy of her bed, acting out a story Stitch Mouth told.

"Balloon Girl had a grand plan. It required all eight of us and a sheet. Balloon Girl and I stacked two beds on top of each other. Balloon Girl climbed to the top, holding the sheet."

Balloon Girl stretched a sheet wide.

"The other children and I were in position, just as we'd planned. The witch came stomping up the stairs. The door opened. Crying out like a mad baboon, Balloon Girl threw herself from the bed and landed on top of the witch, wrapping her in the sheet as they both collapsed."

Balloon Girl launched herself from the canopy, landing onto the pillows below, and wrestled and wrangled the biggest pillow into the sheet.

Stitch Mouth went over and began kicking the pillow Balloon Girl had pinned down. "I began kicking the witch. But the other children didn't help. One child ran down the stairs. Another child crept to the corner, begging to be forgiven. The others stood there, watching. The witch flung Balloon Girl from her back and stood from the sheet."

Balloon Girl flopped over onto the floor, then rose to her knees, gazing upward in horror, as though the witch was there.

Stitch Mouth ended the story. But Balloon Girl wasn't quite finished. She began striking herself in the belly and face.

"That's enough," Stitch Mouth said.

Balloon Girl continued to play out the brutal beating she'd received at the hands of the witch. Stumbling back with another hit, she slammed herself against the wall where her head hit hard and she flopped motionless to her side.

"Stop it!" Stitch Mouth screamed, covering her ears. "Stop it!"

Balloon Girl tilted her head, wondering what was wrong.

"I don't like that part. That was the first time you went unconscious. I know it doesn't bother you. But it bothers me. Well, please don't. Not again, okay? I didn't like that part at all. I thought she killed you."

Balloon Girl shrugged her shoulders.

"Yes, I know she killed you anyway. But I still don't like it."

"Was it bad?" I asked.

Stitch Mouth turned to me. "It was the worst. The witch was accustomed to Balloon Girl and I doing little things, being obstinate when we could, dancing and singing, playing our games. But we had never gotten the other children to help us before. Not that they helped anyway," she corrected.

Balloon Girl's skull face scowled.

"Yeah, that upset me too."

"Why didn't they help?"

"They were afraid."

"Yeah, but they were ready to help."

"I guess the plans of children change when confronted by a witch. Anyway, after that, the witch became much more impatient with us."

Balloon Girl nodded.

I heard the smallest sound downstairs. Like a button dropping to the floor. We froze. Balloon Girl placed a finger to where her lips would be and walked quietly to the bedroom door to listen.

"She's here," I whispered.

"I know." Stitch Mouth gaze was pinned to the open door.

Balloon Girl was there, peering towards the stairs.

Balloon Girl touched the tip of a balloon to the floor. A girl appeared – her formation was as dazzling as the first time, wonderfully magical and tossed with pink glitter. Balloon Girl pointed the girl in the opposite direction of the steps, and the girl took off. Balloon Girl shut the door silently. A few seconds later, a door slammed shut. The girl had gone into another room. We heard rushing feet. The witch climbing the steps. She ran past our door and began opening and shutting doors in her desperate attempt to catch us, not knowing it was the balloon girl she was chasing.

We edged closer to the door.

"Sarah?"

"Yeah?" I whispered.

"Can you carry Balloon Girl?"

"I think so. But why?"

"We will need to run, and Balloon Girl is the slowest."

I lifted Balloon Girl into my arms. "She's light. I can carry her."

Balloon Girl nodded.

"Good. Ready?"

Somewhere down the hall, the witch gave off a shriek of surprise and fury. She had found the girl – not us – and it sounded like the girl had hit the witch with something hard and metal.

"Go."

Stitch Mouth yanked the door open and we scampered down the stairs. The sounds of the witch and the girl fighting continued a moment more. Then there was a snap. We went out through the front door, entering the night outside. I had never been outside in the third circle before. The world was cold and dark and dead. Dead trees in dead darkness. The only sound seemed to be the sounds of our feet and breath, as though nothing else was alive in the world but us.

We ran through the night, making our way across a path that led to another home further away. Street lanterns remained unlit and useless. The darkness swirled like black mist, always thickening. I was huffing. Balloon Girl wasn't heavy, but I wasn't used to running with her weight. And I was afraid. But I kept running, accepting the burning sensation in my lungs and the weariness in my legs as a necessity.

"In here." Stitch Mouth led us into another home. It was dark inside. But the darkness helped, hiding us. Balloon Girl wriggled out of my arms. We went to a window to stare out at the path we had just crossed, searching for any evidence or sign of the witch. We breathed, watching.

"Why aren't you using chalk?" I whispered.

"There's no need. Not yet." Stitch Mouth's eyes were intent, focused on Balloon Girl's home across from us. It glowed in the darkness, filled with light from the lanterns we had lit, which escaped from the windows. Everything was still.

"Why isn't she coming?"

"I'm not sure."

We waited.

"Where is she?"

"I don't know."

We watched.

A tiny creak was heard. The back door had been opened. Rushing steps came for us.

We dashed back out through the front door, heading straight towards Balloon Girl's home again. Stitch Mouth worked at her purse, searching for a chalk as she ran. Balloon Girl was in my arms. My lungs burned immediately. My heart pounded in pain. I ran as fast as I could. I glanced back, thinking Stitch Mouth was just behind me. She wasn't. She was winded, dropping further behind. The witch came out of the front door. We were still halfway to Balloon Girl's home, stuck in the darkness between the two homes with nowhere to hide. The long strides of the witch consumed the distance. I slowed, watching idly as the witch gained on Stitch Mouth.

Stitch Mouth screamed, "Go! Sarah! Go!"

The pale arm of the witch stretched through the air and snagged a fistful of Stitch Mouth's hair, ripping her back so hard she fell to the ground. The witch pounced, her long arms and hair swallowing Stitch Mouth beneath her. Stitch Mouth kicked against the witch, swatting and shuffling away.

Balloon Girl kicked against me and dropped hard from my arms. She flipped to her knees and touched a tip of string to the ground, giving life to a girl who shook off the remnants of her creation and ran immediately at the struggle. Balloon Girl took off after her.

It felt as though I was watching everything from behind glass. Or from above. Watching. Stitch Mouth on the ground. The witch grabbing for her. The balloon girl running. Balloon Girl just behind. Chaos and cries. Huffs and screams. And in the middle of it all, a girl stood, too scared to move. That girl was me. And I hated her.

I ran. Passing Balloon Girl. Passing the other girl.

Stitch Mouth glanced towards me. "No, Sarah!"

The witch didn't even notice.

I screamed, "Get off her!" and I grabbed the witch's hair, taking a huge lunging step past her and yanking her from her feet. The witch flopped over in a long-limbed tumble, smacking the ground with her face. She shrieked, clawing at my ankles through her own blinding hair.

Balloon Girl had dropped another balloon, and now two blond girls were at the witch with me. They jumped on top of the witch, pummeling her in a flurry of small tiny fists which beat her down.

I went to help, but both Balloon Girl and Stitch Mouth were at my arms, turning me away. We returned to Balloon Girl's house. Stitch Mouth drew a door of escape. From the window, I watched the witch as she got up, as she stood, as she attacked the other two girls. The witch dashed one girl's head against a rock. The girl's body went instantly limp. The other girl fought. Fought with everything in her. But it was obvious. Too obvious. And the witch knew. She took her time, the girl's throat in her hands. I couldn't look away. What right did I have, when it was my fault? What right did I have? I cried, hating myself even more. When the witch was finished, the girl hanging from her hands, the witch looked at me and smiled.

Balloon Girl tugged on my arm. We went through the new door, entering an in-between room. Over and over, we repeated the cycle. I only barely kept up. The adrenaline from moments ago had worn out, making me lethargic and heavy. But it wasn't only that. I couldn't stop replaying the sacrifice of the two girls.

We entered Stitch Mouth's house, but she then led us outside into the woods. "We can hear her better from here."

We passed between the trees, staying close together. Even in the darkness, Stitch Mouth looked unnerved, shifting her attention to various spots of darkness. "Don't ever do that again, Sarah," Stitch

Mouth said sternly. "Ever."

Her words stung. "I wasn't about to let the witch take you."

"It's not about me."

"Then why do you still look so afraid?"

"I never said I wasn't afraid." Stitch Mouth turned away, facing the gap between two trees.

My words barely made it out. "I won't let you. Not like that. Not for me. No."

"If I must die at the hands of the witch, then that is something I willingly accept. She could have grabbed you!"

"I don't care! Stop pretending it doesn't bother you! Look at you! You're still trembling. And I saw you!" I accused. "You – you were terrified! You were kicking at the witch just to keep her away. But it wasn't working! It was only a matter of time!"

"I didn't say it was what I wanted. But if I had to choose between myself and you, I would choose to be taken a thousand times of a thousand, Sarah. And I would regret nothing."

"Can't I feel the same way about you?"

My question humbled her. "Balloon Girl and I were sent to protect you. Not ourselves. We do not matter."

"That's so stupid! It's so stupid! You do matter! You matter to *me*!"

"But that's not why we are here."

"You know what? I don't care if you were only sent to protect me! Maybe that's not what I want!"

Balloon Girl raised her hand, then lowered it, telling us to keep our voices down.

Stitch Mouth and I nodded our understanding.

"Sarah, you are the only one who is allowed to kill the witch. So, you are the one who must be kept alive."

My voice lowered and calmed. "When the witch was on you, a part of me wanted to keep running. My body told me *run*. But I froze. It felt like I was watching everything from the outside. I could see the witch. I could see you. I could see Balloon Girl and the other girl running to help. And then, I saw another girl. A scared girl. She was just standing there. That girl was me."

"Sarah –"

"Listen. I saw myself. I saw how selfish my fear makes me. And if I had listened to it, you would have gotten hurt. But I didn't want to lose you. I had to do something, even if it meant I would get hurt. You say I'm not allowed to do something like that. But if you're allowed to do that for me, then I'm allowed to do that for you. You're not the only one who's allowed to care about someone else."

Stitch Mouth was determined to counter everything I said, but Balloon Girl interrupted her by holding up three fingers, which she then closed together.

"What did she say?"

Stitch Mouth hesitated to tell me. But Balloon Girl made the motion again, directing it towards Stitch Mouth more than me.

I said in realization, translating Balloon Girl's gesture, "When we fight the witch together, we can beat her."

"It only worked tonight," Stitch Mouth said.

"Now, you're the one being stubborn!" I declared.

Stitch Mouth shook her head, smirking. "No, I'm not."

"Yes, you absolutely are!"

She admitted, "Maybe a little."

"I want you to say it."

"Okay, I'm being stubborn."

I rolled my eyes. "Not that."

"Okay," Stitch Mouth said. "We were able to beat the witch because we fought her together."

"We can do this. We can beat her," I said, almost believing my own words. "I mean, we just did, right? You're safe. We're all safe. So, there's no reason for you to give up."

"I didn't give up."

"Whatever. You told me to leave you there."

Stitch Mouth nodded her head and blinked her red eyes. "Thank you, Sarah. For saving me."

I hugged her. "Please, don't thank me."

"Now I'm not even permitted to thank you? When did you become so demanding?"

"Just a few minutes ago." I winked. "And that's right, you're not allowed to thank me again. Ever."

"My life just got so much easier," she joked.

"Ha-ha," I said flatly.

I suddenly felt the touch of something on my wrist. Realizing what it was, I flung sticky strands of black hair I had torn from the witch's head. "Gross!" I shouted. "Gross!" I waved my hands in the air.

The hair sailed and landed onto Balloon Girl's skull face, plastering itself there. Balloon Girl shook her head violently, as if spiders were crawling on her. Flicking the hair away, Balloon Girl then stomped it into the soil.

I cried out, "Oops! Sorry!"

But Balloon Girl continued to throw a fit, pacing back and forth between two trees with her hands going this way and that in fury.

Aghast, Stitch Mouth suddenly proclaimed, "Balloon Girl! Those are *very* naughty words! Very naughty! No, I am not your mother, but that does not mean I cannot tell you not to say such things! My goodness! Such filthy words from such a little girl! Yes, I am aware that you are a skeleton but that gives you no right to speak such things! Now you're saying those things just to be mean! No, dying does not mean you can speak however you like! Fine! Talk however you want! But don't say such words when you are with me! Yes, I am aware you have no one else you can talk to. Goodness. If your mother or father could hear how you are talking. Fine! I'm through with scolding you. Fine? Fine!"

I laughed and I laughed. Soon, we laughed together. We spoke for a while. Soon, we didn't think much or talk much about the witch at all, until I said, "We can do this." They looked at me, waiting for me to be more bold with my words. I said, "We can kill the witch. We can kill the witch together."

Stitch Mouth took a deep breath, she smiled. Balloon Girl smiled gruesome, yet beautiful, then patted, then held my hand.

# 40

Balloon Girl had devised a grand plan.

Balloon Girl pointed to a specific spot on the floor, instructing Stitch Mouth to sketch a door there. Then she beckoned me over to the furniture, where I helped her slide a couch across the room so we could jam it against the door. Directed by Balloon Girl, I then draped a sheet over the door and stretched another one over the couch. Pots and pans were placed in small stacks near the entrance like harmless noise mines. The traps were obvious, almost silly, but they set a discreet path that led to the open door Stitch Mouth had sketched on the floor – the true trap. The door was also covered with a sheet, and the end of the sheet was tied to the knob. With everything prepared, we snuck up the spiral staircase and waited, ducked to the floor to watch, and giggling in anticipation.

It seemed to take forever. But finally, the door tilted open until stopped by the couch. The witch peered from behind the sliver of gap, listening and watching with her intent unblinking eyes. She pressed against the door a little harder to squeeze her body through, causing a pot to fall over, which banged loudly. The witch tucked back away. A moment later, she pressed against the door

again, but when the couch wouldn't budge, she drove her body
hard, causing the sheet above to fall on top of her. She flailed in
fury and tore blindly at the sheet. Ripping the sheet from her head,
she kicked it away. Then she kicked a pot in anger. When she saw
us laughing at the top of the stairs, the witch's eyes were
emblazoned and she took a gigantic step, right onto the sheet, and
fell through the doorway Stitch Mouth had created. The witch
dropped down, and the weight of her body whipped the door shut.

*Smash!* Stitch Mouth crushed the chalk. The door vanished,
taking the angry shrieks of the witch with it.

"Oh my goodness!" Stitch Mouth jumped to her feet. "It
worked! That was the best!"

I jumped to my feet as well, joyous and feeling victorious.

Balloon Girl twirled and clapped.

We made our way towards Balloon Girl's room,
congratulating ourselves and each other. Stitch Mouth could barely
breathe with how hard she was laughing, and we all laughed. I
laughed until my belly ached. Stitch Mouth and Balloon Girl soon
began playing dress up, making themselves fancy as though they'd
be attending an extravagant tea party later in the evening. Long
white gloves. Elegant hats. Every single piece of jewelry in the
room. Seeing me off to the side, Balloon Girl became intent upon
dressing me up as well. An ivory touring hat was placed on my
head. Necklaces strung from my neck. My wrists clinked with
ornate bracelets. A lacy scarf wrapped lavishly around my neck.

Hands on her hips, Balloon Girl nodded in approval of my
makeover.

"My mom has a hat like this," I commented with bright red
lips, touching the rim.

Balloon Girl appeared delighted.

I said, taking the hat from my head, "We used to picnic in the
spring, and we'd all dress up to look our best. My father would
wear a suit. I had new dress to wear that my mom and I picked out
specifically for the picnic. It was kind of our special thing. A
tradition we were trying to create. Together." I began telling them
more. Memories were released, setting others free. I told them
things I'd never told anyone. How my father had been in a car
accident. How he changed from the man he had always been. He
didn't remember things like he used to. He became moody. He was

irritable and quick-tempered. Things he had never been. He lost his job and couldn't find another. My mother began working two jobs. Then one day, my father became upset when my mom tried doing something for him, something he used to be able to do on his own, and he shoved her to the floor. My mother scrambled to the wall. I stood there, afraid of what was happening. Afraid of him. My father broke down, seeing what he'd done. He had fallen to his knees. He started crying. My mother said it was okay, that she should have seen how upset he was becoming. He said there was nothing about it that was okay. My mother tried to go to him. I did too. But he waved us away. Told us to stay away from him. Said he hated what he had become. That he couldn't do this anymore. Then he asked us to remember who he had always been before the accident and I didn't know what he meant. He hugged me. He called me his princess and wiped the tears from my eyes and wiped the tears from his own. He hugged and kissed my mother. Kissed her for a long time. He told us he loved us. Then he left. Drove off to the mountains where a friend of his owned a cabin he could stay at until he could find a permanent place to live. He moved there for good. "Like a fortress to lock the monster away," I finished.

I had never told anyone about what had happened to my father or why he had left. Not even Clara. Not like that. In telling Stitch Mouth and Balloon Girl, I had let out a part of me no one had ever seen. I can't explain why, but I was glad when Stitch Mouth and Balloon Girl only hugged me. They didn't try to say anything to make everything right. Then Stitch Mouth asked if I wanted to rest. I said I would. And the two of them helped me up.

When Stitch Mouth gave me a hug to end the night, I noticed something. The sides of her purse were sinking in. It was light on her. Not heavy with tricks. I turned away, because I didn't want to see how much the purse was thinning.

The lantern was blown out. In the darkness, I heard Stitch Mouth whisper to Balloon Girl, "The witch will not allow anything like that to happen again. She will be more wary than ever."

Balloon Girl nodded in the vague darkness. Above her, four balloons remained. Four of eight.

# 41

I touched my bedroom window. My fingertips warmed there, my skin pulsing beneath the afternoon glare. I stared outside, waiting for night to come.

*How many more tricks were left?*

*How many more nights could we spend together?*

I had been depending upon my two friends for safety. But really, they were depending on me.

# 42

I went downstairs. In the kitchen, I spied an array of Danishes carefully constructed into a mountain of glazed and sticky pastries on the counter. "What's all this?" I asked, followed by, "Can I have one?"

"Of course." My mom was digging in the fridge, pulling out different things.

Danish in hand, I asked, "Are you having one of those Pampered Chef parties or whatever?"

"No."

"Oh, so these are all for us?" I joked.

"Yes. I got them for *you*."

I stopped chewing. "For me?"

"Yes. Of course. You've gotten too skinny."

"I'm not as skinny anymore. I'm even gaining a little weight." I pinched at my belly as proof.

"Not enough though," my mother said.

"Enough                              for                              what?"

She paused. "To look like your old self. To look healthy. *"*

"So, these Danishes are for me. Like, all of them?"

"Yes, I got them for you, *Silly*."

My head rang with alarms. My mother never called me *Silly* –
the name Stitch Mouth used so often to tease me – and it clanged
like a bad piano key. I placed the pastry onto a napkin, my appetite
gone.

"Finish the Danish," my mother offered as she opened a packet
of bacon at the stove. "I'm making breakfast. To celebrate."

"What are we celebrating?" I asked, watching her.

"We're celebrating how good you've been doing. You know,
with your schizophrenia symptoms."

"Dr. Tariq said I don't have schizophrenia, remember? He said I
*never* even had schizophrenia."

Pointing her spatula at me, my mother corrected, "But, there
*were* symptoms, Sarah. You know," she said, "sometimes I think
maybe you lied to Dr. Tariq about not seeing that woman."

"I told Dr. Tariq everything."

"Oh, I doubt that."

"You really think I lied to him?"

She took on a condescending tone. "Of course not, Sarah. You
would never *lie*. Anyway, from what I've read, schizophrenia
never truly goes away. Which means that woman in your window
will likely never leave you." She was staring at me with eyes that
had never been hers.

My heart was racing. I wanted to be back in my room. I wanted
to be back with Stitch Mouth and Balloon Girl.

"Don't go," she said sweetly.

"I'm not."

My mother smiled.

"I just have a lot to do," I said, trying to act casual.

She grinned at that. "I'm sure you do."

I shooed a fly from the pastries. Another fly flew across my face
and I swatted at that one, too. "Mom, can you stop talking like
that?"

"Like what?"

"Like that." I didn't want to give away any hint that I sensed the
witch. I had to pretend. But I had to pretend better.

"You'll have to be more specific."

"Like you're a weirdo."

There was a flash of anger. "Anything you want," she said,

turning back to the stove.

I didn't like the feel of her, the way of her, and I definitely didn't want to be in the home with her. But I had no choice. I decided to try and be nice, maybe that would make her stop acting the way she was. "Everything smells great, Mom."

"Good."

"Thank you for cooking."

"You're welcome."

It wasn't working. I tried something different. "I was telling a couple of friends about dad."

Her body went rigid. "That's good."

"I was thinking. Maybe the two of us should talk about him more. Maybe it would be good."

"Maybe." She began lifting bacon with the tongs and placing them on a plate.

"I miss him. I know you miss him too."

She nodded, then cracked eggs and sprinkled salt and pepper on top. "Over-easy sound good?" She sounded more like herself.

"Yep."

I swatted at a couple more flies. They wouldn't leave me alone. I looked around. They were filling the kitchen, landing and flying.

"Those things have been everywhere," my mother commented, carrying our plates over to the table.

"Where are they all coming from?" I asked. I found the flyswatter hanging in the pantry and killed one, smacking it flat against the window, then killed another.

"There's no telling," my mother said. "Anyway, breakfast is ready."

We sat to eat. Bacon, eggs, English muffins. My mother carried over the pile of pastries to join us, like a guest she wanted to include. I took tiny nibbles.

As my mother ate, she didn't take her eyes off of me. She too ate very slowly, and she didn't seem bothered by the flies at all.

Talking about my father worked a moment ago, bringing my mother back out, so I said, "Do you think dad is doing better?"

"I don't know."

"Do you think he still goes bowling?"

"I don't know."

My mother was tossing back and forth between herself and the witch.

"Thanks, Mom. Everything was delicious." I had eaten enough.

"You're very welcome," she said. "Have I ever told how much I love when you call me *Mom*?"

"What else would I call you?"

My mother didn't answer and she didn't say anything more. As I began placing the plates and silverware into the dishwasher, my mom began to hum. She didn't sing the words. But I knew them. She hummed merrily and my mind played the words.

*She's here, she's here*
*Our Mummy dear!*
*Open the door and let her in,*
*Not to do so would be a sin.*

*It won't take long,*
*Only the length of a song.*
*When she's through eating you,*
*We can eat you too.*

I went to my bedroom and locked the door.

# 43

I told Balloon Girl and Stitch Mouth about the strange encounter with my mother. Stitch Mouth nodded. Like she figured something like this would happen. While she sketched a new door, she asked me more questions about what had happened. We went through, and suddenly, we stepped into a home I had never been in before.

A swarm of flies stood thick like a cloud the doorway. They were at my mouth and ears and eyes, eagerly seeking any exposed part of me they could set their little wings upon, so that I had to brush my entire face of them. I ducked further inside the home to avoid them, swatting blindly to keep them away. Pulling in desperate breathes, my stomach lurched as a rotten stench clogged my nostrils and mouth. My foot squished onto something. A pile of bloodied meat. Maggots climbed each other in a wriggling mass. I stumbled away to escape, tiptoeing past horrors I never wanted to touch or see while still avoiding the flies.

Stitch Mouth was behind me, mumbling and waving at the air, "No, no, no, no."

I took another step further in. And my hand lowered from my face. I didn't care about the flies anymore. I had to see. Forced myself to look. I knew where I was. Even if no one told me. Off to the side was a ragged pile of clothes, all children's sizes, some sprinkled with blood. A toppled pile of shoes in a corner. Teddy bears and children's blankets in blue and pink. Bracelets and necklaces. Hats and caps.

"So many children," I whispered.

Stitch Mouth and Balloon Girl remained at the door, panicked and unaware that I was leaving them.

"You lived here," I said to myself. "The both of you."

Beyond the kitchen was a furnace near the back of the house. I went to it. Kneeling low, I peered into the dark opening of the furnace. Layers of thick ash were piled high, pockmarked with flaps of scorched skin.

"Balloon Girl, this is where you died."

I shut the heavy door.

I discovered a stairway, a crooked door at the top. I took a step up. I wanted to go to the door. I wanted to see inside. I knew I'd see beds and that there would be eight of them. Someone touched my wrist, stopping me. Balloon Girl was there, gazing up at me. She shook her head, telling me not to go.

"I need to."

Her mouth moved. I knew the silent words she spoke. *You don't.*

I tried again.

She shook her head. *You don't.*

Balloon Girl drew me from the steps and led me past the horrors and the flies and the things I had seen.

When Stitch Mouth saw me, she ran over and began shoving me along faster towards the door. "We have to go. This is – this is –" She couldn't say it.

I could. "I know where we are. This is the home of the witch."

Stitch Mouth shut the door behind us. She could hardly breathe.

A part of me knew I would return there again.

# 44

With a fresh chalk, Stitch Mouth sketched feverishly at our feet, leading us downward. We descended, burrowing ourselves into the basement of a basement of an even lower in-between room. Stitch Mouth was desperate still, mumbling to herself, trying to figure out what had happened, blaming herself. Balloon Girl touched her arm. The chalk dropped. Stitch Mouth fell into a gasping and hyperventilating fit. Her hand went to her chest, her shoulders shaking. Between the tight breaths, she began to utter, "No, no, no, no, no, no, no, no, no, no."

I lowered myself to her. "Stitch Mouth. We're okay." But she couldn't see me.

Then she shrieked, seeing something I couldn't, and began sobbing horribly against the wall.

I tried to console her. To help her.

I couldn't.

Balloon Girl stepped forward and slapped Stitch Mouth hard across the face.

Stitch Mouth asked, hand to her cheek, "Why'd you slap me?"

*It was the only way to help you.* A voice, quiet as a distant echo.

"Wait, who said that?" I asked.

They turned to me.

"Balloon Girl? Was that you?" I asked.

*You can hear me?*

"Yeah. If that's you."

*Well, we are the only ones here. So, it likely was me.*

I asked the hollow eyes of Balloon Girl, "That's you?"

*Yes.*

"Really?"

*It always has been.*

"That's amazing!" Then I asked her, "Is Stitch Mouth okay?"

"I'm right here, Sarah," Stitch Mouth said, still rubbing at the reddish glow on her cheek.

"I know," I said.

"So why did you ask Balloon Girl?"

"Well, because you look terrible, and sometimes, even when you're not okay, you pretend you are anyway."

*She knows you well.*

"I'm fine," Stitch Mouth said, irritated at being the topic of concern.

"You didn't seem fine. Are you sure you're okay?"

Stitch Mouth's eyes flashed red with a sudden fury. "Stop asking! I'm fine!"

*Stitch Mouth, you cannot blame her. You scared the both of us. You were still in the home of that witch, reliving the moment –*

"Shut up," Stitch Mouth commanded.

Balloon Girl bowed her head. *I'm sorry. You had us both concerned, that's all I was saying.*

"I'm fine now."

*But you weren't. You were acting like a baby.*

"I was *not!*"

*Now you sound like a baby.*

Stitch Mouth huffed, arms crossed. "Well, I'm very glad Sarah gets to hear you now. Now I'm not the only one who has to hear how mean you can be. And stop looking at me like that. I'm fine." But a spasm of nerves interrupted her, shaking her, telling us she was lying. Stitch Mouth gritted her teeth into an angry smile in an effort to regain control.

*That's more like it. No, not that smile. The other smile. Nope. The other one. Wait, wait. There we go!*

Stitch Mouth smiled a ridiculous fake smile. "Is this better?"

*No. I don't like that one either. I like the angry smiling face.*

Stitch Mouth scowled with a grin thrown in. "This one?"

*Yes! It brings out the color of your eyes.*

"That doesn't even make sense," Stitch Mouth said.

*Sure it does. All I'm saying is that your smile, the one you use to make us think you're happy, is stupid.*

"My smile isn't stupid." Stitch Mouth sounded hurt.

*I'm sorry. It's not stupid. But I like the angry smile more. I like it the best.*

Stitch Mouth placed the chalk back into her purse. "I don't have to be like you, Balloon Girl."

*But you don't have to wear your smile like a mask.*

Stitch Mouth's shoulders sagged. "Then what else should I do? Tell me that. Cry? Lose control like I just did? Because that's what will happen if I don't."

*We only want to see you smile when you're happy. It's my favorite. I'm tired of your vain attempts at being more mature than us. Besides, Sarah is the oldest between us, and I'm two months older than you, so you're the youngest of us. So stop trying to act like you're the oldest or something.*

Stitch Mouth twirled in frustration. "Oh my gosh! That doesn't even matter! The both of us are like a hundred years old! But of course – there you go! Doing like you always do! As if two months means you're that much older!"

*Well, I am older.*

"Not when we're decades and decades old!"

*Well, I'll always be older, whether you like it or not. And when you're a thousand years old, I'll still be a thousand AND two months.*

"Oh, my gosh! Sometimes I just want to punch you in your dumb skull face!"

*Do it then.*

"Maybe I will."

*Maybe I'll unlock the rest of these balloons and watch them pummel you.*

"You would," Stitch Mouth accused.

*That's right. Good luck punching me when that happens. I'll probably just sit back, watch, and eat something.*

"So food can just drop out from your ribcage," Stitch Mouth teased.

*That was mean.*

"Come here," Stitch Mouth said.

They hugged. *You weren't doing very well for a moment.*

"I know. Returning there forced me to remember. But I'm okay now."

*There. That is the smile I have always loved. The one your mother gave you. The one your father taught you to keep.*

"I miss them so much." Stitch Mouth faltered.

*I know.*

Balloon Girl pulled Stitch Mouth to her and Stitch Mouth sunk her face into Balloon Girl's shoulder, and she began to cry.

# 45

*Stop gawking at me like that, Sarah. You're making me feel weird.*

"Oh, sorry. It's just amazing that I can hear you now. Why can I all of a sudden?"

*I have no idea. But I'm glad you can. It was so boring being left out of every single conversation between you two. All you two do is talk about sad things all the time.*

"Don't listen to her," Stitch Mouth said. "She's almost always like this. She hides how she feels through her sarcasm. If she's scared, she's sarcastic. If she's angry, she's sarcastic. If she likes you, she's sarcastic."

*And if I don't like you, I'm sarcastic as well. So, you can never really know.*

Stitch Mouth said, "Oh, please. I know you like me."

*Or do I?*

Stitch Mouth rolled her eyes. Balloon Girl laughed. It was light and sweet.

I said, "You have a really beautiful voice, by the way. I guess I'm the only one who doesn't always sound like she's singing."

*That's strange, Sarah, because to us, your voice sounds very much like a song as well.*

"Really?" I was so excited.

*No.* Balloon Girl laughed at my disappointment.

"Sorry," Stitch Mouth apologized for Balloon Girl. "You may end up preferring her mute. I do sometimes."

*What fun would that be?*

"I don't mind," I said, smiling. "I'm just thrilled now that the three of us can talk together. But when I first met you – and you were standing in the corner looking super creepy – I figured you had some gross demon voice or something."

*You mean like this, rahrahrahrahrahrahrah!*

"Oh my gosh! That sounded just like a heavy metal band!"

*I have no idea what you're talking about. But I like it already. And as for what you imagined my voice to be –* she tilted her arms out before her – *I can't blame you.*

Stitch Mouth interrupted, "If you think I can sing, you should hear Balloon Girl."

I clapped. "Can you sing something now?"

*Not a chance.*

My anticipation deflated. "Why not?"

*After returning to the home of that witch, there is very little I feel like singing right now.*

Stitch Mouth huffed. "After all the trouble you just gave me! Now you're the one who's too traumatized?"

*I have feelings, too.*

I laughed and Stitch Mouth did too.

Balloon Girl then commented, *The house of the witch has changed. We never saw it like that.*

"Thankfully," Stitch Mouth said.

*Yes. She's been feasting for years.*

"Why did we end up there?" I asked.

Stitch Mouth shook her head with obvious concern and shrugged her shoulders.

*We don't know. Either the witch has more powers than we know. Or, it was simply something that happened.*

Stitch Mouth nodded, still contemplating. She touched her purse.

*Don't, Stitch Mouth.*

"Don't what?"

*Don't second guess yourself. You have done wonderfully these past weeks in keeping us safe. We still trust you.*

"I'm not so sure you should," Stitch Mouth said.

*Sarah, do you still trust Stitch Mouth to do as she has done?*

"Absolutely."

*There, it's settled. The two oldest girls in the room have voted, and we still trust the youngest littlest baby girl.*

I laughed.

Stitch Mouth tipped her hip in playful aggravation. "You're always so tricky."

*What did I do now?*

"I mentioned singing and you changed the subject. You're such a tricky little girl."

*Tricky little girl who's two months older than you.*

"Yes, yes. You know what will help cleanse away the feeling of that place, don't you?"

*I think I do.*

"A song. And I have the perfect one," Stitch Mouth said.

"Which one?" I asked.

"The song we sang the night we died."

*Don't look like that, Sarah. We like it. It's our favorite song because we made it up together, even if it got us tortured and killed.*

Stitch Mouth giggled.

"I just want to listen to you two sing."

*Oh, so we should just sing for you?*

"Um, yeah."

*While you sit and listen?*

"Um, yeah." I smirked.

*Not a chance.*

I laughed nervously. "I forgot how to sing."

"Nonsense! You can never forget how to sing!"

"I think I did."

"Such nonsense!" Stitch Mouth began tugging at my hands.

*Are you two done? Stand up and sing Sarah. For all the trifling ways in which we spend our nights in fear of the witch, there is only one way to let her know that we are not afraid.*

We took positions in front of the fireplace of Stitch Mouth's home.

"This is where I used to sing with my mother. When my father and brother would listen."

Balloon Girl nodded, then said, *the witch always wanted us to sing songs to her stupid ugly face before we had to go to bed. It was some dumb song about how the witch was some super great mom and blah blah blah she's such an ugly cow. But we made up our own version. Stitch Mouth, you begin.*

Stitch Mouth brought two fingers to her lips in sudden remembrance of the loose cage over her mouth. When she lifted her chin, her chest lifted as well. Her voice had always been beautiful, discovered in the slight evidence of each word she spoke, but this time, when she sang, the fullness of her beauty unfolded like a flower in perfect bloom. Balloon Girl harmonized with her, and yes, her voice was possibly even more beautiful than Stitch Mouth's. They sang:

*She's ugly, oh so ugly, our mommy dear,*
*Ugly as a donkey's rear.*
*She wants to be our mommy,*
*But she's nothing but a witch.*

*She's ugly, oh so ugly, our mommy dear,*
*Ugly as a donkey's rear,*
*She wants to be our mommy,*
*But she's just a mangy bitch.*

"That's a female dog!" Stitch Mouth burst out, hands over her belly as she laughed. Balloon Girl laughed just as hard, bone legs jostling.

I laughed with them. "Yes, I know what it is. But that's not what I was expecting."

*What were you expecting?*

"I don't know. It's just, your voices are so beautiful. And that song was ridiculous."

*Exactly. You should have seen the stupid look on that witch's cow face when we sang it at the top of our lungs. She was all like –* Balloon Girl's face dropped and her jaw flopped open as she mimicked the stunned fury of the witch.

Stitch Mouth laughed hysterically.

*The witch couldn't believe we would do such a thing.*

Stitch Mouth asked, "Did you like it? Our song?"

"Very much," I said.

*It's funny, isn't it?*

I chuckled. "Yes, it's very funny."

Stitch Mouth said, "It's probably not the funniest, but when we were living with the witch, anything helped. As Balloon Girl said, you should have seen the look on the witch's face. It was the best. Do it again, Balloon Girl."

And Balloon Girl did, mimicking the sagging face and Stitch Mouth laughed so hard it gave her hiccups. When she couldn't stop, Balloon Girl offered, *Should I slap you again to help you?*

"No! *hic*–you stay–*cup* right there! You–*hiccup*–evil little girl!"

*And now, Sarah, you must sing with us.*

And I did.

Our voices intertwined, and Balloon Girl and Stitch Mouth's voices lifted my own, like two brave birds escorting a timid bird towards the sky.

"Wonderful!" Stitch Mouth cheered.

*It really was.*

Stitch Mouth then said, "I'd like to make a request. I have a song that I've wanted to share with both of you."

*A song I have not yet heard?*

"Yes."

Stitch Mouth looked away towards her brother's room. "It was my brother's favorite. I wrote it for him on his birthday as a surprise. No matter how irritated I was with him, or how angry he was with me, I would sing it to him each night. It was also the last song I ever sang to him."

*Are you sure you want to share it?* Balloon Girl cautioned.

"Yes. With all my heart."

The song Stitch Mouth sang was the simple story of a brother and sister, carried by a sweet and sullen tune, like a sun shower song. The song soon grew roots inside of me – both the words and melody – a gift Stitch Mouth placed directly into my heart. When she finished, Stitch Mouth said, "I'd like to spend some time in my brother's room, if that's okay."

*Of course.*

Stitch Mouth left us. She closed the door quietly.

Balloon Girl and I rocked side by side in our chairs.

*Sarah. Do not say anything, other than whispers. Stitch Mouth must not hear us, do you understand?*

I nodded, looking at her.

*Stitch Mouth has not always been truthful with you. We did not die on the night of our song.*

"You didn't?"

*No. I was beaten unconscious. And when I woke, I staggered to Stitch Mouth's bed, only to find that she had been strapped to the mattress and her mouth had been sewn shut. She smiled when she saw me, and told me she was okay, because that is who she is. For days, she could hardly eat, so I chewed her food into smaller pieces and fed them to her, and would rub her brow each night till she fell asleep. Those days continued and Stitch Mouth slowly healed. And every time the witch came in, Stitch Mouth smiled as big as she could just to prove she didn't care about her stitches.*

*One day, the witch left, seeking another child. A few days later, she returned. She unlocked the door and told us all to come downstairs because she had a gift to share. A gift for Stitch Mouth. The witch said, "If you love smiling so much, you'll love smiling after you see what I've brought you." Downstairs, stood Stitch Mouth's brother. In a combination of joy and fright, Stitch Mouth clapped her hands to her mouth. I could see how she wanted to run to him. But she stayed there, trying not to let the witch see anything. Her brother cried at the sight of Stitch Mouth and would have run to her, except the witch had gone to stand beside him, digging her fingers into his shoulder. Stitch Mouth begged for the witch to let her brother go, promising the witch anything she wanted. "If I do, will you promise never to sing one of your songs again?" the witch asked. "Of course," Stitch Mouth said, crying. I promised too. "Good," the witch said. Then, without warning, the witch slit the boy's throat. Stitch Mouth ran to her brother as he fell. She held him. The witch at least let her do that. Stitch Mouth kissed her brother through sewn lips, weeping over him as he died there, curled in her arms.*

*That was the night we died. I knew Stitch Mouth couldn't go on. Without her, I couldn't go on either. We kissed each other and embraced. And the rest you already know.*

# 46

My mother woke me, banging on my door so hard the knob rattled. I leapt from my bed, thinking the house was on fire. "What's wrong?"

"Thank God, thank God," my mother called to the ceiling. She began pacing in circles. Her nightgown was on. Her hair in tangles. She was sweating.

"What is it?" I asked, confused by the sudden change in her.

My mother touched at my face and arms as though making sure I was really there. "I had such a terrible dream."

Thinking of the house and the flies from the previous night, I cringed. "What dream?"

She sat on the edge of the bed and stared at her hands. "I was in a kitchen. It wasn't our kitchen, but it still felt like home. Something was cooking. Everything smelled wonderful. Spices and black pepper. Cumin. The counter was covered with fresh vegetables. Like from a garden. There was a pot on the stove. The lid began to rattle, so I scooped up a handful of vegetables to drop them into the boiling water. I removed the lid. Inside the pot, was your head. Your eyes had boiled away. Your skin had loosened. But it didn't bother me. I just dropped the vegetables in like it was what I was supposed to do. When I turned towards another counter, I saw the rest of your body. Which had been cut up into neat piles." My mother stopped.

I could tell there was more. "Then what?" I asked, suddenly sweating.

She hesitated. "Well, I grabbed an empty bowl and filled it with...parts of you...and I started eating. A woman came down the stairs and asked if she could join me. I said, of course. We ate together. She said everything tasted delicious." My mother looked away in shame.

"The witch," I whispered.

She couldn't accept it. "Nonsense, Sarah! Just because there was *some* woman in my dream doesn't mean it was the same one you claim has been coming after you!"

"Then why did you come and tell me about it? Obviously you thought it was her."

"No, I didn't."

"Then why didn't you want to tell me that part?"

"I – I don't know."

"You don't think that sounds a lot like my dreams? You don't think there's not some sort of similarity, Mom?"

She shook her head in refusal. "It was just a dream."

"Then why are you so upset?"

"How could I not be upset about a dream like that?"

"Then why tell me?" I asked again.

"Who else can I tell? And I don't even know why it upset me so much. Maybe I shouldn't have told you at all!"

"Oh, great! You have a dream about eating me and now you don't even know why it upset you!"

"That's not what I meant! I meant that it was just a dream so I should know that it's just a dream. I should have been more rational. Dreams are dreams. That's all they are. Stop looking at me like that, Sarah! It's not like I'm going to *eat* you!"

I looked towards my window and then my bedroom door, expecting the witch to be at either. I wanted Stitch Mouth and Balloon Girl at my side. "Ready for a heavy dose of crazy, Mom?"

My mother stood and crossed her arms over her chest. "Sure!

Fine! Go ahead."

"Maybe, since the witch hasn't been able to catch me, she'll eat me through you somehow."

"That is revolting! I would never!"

"You don't know the witch like I do!"

My mother let out a heavy sigh of aggravation. "Since when did she become a *witch* anyway?"

"Ready for even more crazy?" I laughed a little. "I know she's a witch because Stitch Mouth and Balloon Girl told me. And they're the reason I HAVEN'T DIED!"

My mother paced in tight angry circles. She was about two seconds from pulling out her hair. "What is going on with you, Sarah? Stitch Girl and Clown Face!"

I was offended. "Stitch Mouth and Balloon Girl! Get it right, Mom!"

"I don't even know what to say!"

"I bet I know what you're thinking though."

"Oh, and what's that? Did your make-believe friends tell you what I was thinking?"

"Now you're making me angry, Mom! They're not make believe! Say anything bad about them again and – and –"

"And, what, Sarah? What?"

"Forget it!"

"What was I thinking, Sarah? Tell me!"

"It's obvious! You were thinking about taking me to the mental hospital."

"Of course I was! You need help!"

"I already have help. And my friends are way better than all those people at the hospital."

"Really? Really, Sarah? Having make-believe friends who help you fight away a make-believe witch doesn't sound like help to me! Do you know what it sounds like? Like absolute lunacy!"

"Actually, it's the truth."

"Now you're concerning me." She stopped her circles. "Please, answer me honestly, do I need to take you?" She was trying to sound reasonable. I don't know if she really thought I'd say yes.

"To the mental hospital? Not a chance. But *you* might have to go there for a visit yourself soon enough if you keep having those dreams about eating me."

"Oh please, Sarah, having *one* dream does not make me insane."

"I'm not insane either, Mom. I never was."

"Sarah, I had one dream. You saw things and you are *still* seeing things, and now you're seeing even more things! What are their names again?"

"Thing one and thing two."

She grinned in anger. I thought she was going to smack me. But then her voice and eyes suddenly changed. "There you go again, lying to me. My *silly* little lying Sarah." She was alternating between herself and the witch again, transitioning each time she blinked.

"Stop talking like that, Mom."

Her grin looked distorted, as though the witch was trying to wear my mother's skin. "How many more tricks do you think you have left?"

Her question stole my breath. But she wanted me afraid. I remembered my promise to Stitch Mouth and Balloon Girl. I remembered all the stories that had taught me to hate her more than fear her. "We have more than enough."

She patted my leg. "Oh, Sarah. Such a pretty little liar."

"Mom! Mom!" I snapped my fingers in front of her eyes. "Mom! Mom!"

"What, Sarah? What?" But even though my mother sounded annoyed with what I was doing, she seemed confused, like she wasn't sure where she'd been for a few seconds.

I took my mother's hands. "Mom, please, if you keep having dreams like that, please tell me."

"They're only dreams, Sarah." But this time, she didn't sound convinced.

"Just tell me, okay? This isn't like you. These dreams and the way you've been acting."

She shook her head at herself. "I know. I'm sorry. You're right. I don't know what got into me. I've been acting different lately, and I don't even know why. And that dream. It was horrible. I'm embarrassed I even had a dream like that. I'm sorry."

I hugged my mother tight, trying to keep her with me, hoping she could stay with me just a little longer. There wasn't much time left.

# 47

"Stitch Mouth. Balloon Girl."

"Yes?"

*What is it?*

"The witch is trying to get to me through my mother. I have to keep my door locked all the time, and even then, I can still hear her trying to open it at times. She's been humming the witch's songs. She's been trying to fatten me up. And now she's dreaming about being in the witch's house and eating me. But I don't think she even knows what she's doing. It's like she's not herself."

"How long has this been happening?" Stitch Mouth asked, sounding very much like a nurse concerned over symptoms.

"I'm not really sure. Maybe the whole time. But it's getting worse. I don't know what to do. I can't hurt my own mom, but I'm afraid that she's going to hurt me."

*We have to convince her to fight back. We have to convince her the witch is real.*

"Well, that's never going to happen," I said. "Any other ideas?"

"Balloon Girl is right. We have to convince her the witch is real."

*It's the only way. If she does not believe, then the tentacles of the witch will sink deeper and deeper. She has to be the one to fight back. It won't take much. The witch is weakest in this world.*

"Okay, but how do I do that? Every time I bring the witch up my mom wants to take me to the mental hospital. Today, I even mentioned you two. She wanted to drive me to the hospital immediately. Big surprise, right?"

"You mentioned us?" Stitch Mouth was flattered.

Balloon Girl brushed her skull with a bone hand. *Did you tell her how beautiful we were?*

I laughed. "No, I can't say I described you at all."

"But you can't tell her because she won't believe you," Stitch Mouth cautioned.

"I already said that."

"Which is why you're not the one who is going to tell her."

"Who will? You two?"

Stitch Mouth decorated her smile with a wink.

*This is going to be fun!*

If there had been food in my mouth, I would have choked on it. If I had been drinking something, it probably would have shot out through my nose. "Yeah, um, no. That's definitely not going to happen."

"Why not?"

"For obvious reasons." I held my hands out to the both of them, displaying the blatancy of why not.

*Oh, Sarah, don't you see? This will be fun.*

The idea was ridiculous and nerve-wracking. I couldn't help but laugh. "If you say so."

Stitch Mouth jabbed a finger into my ribs. "I do. And so does Balloon Girl."

I shied away from her pokes. "Well, I guess it can't make anything that much worse. If anything, she'll just think it's another crazy dream."

*A crazy dream with two very intelligent, very beautiful, little girls. With one being two months older than the other.*

Stitch Mouth laughed, then opened the simple door of my bedroom. The hallway ended at my mother's bedroom. No chalk necessary. My mom was about to get the shock of her life.

# 48

"Mom."

My mother's eyes opened in a sleepy daze. "Is everything okay?"

I walked towards her bed. "Everything's okay. I wanted to talk about something."

"Can't it wait until morning? I have to work tomorrow."

"It can't *happen* in the morning." Kneeling beside her bed, I brushed a few strands of hair from her face.

She tried to lay back down. "Sarah, it's late. Let's just talk in the morning."

"Like I said it can't *happen* then. I just need to explain a few things, okay?"

"What things?"

"You know how you've been having those dreams? And you've been acting different too, like, you haven't quite been yourself?"

"Yeah, sure. But what is this about? Why are we talking about this now? Did you have another nightmare?"

"No." It was now or never. "Like I said before, they're not just dreams you're having, and it's not just a coincidence that you're dreaming about the same witch that's been haunting me."

"Sarah, please, let's not bring up that woman of yours right now."

"Actually, I don't want to talk about the witch either. But there is someone else I want you to meet."

That was their cue. The door slid open again. The darkness of the hallway gave way to the subtle light from the light of my bedroom at the other end. Feeble light. First came skeleton feet. Then red shoes. In a way, I had an opportunity to see Balloon Girl and Stitch Mouth for the first time. They were ghastly. Horror girls from some dark tale about demons and their demon children. I couldn't help but smile.

"Hi," Stitch Mouth greeted.

"Sarah!" My mom clambered out of bed, shoving her way past me to snatch up a shoe to defend herself with. Tucked to the corner, she reached out to pull me back while waving her shoe at Balloon Girl and Stitch Mouth. "Stay back!"

*Oh, boy. Maybe this was a bad idea.*

I introduced, "Mom, these are the friends I was telling you about. This is Stitch Mouth. This is Balloon Girl." The girls curtsied at the mention of their name.

My mother didn't hear me. "I – I – I – I'm dreaming. That's what this. It's a dream. Just like all the others. Just a dream. Just a dream." My mother closed her eyes and shook her head vigorously, maybe thinking she'd wake up in bed or that she could tap her heels and disappear. Then she slapped herself across the face.

"Mom, stop! Oh my goodness!"

She looked at me, trying to figure out if I was really me.

"Mom, it's not a dream. This is where I go every night. This is where the witch is always trying to catch me."

"Witch? There's no witch! And those two things aren't real! All a dream. All a dream. All a dream."

*That woman is not right in the head.*

I waved at Balloon Girl, telling her to stop, then turned my attention back to my mother. "Mom. I'm sorry. It's not a dream. You can't just wake up. And please, stop shaking your head like that, it makes you look crazy."

My mother stopped, looked at me intently. "How do I wake up?"

"You already are awake. But you woke up in a different place."

"What place?" My mother refused to even glance at the door where Balloon Girl and Stitch Mouth still watched quietly. I was glad they weren't offended by how my mom was acting, even though it was embarrassing me.

"Never mind that, Mom, please. I want you to listen."

"I'm listening, I am. I am. Just, make those *things* leave." She flicked her hand their way.

That made my blood hot. "They're not *things*. They're my friends. They're the reason I'm alive." I took her hand and pressed it to my face, convincing her of my realness. When she realized how very real I was, I oriented her towards the door, tilting her just enough so that she would have to face Stitch Mouth and Balloon Girl. "But I don't want to explain anything to you. I want them to. Well, really, I want Stitch Mouth to because she's the only one who you'll be able to hear."

*I'd probably say something I shouldn't.*

Stitch Mouth giggled at Balloon Girl's comment, but when my mother gasped, Stitch Mouth put a hand to her mouth. "Sorry," she said.

I stood behind my mother, hugging her. My mother's tears fell to my arm. I told her she was safe because I was there. With a low wave, I beckoned Stitch Mouth and Balloon Girl to take another step inside. My mother trembled when they did, but I held her tighter and gave her another promise.

"Mom, will you let Stitch Mouth talk to you?" I asked.

My mother nodded like a ransom victim.

"Go ahead," I said to Stitch Mouth.

Through the hours, Stitch Mouth explained everything to my mother. Stitch Mouth took her time, maintaining her courtesy and her sweetness. My mother eventually asked questions. They sounded a lot like mine used to be. As the questions and answers came and went, my mother relaxed in my arms, and before the night was over, we were sitting side by side on the bed, and my mother spoke with Stitch Mouth in a way that told me she was listening. Before the night ended, my mother asked, "When I wake up, how will I know this wasn't a dream?"

Stitch Mouth walked over cautiously, as though approaching a wounded animal, and handed her the purple bow from her hair. "Here. When you wake up, this will still be with you. I just ask that you return it to Sarah. My dad gave it to me. It's my favorite."

"Sure. Of course," my mother said.

"And remember –" Stitch Mouth cautioned "– you must fight the influence of the witch. We draw her away at night. But in the daytime, you must recognize when she is trying to change the way you see Sarah. We have to close off the witch's options, and we need your help to do it."

"Yes. Of course."

"Good." Stitch Mouth smiled. Then she turned to me and touched my face. "Goodnight, Sarah."

I stood and kissed Stitch Mouth's cheek. "Goodnight."

*Goodnight, Sarah.*

"Goodnight, Balloon Girl."

*I don't want you kissing me anyway.*

I went to her and kissed her cheek as well. "Goodnight, Balloon Girl."

*Goodnight.*

They left. I stayed with my mother to explain a little more. When the sun rose, my mother and I woke in our own beds. We met at the center of the hallway. My mother handed me the bow, shaking her head in disbelief before hugging me and weeping at how sad she was for never believing me.

# 49

Traps were prepared. We stood at our stations. Balloon Girl was in the kitchen, bent behind a cabinet. Two other balloon girls crouched near her. Stitch Mouth stood where the door would open. I was tucked into a corner, cradling an axe in my shaky hands. The longer we waited, the heavier the axe felt.

Then we heard her. Leaves crunching. The front door gave a creak. Pale fingers wrapped the edge of the door. A foot touched. Dangles of black hair drifted inside. A body followed.

Rushing feet and a holler of rage. Balloon Girl and the other girls collided into the witch, grabbing at her and tugging her to the center of the room. Stitch Mouth ran at the witch's back while she was occupied with the other two girls and slammed against her. I stepped from the corner, watching. Waiting for my moment. The witch was hissing and swinging, swatting at the girls. Her back was to me. I took another step. Lifted the axe. So heavy. I swung. The axe struck the witch in the side of the head, but only knocked her to the floor. I had hit her with the flat side of the axe, not the blade. The girls scurried over the witch's body. Stitch Mouth held a leg. The balloon girls secured arms. Balloon Girl remained at the head of the witch, wrenching at her long black hair to expose her neck and face. The witch was woozy from my blow, uncertain, laying there. Traces of blood trickled from her scalp, wetting her hair.

I stood over the witch and raised the axe to the ceiling. I imagined the witch's house. All the death. My friends. Stitch Mouth's brother.

The eyes of the witch met mine. "Please, don't."

Her plea struck my nerve. The axe weighed a hundred pounds over my head. The witch wouldn't look away, just held me with a pitiful gaze that transformed her into something human.

The axe wobbled.

"Do it!" Stitch Mouth screamed.

*Do it, Sarah! Now!*

In a sudden burst of violence, the witch ripped herself free. I swung the axe at her retreat. But it split into a floorboard, causing my arms to hurt with the reverberation. The door flew open. The witch escaped.

I looked around at everyone. Their heads hung low. They wouldn't look at me. I had failed them. I had failed all of us. We stood together in the aftermath of what could have been, my failure.

"It's okay," Stitch Mouth finally said.

"No, it's not."

*It's okay, Sarah. We'll get her next time.*

Sounds from the woods interrupted us. Crunching leaves and the noise of feet.

*She's coming back!*

"The witch is not alone," Stitch Mouth stated in confusion, eyeing the windows around us.

A bang jolted the door, startling us. A face appeared in the nearest window, dark and disfigured. It disappeared again. Fists banged on the walls like hail. We were surrounded. Stitch Mouth ran to the center of the floor. The rest of us went to her, huddling together. Squeals of victory erupted outside. The axe was in my hands again, but it felt like a hindrance.

Balloon Girl sidled closer to my side, looking from window to window to door. *Be ready, Sarah.*

A crash came from Stitch Mouth's bedroom. The window had been shattered. Shoes on broken glass. Someone was climbing through. I thought it was the witch. But then her hair drifted past the window across from us.

"Return the girls," Stitch Mouth commanded to Balloon Girl.

*What?*

"Return them!"

Balloon Girl did as she was told, and the two girls became balloons again.

Stitch Mouth bent to the floor, holding a piece of chalk made of sparking glitter. She tapped the tip to the floor and began to spiral it outward. The chalk circled faster and faster. Winds arose at our feet. Glitter brushed the floor. The circling gusts rose, touching at our ankles, continuing to expand, as it rose until it whipped my hair about my face. A miniature tornado had formed, growing more and more violent in purple-streaks. A chair crashed against the wall, flung by the winds. The table flipped over and continued until it too hit the wall. Clothes tossed the air before scuttling to the fireplace where they flew up into the night. Balloon Girl's remaining balloons fought against her grip.

Stitch Mouth stood in the heart of her storm. She was smiling.

The walls began to shake. Boards wobbled, loosening, and one flew off into the night. Another peeled away. The winds ripped and swirled. Stitch Mouth called out at the top of her voice, "We need to go!"

With the same glittering chalk, Stitch Mouth sketched a door she opened. Balloon Girl and I jumped down, landing on top of my mattress. I stared up and watched. Stitch Mouth blew a kiss to her home. Then she dropped down as well. The chalk crushed. The door on my ceiling disappeared. The winds as well.

My hair was tangled around my head like a bird's nest. My clothes were ruffled. "Wow," I said.

Balloon Girl touched my arm and shook her head.

Stitch Mouth sat up neatly and closed her purse. She reset the bow in her hair and flattened out her skirt. Stitch Mouth was about to stand from us, but Balloon Girl reached over and pulled Stitch Mouth into a hug. Stitch Mouth dropped her head to Balloon Girl's shoulder. "It's okay."

"We can't go back to your home, can we?" I asked.

"No."

Her home. The place we spent most of our nights. A place of safety and enjoyment for me. A home filled with memories for Stitch Mouth who was able to talk about her family as though they might return. Destroyed by Stitch Mouth's own hand. And of course, she had done so for me. For me. Always for me. It made me sick. Sick of all the loss. Sick of the witch. But most of all, sick of me.

"Your home is gone," I said.

"I had no choice."

I was becoming hysterical, "You've lost your home! Again! And those girls! The balloon girls! They die for me! It's all I can imagine, them being ripped apart! Dying!"

*What do you want, Sarah? Everything has a cost.*

"But I'm so tired of being the one who never has to pay!" I broke down crying. "If I had done something earlier, then none of this would have happened! Stitch Mouth would still have her home! Those other balloon girls never would have died! I never wanted anyone to get hurt! Not for me! Not for me." My face was in my hands. I couldn't look at them.

*Enough, Sarah. Wipe your tears. Save your anger for the witch.*

Stitch Mouth stood and came over to me. She hugged me. "It's okay, Sarah."

"But you loved going to your home."

"I did."

"And you're okay?"

"I am."

"Promise?"

"With all my heart."

I think it was the only time she ever really lied to me.

# 50

If the witch was made wary by what had happened – had almost happened – we became even more wary. We took fewer paths and fewer doors, both to conserve what we had, like last rations, but also because we were unsure of what the witch would do next. In the past, we had run from her, we had tricked her, but now, we had tried to kill her. And someone else was with her. She wasn't alone.

The following night, we stayed to the in-between rooms. Stitch Mouth kept at least two pieces of chalk pinched between her knuckles to ensure we had our best options readily available. And we spent the night in silence. In part, to be ready, and also because none of us had much to say. I had already apologized enough times to earn a sharp *No more, Sarah!* from Balloon Girl, and this time, Stitch Mouth didn't intervene. I wanted to apologize every time I took a breath. But what would that have done? When it came to the other people who were at the house that night, their surprise being what forced Stitch Mouth to do what she had done, we simply didn't bring it up, because no one had an answer.

Traveling along like weary sojourners, we turned at the corner of an in-between room and stopped. The witch stood at the other end, blackened by shadows. Her head tilted just slightly, almost at the ceiling. Her arms hung long at her sides. We stood at opposing ends of the hall, silhouetted in a darkened standoff. No one moved. We were held there by the peculiar way the witch waited. Then the witch bent her way back through the door she had entered and shut the door.

# 51

"We haven't seen the witch for a few nights now. Not even at my window."

"I know."

"Why not?"

"I believe she is planning."

"What do you think she's planning?"

"I'm not sure."

# 52

I stepped through into the in-between room first, with Balloon Girl and Stitch Mouth remaining behind me, looking and listening for the witch. The door slammed shut. Fingernails raked my bare shoulder and I screamed out in terror and pain. I tore away. Warm blood. I shrank, tucking myself to the corner. The witch's hands went for my throat and she lifted me to my toes, stretching me against the wall, smiling at my grimace. Balloon Girl and Stitch Mouth's yells and bangs reverberated uselessly against the door as the witch held it closed with her heel. Her grip tightened around my throat. I flailed against the wall, losing air, crying in pain. My neck gave off a pop. My lungs screamed at me to breath. The witch brought her face to mine. Her breath sank down my face and down my shirt. Her eyes absorbed me.

"I have you now. So long. Worth it. Sweet flesh." Her nail crossed my belly. "Tasty. Sweet. Flesh."

I began to cry.

"Yes. Cry. Salty." Her tongue slithered over my face.

"Friends. Not here. Can't save you. Tricky friends."

"I hate you," I said. "I hate you."

She mocked my sadness. "Makes me so sad."

"I don't care if you kill me," I said. "I don't care anymore."

"You will."

I forced a smile through the grimace. "You can't take our friendship. Ever."

She smiled more darkly. "I can." Then she began choking me again. My eyes rolled toward the top of my head. Everything became distant.

A green rectangle glowed on the wall across from us. I faked further pain, hoping the witch would stay intent on hurting me. She laughed darkly at my expression, pleased by how I cringed. The girls burst through the new door like a miniature army troop. The witch spun and shrieked, releasing me. I dropped to the floor, coughing.

Stitch Mouth was at the witch first, but the witch decked her against the wall. Balloon Girl was next, but she was kicked to the side. A balloon girl dove, knocking her shoulder into the belly of the witch. The witch scrambled in an attempt to get back to her feet, but the girl kept coming, tussling her way to the witch's chest, punching as she rose. Stitch Mouth was up again, shaking away the daze, and she ran at the witch again. Balloon Girl just behind her.

The witch dropped beneath their assault, falling near my toes. She was so close, I could touch her. Her eyes flicked up to me just in time to see me lean over to put my hands around her throat. It was my turn. Her neck was thin and balmy. I hated the feel of her. The girls took positions on her limbs, faceting her down. My grip tightened. The eyes of the witch drew in a panic. My hands continued to work. Squeezing. Pressing. The witch lurched and bucked, but the girls held tight, causing the witch to grow more faint as she burned the oxygen she didn't have.

I couldn't believe it. The witch was in my hands. Her eyes were dimming. Her struggles weakening. She was going to die. I began to cry. The overflow of emotion, of all that had happened, of all that been done, it came out in a mixture that could not have been named, but it poured from my eyes. Stitch Mouth and Balloon Girl were intent on their duty, but they glanced my way to ensure I was okay, that I could go through with it. I could.

Balloon Girl nodded at me. Stitch Mouth held a look of slim concern for me, hoping I was okay to do what I was doing. The witch wilted. I couldn't watch. I looked up and past them, focusing on the door which had been created to save me as I finished. I saw the chalk on the floor. It would be the last chalk we would ever need. I kept my eyes on these things, not wanting to look at what I was doing.

The witch became limp. I looked down. Her blank, empty eyes stared up at me. I released my grip. Suddenly, the door burst open, causing the four of us to turn. A boy stood there. He was tall and pasty, almost sickly. His clothes were small and his hair matted. He looked at us. He looked at me. He saw the witch between my knees. A twist of rage contorted his face before he launched himself at us. He backhanded Stitch Mouth and punched both Balloon Girl and the other girl before kicking me in the face. Slammed back against the wall, my vision blurred with pain, blood in my mouth. The boy hovered over the witch, then dropped to her side, where he began slamming a fist onto her chest. "Mother! Wake up!"

The four of us had scattered to different corners, and we watched from where we were, disoriented by the confusion, but still hoping it was finished. The boy growled and hit the witch again. "Wake up!"

The witch convulsed back to life. She looked up at the boy, confused, then astounded. The boy helped her to her feet, an arm around her waist. Regaining her senses and her strength, the witch's hatred returned. But we were scurrying our way back out through the green door. Stitch Mouth sketched a pink door, leading us into Balloon Girl's home where she crushed the chalk immediately. We were too stunned to keep running. And we had to talk.

# 53

"We almost had her," I stated in disappointment.

*Not we. You.*

"You did have her," Stitch Mouth corrected the both of us. "The witch was dead."

I still didn't know how to feel about coming so close to what we had craved so desperately for so long. It felt more like failure, yet Stitch Mouth and Balloon Girl weren't disappointed at all.

*How did it feel?*

"I don't want to think about it."

*Tell me,* Balloon Girl asked with anticipation.

I measured the multiple sensations running through my body. The drained feeling in my arms which proved how hard I had been squeezing. My tired hands. The way my fingers wouldn't stop trembling. The sick feeling in my belly. The moment had been horribly personal. The witch in my hands. Her struggling efforts to stay alive. Her final twitch. The blankness in her eyes. It felt like something I was never meant to do. Had been forced to do, but never wanted.

"I hated it. It felt terrible. It felt *wrong.*"

*Really?* Balloon Girl sounded worse than disappointed.

"You make it sound like all of those feelings are wrong!"

*It's just – personally – I thought it would have felt wonderful.*

"It didn't. It felt *nothing* like wonderful."

*Are you sure?* Balloon Girl asked, as though I may have been confused on what we were talking about or how I actually felt.

"Enough, Balloon Girl," Stitch Mouth said. "Leave Sarah alone. Asking her repeatedly won't change the fact that Sarah did not enjoy what she was forced to do."

*Well, it's surprising, is all. I would have thought it felt much better than terrible and wrong.*

"Sarah is not you."

*I know.* Balloon Girl nodded. *And Sarah, I am not asking you because I'm being sarcastic or to tease you. But after all the witch has done –*

"I was just trying to get through it. I wasn't thinking about anything that the witch had done. Not what she had done to the both of you or to Stitch Mouth's brother." I tensed.

Stitch Mouth's eyes widened – her secret had been exposed. She turned on Balloon Girl. "You told her."

Balloon Girl lowered her face. *I had to.*

Stitch Mouth looked too shocked to be angry or hurt. "You had no right."

*Forgive me. But Sarah had to know. Do not pretend that your brother's death was yours alone to witness. I was there too. And it was the moment that sealed our deaths. It was when you left me, and I knew you'd never return. Sarah had to know.*

"Why?" Stitch Mouth wanted an answer.

*You love her as you love me. Such a secret must be known because Sarah loves you as well. Knowing what happened to your brother, to you, will empower her resolve to do what she must.*

"I don't know what to say," Stitch Mouth said.

*Say that you forgive me.*

"There's nothing to forgive."

*You're not upset?*

"No."

Before we could say anything more, the most amazing thing

happened. A sunbeam traced the floor.

"The sun." I pointed.

Stitch Mouth's mouth opened in speechless awe.

*It's beautiful,* Balloon Girl said in a whisper. Then she walked beyond us, stepping into the growing golden pool. *It's beautiful.* Balloon Girl raised her hands out from her sides, taking in the fresh warmth of the newborn ray. *And warm.*

Dawn of the third world rose through the window as we stood and watched. Soon, the house was filled. Everything sparkled.

Rising to her toes, Balloon Girl danced elegantly between the windows, passing in and out of the glittering rays.

Stitch Mouth extended her arms before her, accepting the sun into her palms.

"Why is the sun rising?"

"Perhaps this world is rejoicing at how close the witch had come to death. At least, that's what I'd like to think."

*You were close, Sarah. You can do this, because you already have. And this marvelous sun! What a night! What a day! I must dance.* And she was off again.

Stitch Mouth stated, "The boy."

"You don't sound surprised," I said.

Stitch Mouth took a moment to try and relay something she didn't know how to convey, or didn't want to. "When I first saw the boy enter, it took me a moment to recognize him."

"He lived in the house with you? Back when you were alive?"

"Yes. There was something different about the boy."

"What?"

"He was the only child who never cried at night."

"He liked it there?"

"Not necessarily. But the home he had come from was a place of beatings and *other* abuses, and so, while it may seem unthinkable, the witch had brought him to a house better than his own. The boy was always disturbed though. He enjoyed watching the beatings the witch gave to us. He's as bad as she is."

"But he's a kid. Like us."

*If you think he is anything like us, then you are a fool.*

"That is too harsh," Stitch Mouth corrected.

"No, Balloon Girl is right. I need to know these things. But it makes me think – all the boy wanted was to not get killed, right, and that's why he did it? Can we really blame him?"

"Yes. We can blame him." This time it was Stitch Mouth who was upset.

"What? Why?"

"It means that he has taken on the witch's tastes. Therefore, I am certain he has helped her in taking other children as well."

"But maybe he only did it to live longer," I reasoned. "Before you came to protect me, I was scared, too. I was even willing to go with the witch just to get her to leave me alone. Which sounds stupid to say, but it's true."

Stitch Mouth turned on me, her red eyes blazing in the new sun. "I would choose death again and again before becoming anything like the witch! Are you saying that if Balloon Girl and I had not come to you, you would have become like the witch, just so you could live a *little* longer?"

*Leave her be, Stitch Mouth.* Now it was Balloon Girl who intervened.

"No. Sarah, if that boy chose to accept a life like that, then he chose no life at all!"

*Enough, Stitch Mouth.*

"But she's so powerful, that's all I was saying. And he was just a child."

"We were children as well."

"I know," I said in shame. "I didn't mean to make you so angry."

"No, Sarah. I am not angry with you. I am disgusted by the power the witch has over children in far more ways than I ever wanted to imagine. And I want it to end."

"We'll probably only get one more chance," I admitted.

*Third times a charm. And we have a few chalk left and two balloons – enough to finish this. But we should try something new. I believe, after all this time, we need a completely different tactic, a different approach.*

"And what is that?" Stitch Mouth asked.

*We need to kill her with kindness.*

"Here we go."

*Here me out. We need to consider the witch's feelings. So, this is what we do. We invite her to a tea party. We get all dressed up. And we tell the witch we are willing to love her and appreciate her for who she is. I'll pour her some tea for all of us. Then we shove puffed pastries down her throat until she suffocates on them.*

"I don't know if that is what people mean when they say, 'kill them with kindness,'" I said with a smile.

*Are you sure?*

Stitch Mouth laughed. "I knew it was leading somewhere ridiculous."

*You don't think it would work?*

"I don't think so."

"Whatever we plan, we must consider that boy," I said.

Stitch Mouth turned to me. "Yes."

"Stitch Mouth?"

"Yes?"

"I'm afraid," I admitted.

"Me too."

"This would have been a lot easier if we had more chalk and balloons. But I took too long."

"Maybe. But maybe not."

"It would have been easier, and you know it."

"Yes. I know."

"But by using the chalk like we have been, we got to spend a lot of time together. That's what I loved the most."

"I have loved it as well."

"Is that bad of me? Selfish of me?"

"No. I have no regrets, Sarah."

*I have loved it too. No regrets, Sarah. None at all.*

"Do you know what I'm worried about the most?" I asked.

*That the witch can breathe fire?*

I laughed. "No. Something else."

*That would be bad though.*

Uninterested in any more banter, Stitch Mouth's red eyes shimmered with curiosity. They were beautiful. "What worries you the most, Sarah?"

My bottom lip trembled. "That when it's all over, we won't be able to spend time together."

They both nodded.

*We don't have much time. And we must prepare for the boy.*

"Stitch mouth, exactly how many more chalk do you have left?"

She didn't even need to look. "Three."

"Oh, wow, you were almost out!"

She smirked. "Yes."

"And Balloon Girl only has two balloons. But I don't want you to use them."

*Sarah, this is no time to be a fool. I will use the balloons. And you will not refuse me.*

"But –"

*No. They sacrifice willingly. And we will need them.*

"Okay." I gave in. "Tomorrow, I'll think up a plan to beat her. I'll be ready. But first, how many other children do you think the witch had with her that night when we were surrounded?"

*There seemed to* be *three*

Stitch Mouth agreed.

"Why don't you think she's brought them before?" I asked.

*The witch has always enjoyed the chase. I believe we forced her to realize she could not defeat us on her own, especially after how close we came to killing her.*

"We finish it. Tomorrow." I shivered at the use of that simple ominous word the witch had once said to me.

*Tomorrow.*

"Tomorrow."

THE WOMAN IN THE WINDOW

# 54

"What's with the scarf?" Emma asked, flicking at the tassels.

"No. Yeah. I was cold." A scarf hid the bruises the witch had given me.

"I know, right? It was freezing this morning."

"Was it?" I was in and out of the conversation, forgetting almost instantly anything outside of what I needed for my plan.

She laughed. "You just said yourself that it was."

"Oh, yeah."

"What's with you?" Emma asked through a chuckle, distracting me from my schemes as I worked through countless plans and possibilities through the pages of my notebook. It was tough. The last thing Stitch Mouth had told me the previous night was, *You know the witch well enough to finish this.* It helped. But not as much as I'd hoped.

I answered, "Oh, nothing. Um, I was thinking about the assignment. The project and stuff."

Emma laughed. "What assignment? It's the last day of school!

We're graduating tomorrow!"

"Oh, right. Yeah. I was. Um, kidding."

She laughed. "Great joke, Sarah. Like, the funniest ever. Well, when you're done with your *assignment*, maybe we can hang out sometime. We haven't hung out, in like, forever."

I scribbled a few notes.

"Sarah?" She snapped her fingers. "Earth to Sarah."

"Yeah," I said. "Hang out. That'd be great. I hope we can."

"Hope we can?" she asked.

I looked at her. "That I'll be able to."

"Are you grounded or something?" Her eyes touched a glance at my notebook and the notes that read *lead her this way, corner her, use a knife.* A planned out real life pre-murder scene to *Clue.* Emma realized what I was doing. "It's that woman, isn't it? She hasn't left you yet?"

"No."

"I'm so sorry!" Guilt was in her eyes, guilt and hurt for me. "You've been acting like yourself again, at least some, so I figured that horrible woman had left you. That's why I haven't brought her up. I just wanted to, you know, forget about what happened and whatever."

"I don't blame you," I assured with a smile. I felt bad because she really looked upset at not being a good friend. But she had been.

"I'm so sorry," she said again. "I could have at least asked. But it was scary. And you were better. I just thought."

"It's not your fault. It's mine for not saying anything. Believe me, I don't like talking about it either."

"That was totally freaky, right?"

"Totally." I asked, "When did we start saying *totally*?"

"Just now." Her smile rose then dropped. "So, what are you doing?"

"I'm going to kill her tonight."

"Whoa! What? When did you step out into the spotlight as *Sarah badass*?"

"I'm not. And I'm not trying to be. It's just – I can't let her haunt me forever. I can't, I don't know, I can't let her keep going. She's hurt so many people. I have to try."

Emma held back any words of second-guessing – any

inadvertent sabotage she might have been ready to say – and instead, a hint of anticipation flashed through her eyes. "How are you going to do it?"

I chuckled miserably. "That's the part I haven't figured out yet."

She threw a hand over her mouth then waved it at me. "I'll totally shut up then. Oh, my gosh, I can't even believe you've been going through all this while everyone else has been complaining about tests and whatever."

"That doesn't matter." No matter how much I tried, I couldn't focus. I shut the notebook. "You know what? I think I need to take my mind off of it."

"Are you sure? I totally understand if you can't talk."

"Totally." I winked.

"Okay, okay." Emma thought a moment, as though we were on a first date and had stumbled into an awkward patch of conversation. "Okay, so, do you have big plans for graduation, or nah?"

"Kind of. My mom set up banners and ribbons all around the living room and kitchen, and there's a stack of invitations my mom's been getting back from family and friends. People who have RSVP'd or whatever." Ever since my mother had met Stitch Mouth and Balloon Girl, she had become herself again and had stopped treating me like some evil identical twin of myself. Periodically, she'd ask how things were, hinting that she was curious about the witch, and she even asked one morning about Stitch Mouth and Balloon Girl, which I absolutely loved. I asked Emma, "What about you?"

"Same thing. Banners, ribbons, fru-haha. My dad's new fiancé is coming, which could be drama. My mom hates seeing him happy."

"Hopefully everyone will remember that it's *your* graduation."

"Totally."

"I hope we never turn out like that."

"Totally!"

The bell rang. And with it, high school was over. Emma escorted me outside. Before she got on her bus, she squeezed me into a hug. "See you at graduation tomorrow."

"If –"

"No. I'll see you at graduation tomorrow." She winked at me. "Sarah badass."

On my walk home, I thought about the night ahead with a fresh wave of contemplation and ideas. Talking with Emma had helped. Tomorrow had come.

# 55

I went to sleep early after telling my mom I wanted to rest up for graduation. But she knew better. Brushing her fingers through my hair, she said, "Stay close to those friends of yours." Then she asked, "Can I help?"

It was something that had never crossed my mind, and yet, now that she asked, I wondered if her help was something I should have considered earlier. But I had a plan. A plan which didn't include her. "No. But thank you."

"I love you."

"I love you, too."

A gentle kiss woke me. Stitch Mouth was there. There was no hint of fear at all in her beautiful face. She kissed me one more time.

*Ready?*

I sat up. "I am. And I have a plan." They listened intently as I began, "Balloon Girl's home is the best place to go because of all the rooms. Another home would only confuse us as much as the witch. And again, I think we can use the rooms to our advantage." Their nods encouraged me. "When we get to the house, Balloon Girl, you'll set loose the last two balloons and have them go to the top of the stairs. The three of us will be up there too, but first, I'll grab a knife from the kitchen."

"Are you okay with using a knife, Sarah?"

"I have to be."

They nodded again.

*A knife would be perfect. Let her feel a blade, just as she has used it on others.*

Stitch Mouth nodded.

"Okay. Good. Remember that time when the witch went past us in the hallway and we went the other way?"

*Yes.*

"It will be something like that. I'll be in Balloon Girl's bedroom with a balloon girl, and Stitch Mouth and Balloon Girl, you'll be in the room across the hall. Balloon Girl, can you make sure the other balloon girl isn't seen by the witch?"

*The girls are as sneaky as me, so, yes.*

"Okay, that's what I was hoping. When the witch comes up the stairs and goes into the bedroom where the balloon girl went, the three of you will cover her with a sheet to give me just enough time to run in with the knife to stab her or something."

*What will my other balloon girl be doing with you? Why not have her begin with us?*

"She'll wait for the other children. She can hold them off at the stairs if they come."

*Good. Anything else?*

"No, not really." I could instantly sense the countless shortcomings I'd ignored and every which way the witch could adapt to everything I had thought of. I shook my head. "I feel so stupid. I thought of plans all day. You'd think I'd have something better than that."

*It's perfect, Sarah. It will work.*

"I adore your plan," Stitch Mouth assured. "As Balloon Girl said, it's perfect."

*My home is the best place because it gives us time to prepare as well, and it also provides confusion with all the places we could hide. More importantly, it gives us time to run if we must. The four of us should be able to hold the witch down long enough for you to do what you must. To stab her. Or something,* Balloon Girl teased.

"But what if the children come again?" I asked. "Do you think it's enough to have the one balloon girl at the top of the stairs?"

"Yes. It's narrow and all we need is enough time for you to do what you must."

*To stab her or something.*

"Oh, stop." Stitch Mouth swatted at Balloon Girl.

*I don't care what or who the witch brings with her. If she brings ten children, a chicken, and a one-winged donkey named The Great Circling Ass, it does not matter. The witch dies tonight.*

Stitch Mouth reached into her purse. "It is time."

# 56

Balloon Girl touched the last two strings to the floor, unlocking girls who twirled in glitter and gave me nods to tell me they were ready. I dashed toward the kitchen, prepared to grab the biggest knife I could find. Pulling open a drawer, there it was. A sharp butcher blade as long as my forearm. I told myself I could do this. I picked it up and shut the drawer.

The girls were waiting near the entrance. I ran back to them. As I did, the knife changed to my touch and felt light and smooth. I looked down to find that the knife had turned to plastic in my hand, dull and white. I stared at it in dumb confusion. Then, beginning at the ceiling, plastic began spread over the entire home, transforming edges and walls. Everything plastic and colored white.

"What? What's happening?" I fumbled with my plastic blade, then dropped it to the plastic floor.

Stitch Mouth pulled in a meek breath of defeat. "I don't know."

Balloon Girl shook her head.

I turned and turned, spinning in horror. "Why?"

"We have to go," Stitch Mouth said, fumbling through her purse.

"Where? You hardly have enough chalk!"

"I have enough for now. We need to go!"

Balloon Girl whipped her head towards the nearest window. *They are here!*

Windows pulled open.

*Run! Upstairs! Stitch Mouth! Get us out of here!*

We raced towards the stairs as eager bodies emerged through the windows. A plump girl in a dress. A boy climbed through another window just ahead. They shrieked in glee and began clambering through more frantically as we passed them, like the smell of us excited them. I was at the spiral staircase first, Balloon Girl in my arms, the two balloon girls behind us. A few steps behind, Stitch Mouth was slowed by her search for a new chalk that would be our escape, lifting her eyes from her purse in short spurts only to yell and point, "Go! I'm right behind you!"

A child lunged, grabbing hold of Stitch Mouth's purse and causing her to stumble backwards from the force. Stitch Mouth fell. The remaining chalk scattered away. Stitch Mouth worked her way back to her feet, but a boy jumped on top of her.

*Go to her!*

Before I could do anything, a balloon girl dove against the child who had mounted Stitch Mouth, allowing Stitch Mouth to wriggle free and rise.

I carried Balloon Girl up the stairs. Stitch Mouth followed. The other balloon girl was up ahead, waving frantically for us to hurry. I glanced behind. The balloon girl who had saved Stitch Mouth was having her head stomped by three children. I wanted to go to her.

*Sarah!*

I ran up the stairs. We entered the first room. Stitch Mouth shut the door.

I placed Balloon Girl to the floor. "Chalk, we're out of chalk!" I stated. "What do we do?"

*We wait out the night. It's our only choice.*

My fear craved a weapon. Something blunt or sharp, it did not matter. With my eyes, I searched the room for any sign of anything or some idea on a new plan. But again, everything was plastic and light, as though the witch were already three steps ahead, reading my thoughts before they were even mine to think. The children could be heard racing up the stairs. They began banging against the door in a fury, causing us to brace ourselves against the door, backs to it, pressing. The banging continued in loud thuds that filled the plastic room with muffled noises that drained my hope and caused my heels to dig deeper. The night had just begun.

The door gave off a pathetic sound. Something weak and surrendering. It was breaking.

*We cannot do this all night.* Balloon Girl's voice was quiet and defeated. She looked at Stitch Mouth.

"I know," Stitch Mouth said.

*I had hoped –*

"Me too," Stitch Mouth said.

*I love you, you know.*

Tears coursed down Stitch Mouth's face. "I love you, too."

*With all my heart.*

"With all my heart."

*I want you to know, I have no regrets.*

Stitch Mouth nodded, smiled, and cried. "No regrets."

"No," I said, trying to regain their attention. "It's not over! We can do this! We just have to wait out the night."

They ignored me.

*You have one last chalk, don't you?*

Stitch Mouth smirked through the tears. "Of course, I do."

*I thought I was supposed to be the tricky one.*

Stitch Mouth smiled, looked down, looked up again. "I learned from you."

Balloon Girl was crying. Her small bones rattling. *I care not about the witch. I care about you. And losing you again.*

"You'll never lose me."

*You'll never lose me either. One last time, I love you.*

"I love you, too."

*Use it, my friend. And goodbye.*

They wrapped themselves in each other's arms. They kissed. Stitch Mouth stood and stepped from the door. "Sarah, help Balloon Girl and the other balloon girl hold the door for as long as you can. I have one last chalk. When I call to you, come to me."

"We can still do this," I said, crying.

"Sarah." Her face was dry, purposeful.

"We can."

"Sarah." She shook her head.

"No. Please. No."

"When I call to you, you come to me. Understand? Tell me you understand."

*Tell her, Sarah.*

I nodded.

Stitch Mouth removed a translucent chalk from a tiny fold in her skirt.

"We can hold the door," I said to Balloon Girl.

*No. We cannot. Even if we'd like to think so. Sarah. You need to do what Stitch Mouth said.* All the levity, all the playful sarcasm I had ever heard from Balloon Girl, was gone. She sounded tired and sad. Like those were the things she always was.

"Please don't do this. There's another chalk. Please."

*Enough.*

"Come, Sarah!" Stitch Mouth called. There was an open door behind her.

The plastic door was breaking at our backs.

"Not without you two," I said.

*Okay.*

"You'll go through with me?" I asked in disbelief.

"Yes. We'll go! Now, hurry!"

"Balloon Girl, you'll come with us?"

*Yes! I'll be right behind you. Go!*

The center of the door split apart, large enough for fingers to dig through. My hair was yanked by eager fingers. I ripped my head away, losing a chunk of hair.

*Go, Sarah! Now!*

The door peeled apart further as their fingers wrenched at the two halves, other hands seeking inside.

"Sarah!" Stitch Mouth screamed. "Now! I'll be right behind you!"

I dashed across the room and threw myself through the door Stitch Mouth had made. "It's too small," I said, pressing myself back out, "It's only big enough for me."

Stitch Mouth thrust her body against me, knocking me all the way in. Then she shut the door. The walls were tight, congested against me, like I was in a moving box made for me. I had to shimmy around to face the door. The door was clear. When I went to open it, my hand slid over the smooth surface. There was no knob.

I banged on my prison. "Stitch Mouth! Let me out!"

Stitch Mouth knelt down to face me, red eyes sad and resolved. "I'm sorry, Sarah."

"You promised! You promised we'd all go through!"

"I'm sorry."

Across the room, I saw behind Stitch Mouth, the door split in half and tear away completely. The filthy faces and wide mouths of the children shoved and clambered against each other to be the first one through.

Balloon Girl and the last balloon girl stepped back from the plastic door and turned towards the children. Outnumbered and small.

*Come, you rotten children of that whore witch. Come to me and I will give you a taste of what you deserve.*

The children smiled, separating themselves to circle Balloon Girl and the other girl. The came closer. Balloon Girl lunged at the first child, a boy, knocking him to the floor and he fell to his back, arms swatting the air as Balloon Girl climbed him. She dug a hooked finger behind his left eye and ripped it from his face. It popped out like ball. The boy writhed and screamed, grasping at his wound, and Balloon Girl did the same to his other eye then dug her thumbs into those two empty sockets. The other balloon girl was at the next child. She grabbed the boy's hair in her hands and took a great step backwards, taking his own momentum, slinging the boy head-first into the floor where his face crunched, breaking his nose and he squealed.

The blind boy remained where he was, crying about his missing eyes. The boy with the broken nose held his face in both hands while the balloon girl kicked the back of his head. Only the pudgy girl was left. Her face and neck were streaked in dark filth. Her fingernails were black with dirt and her hair was plastered to one side of her head. She backed away as Balloon Girl and the other girl cornered her.

I gave the door a thump of victory. Stitch Mouth nodded and smiled. Balloon Girl had done it.

The witch stepped through. She kicked Balloon Girl to the floor and batted the other balloon girl away. The children of the witch rose at her appearing, even the blind boy, who cried out, "Mother!"

Balloon Girl scrambled to her feet. The other balloon girl tried to as well, but was driven to the floor by the girl and the other boy. They beat her to death and smiled while they did.

"Let me out!" I screamed. "Let me out! I can help! Stitch Mouth! Stitch Mouth! Please! Please!"

Balloon Girl stood in rebellion to the witch.

"Go to her!" I screamed to Stitch Mouth. "Help her!"

"You don't think I want to?" Tears of pain and anger streamed down Stitch Mouth's face.

"Why, then?"

Stitch Mouth remained silent, watching the end of her friend.

Balloon Girl became a torrent of malicious rage, clawing and biting at whoever was closest when the two children came at her. But she was too small, they, too big. Balloon Girl was tackled and pinned to the floor. They held her down. Cursing at her, spitting at her. The witch bent to Balloon Girl and took up one of her wrists, examining it as though something of concern was there.

*My father should have killed you when he had the chance.*

"Yes. He should have. Didn't though. Just like you." The witch ripped the arm free. Balloon Girl grunted in pain, breathing fast and heavy and doing everything she could to make sure the witch would not have the satisfaction of hearing her cry out or beg.

*You killed me once! So, I'm sort of used to it! But I know something you don't know! Hahahahaha* she laughed *Sarah is going to kill you! Too bad you can't hear me say that, or I'd scream it into your stupid face! You stupid – ugly – witch!*

"I can hear you," the witch said casually.

*What? What?*

"I–can–hear–you. How do you think I knew? I knew. Knew."

*No.*

"Yes." The witch tore the other arm away. "Won't cry, will you? Naughty girl. Always so naughty."

Balloon Girl was gasping. *I wanted to be the one to kill you. For everything you did. To us. To all the others. But that's okay. My last regret is that I won't be there to watch you die.*

"We both have regrets. No more flesh. Bones will do. Pain will do. Pain for you."

The witch reached down and ripped Balloon Girl's leg away.

Balloon Girl screamed in pain, crying now, crying, even though she didn't want to, sobbing and crying. *I hate you! I hate you!*

"So naughty. Always lying. Lying about me. Your voice. So beautiful. Came back alive. I could hear you again. Hear you through the walls. Led me. Followed your voice. Heard you. Your plans. Such a grand plan. Stab me to death. Silliness. Not me. Never me. Eternal. Eternal here. My world. Not yours. Only mine. You told me. Maybe you're not so naughty after all."

Balloon Girl turned her head towards us. *I'm sorry. I didn't know.*

Stitch Mouth blew her a kiss.

*No regrets?*

"No regrets."

The witch grabbed Balloon Girl by the skull. "All done. Over now. Your parents couldn't keep you safe. And not your friends. You wanted me to die. Six or seven times. I get to kill you twice. Two times."

Balloon Girl sang.

*She's ugly, oh so ugly, our mommy dear,*
*Ugly as a donkey's rear.*
*She wants to be our mommy,*
*But she's –*

With a shriek, the witch snapped Balloon Girl's skull from her body. Ending the song. Balloon Girl's sockets, somehow filled with life, were now just dark lifeless holes which stared at nothing, not even at the witch who took a moment to look at them.

"No!" I managed through my sobs. "No!" I held my face in my hands. "No."

Stitch Mouth whispered so only I could hear, "I have loved this, Sarah, more than you know. And I am so very thankful for everything. Being with Balloon Girl. Enjoying her sarcasm and love. Returning to my home. Remembering old stories. Becoming your friend. Stop looking at the witch, Sarah. I know she's coming. I don't care. I want this moment with you. My friend. It's okay. Look at me. You don't have to be afraid of her anymore. You can still do this. Balloon Girl believed. So do I. Do this, Sarah. Do it. And I don't mean to sound so selfish, but do it for us." Stitch Mouth pressed a kiss to the door. "These have been some of the best times of my life. No regrets. Say it, Sarah. Say it for me."

"No regrets," I whispered. Thinking back to the many lovely moments we shared, I said more bravely, "No regrets."

She smiled sadly at me. "I have one last request."

"Anything."

"Will you say something that will strengthen me one last time? For what I have to do?"

"I love you," I said, tear ridden and broken.

She closed her eyes a moment and breathed and smiled. Fresh tears came to her red eyes. "I love you, too."

Stitch Mouth turned just as the witch drew near. The children were behind her. The witch hissed through her teeth. The children laughed. I cried. A song rose. A song rose about it all. Stitch Mouth lifted her voice higher than I had ever heard as she took up the second verse of Balloon Girl's song.

*Nothing but a witch.*
*She's ugly, oh so ugly, our mommy dear,*
*Ugly as a donkey's rear,*
*She wants to be our mommy,*
*But she's just a mangy bitch.*

The witch clutched Stitch Mouth by the throat. Stitch Mouth's voice stopped, but her lips still moved with the silent words as she continued to sing and smile despite the pain. Soon, her body convulsed. Before she died, Stitch Mouth slapped the last fragment of chalk against the wall. Everything disappeared.

# 57

My mother heard me weeping. She came into my room. "What happened?" I shook my head, unable to speak. She climbed into bed with me. I sobbed against her as she held me. She didn't ask or say anything. Just rocked me in her arms. After a while, she said, "I'm going to call everyone and let them know I've cancelled the party." I would have said thank you, but I turned towards the corner and cried.

# 58

Twilight came. I was in my mother's bathroom, holding the orange prescription bottle. I hadn't ever used them before. Those pills. Did he know I would use them this way? That I would need them? I tossed six small white round pills into my mouth, hoping it was enough. I returned to bed. Laying there. My body soon tingled, and I plunged into darkness.

# 59

*11:59.*

It had worked. My room was dark, silent.

The corner was filled with the absence of Stitch Mouth, of Balloon Girl. I hurt with how much I missed them. I wanted them. *No regrets.* I held my tears. They would be no use to me that night. There was no place for them.

When I went to the window, I wondered briefly what the witch would think of me. Because I knew she was coming. Did she imagine me cowering in the corner of my room, maybe tucked away miserably under my sheets? Did she think I'd be running ahead of her as fast as I could, with no more protectors to aid me?

She would find me doing neither.

Hatred had found its way into my blood. It was warm. Strangely safe.

Outside, my neighborhood had been replaced by the woods and a world which had consumed my home and brought my world into the witch's. Her world into mine. My heartrate rose as I unlatched the window, opening it fully. The gray air from the other side of my wall sucked life from my room and provided its own presence, which was cold and stale. I climbed through. I had to hurry. The race had begun.

Pale trees stood naked and gangly, glowing weakly in the feeble eternal moon of the third world. The air was gray, and so was I, along with everything around me, as though color couldn't live there, the evidence of lifelessness all around. Ahead of me was a path which had been trampled down by the recurring visits of the witch these past months, easy to follow, easy to see. Without meaning to, the witch would lead me to her house.

I entered the ghostly forest, staying to the side of the path, close enough to see it, but not be seen. I touched at the trees as I passed by them, like blind guides, using them as a covering before dashing my way between the gaps to ensure I stayed hidden. Deeper in, I stopped dead, sidling behind a tree. I heard her.

I peeked around the curve of a tree and saw the witch walking along the path. She was alone. She was almost strolling. A wicked grin of victory on her face. Her long hair trailing her. Further down the path she went, passing in and out of my vision between the trees. She had no idea she was being watched or of what I was doing. She'd know soon enough.

When she could no longer be heard, I worked my way further. The trees tightened around me. Bark brushed my body as I squeezed between tree trunks. Low branches attempted to snag at my hair and face, causing me to hunch as I traveled faster. I had to hurry. The maze of trees thickened even more, as though greedy to fill the air. I had to work to keep the path in sight, and at times I had to backtrack to regain a view of it. I became afraid of not finding the house, or of being lost in the woods forever. But I followed the path. Then I came upon a clearing. Her house was there.

It was smaller than I imagined – almost too small, compared to the hideous sights I had witnessed inside just weeks ago. Having been there, I knew the front door would open to smells and tastes and flies. And children. There would be children locked away in a room, children who had helped the witch for years and had been responsible for the deaths of my friends.

My breath tightened. I told my lungs to breathe. My arms

trembled. I told them to calm. I needed them to be steady. I went to the house, crossing the open space of air and land, feeling as though a spotlight was on me and I felt small.

I opened the door. Flies came at me, black and winged. Stepping through the mass of them, I shut the door silently behind me. Swatting the air and dodging the gore at my feet, I rummaged through splintered drawers and soon found what I hoped to find more than anything. If the witch had a furnace, then she had to have – matches. There they were. Another help the witch had unknowingly given me. Thank you. I went towards the stairs, sifting through piles of clothing and cloth along the way to collect the driest scraps and pieces I could until gathering up what I thought would be enough. Just to be sure, I grabbed a teddy bear, one with long fur, wondering strangely if the child would mind.

My heartrate thumped faster and faster. I ignored it. I took a step up, eyeing the door above me. The next step creaked with my weight. I winced.

"Mother? Are you back already?" a child called from behind the door.

I took a hurried step. Then another.

"Did you bring that girl? I want to punish her for what they did to my eyes."

"I want you to cook her tonight."

"We'll eat her, mother!"

"We'll feast!"

I continued to climb.

"Who's there? Mother? Mother, is that you?"

The door knob rattled as they began to sense what was coming. It rattled harder. "Mother?"

I set the driest articles of clothing at the base of the door and ripped at a sleeve with my teeth to gain strands of thinner thread. My pile grew, the teddy bear on top. I struck a match. The orange flame sputtered at the tip of a single hanging thread. Then it caught eagerly. The flame rose, climbing upward and flaring outward until a ball of heat had formed. It fattened even more as I continued placing more items, all of which burned well. The fire became too much, hot and scalding, but my hand stayed to its task until I was certain the blaze was beyond the point of ever being stopped.

The children began to scream. "Mother! Mother!"

They banged on the door. But it was too late. Black smoke had congregated at the ceiling, spreading and making its way through the crevices of everything that would allow it to enter that room with eight beds. Smoke seeped beneath the door. Entered at the sides. The children began coughing. "Let us out! Please!"

I had prepared myself for that. Prepared myself for any wavering of my will. I remembered the clothes that fed the fire and the unknown victim children who had worn them. I remembered also all the clothes I couldn't even use because of how blood-soaked and stained they were. The innocence that had been taken. Balloon Girl. Stitch Mouth. Stitch Mouth's brother. Countless others. Countless more, if not for the flame.

The fierce heat forced me down a few steps. I returned downstairs as the blaze roared and popped behind me. Flies followed me outside, escaping into the black night sky and disappearing into the air.

I stood near the home, watching, waiting. Pops and things falling could be heard from inside. A beam crashed, taking with it a wall. The blaze made its way to the roof, consuming the home. Billowing smoke darkened the black sky as it rose from the hot orange inferno which continued to feed on whatever it could. Then I heard her. The witch burst from the woods and came to a sudden halt. For a dark moment, she stared at the blaze as it colored her in orange waves.

"You!" she screamed.

I took a step towards the woods. The witch mirrored my slow step and then the next. I dashed into the woods. Skipping over roots and rocks, I paralleled the path again, running back towards my home. The witch was behind me, gaining. I took a sharp turn, heading for a thicker congestion of trees. Low branches lashed at my face. Tree trunks gashed my arms and thudded against me. I traveled deeper, the relentless steps of the witch not far behind. Closer. I side-stepped, cutting behind a tree and then another, zig-zagging back and forth, causing my body to disappear from her sight. She stumbled and cursed her way after me, losing me once, until she saw me again, running ahead. She took chase. My lip split open with the whip of a branch. Another cut across my forehead, causing blood to drip into my eyes. My arms were raw. I dashed behind a tree again, but this time, I stayed, controlling as best I could the rampant efforts of my lungs to pull in deeper breaths. I listened.

The witch came fast. Her fevered hatred blinding her. She came quick, thinking I was further ahead. Closer. She was about to pass me completely. I jumped onto a bough and yanked on it with all my weight. The branch bounced low, snagged the witch by the hair. Her feet flew out from beneath her as her head was ripped back by the unmoving tree. I circled behind her as fast as I could and began entangling her hair into secure knots through the spindly branches, tightening my final trap.

The witch had been caught.

She wrenched around, shrieking and screaming, kicking at the air, clawing for me. I secured one last clump of hair and circled in front of her. She lunged for me, but I was out of reach. I stood before her. Suddenly, the witch relaxed. She began laughing, as though it was all very amusing to her.

I revealed no emotion. Said nothing.

The witch stopped laughing, then considered me carefully. "You have me. Smart. Cunning. Sarah. Never thought. Here I am. What you wanted. What will you do?"

I removed a match as my answer.

Panic flashed across her face. She shook her head dutifully. "Sarah. Don't. You can't. Couldn't live with yourself. I should know. Would know. Hate yourself. Don't."

I wanted to say so many things. Ask questions about my friends. About the other children. Scream at her. Fling judgments until they covered her. But I didn't want her to see me cry, and I knew I would. With nothing to say, I took a step closer.

"Sarah. Don't. Regret. I never wanted to be like this. No one cared. My babies. No one cared!"

I wanted to ask how she could blame anyone but herself. I wanted to ask how she could beg so casually after all she had done. I pinched the match between two fingers and lowered it to the box to strike it. The flame came to life.

"Names. I'll tell you their names."

It was the last thing I expected her to say. The match dropped cold to the leaves. The witch had a thousand confessions to offer, and I wanted to hear them all. I wanted her to beg for forgiveness and prove she still had some shred of humanity left to her. And yes, I wanted to know the true names of my two friends.

The witch tried to take advantage of my hesitation. "Sarah. Yes. Tell you everything. You've only heard one side to the story. Their side. They were tricky. Very tricky. Your two friends. You don't know. They treated me terribly."

I struck another match. She shrieked again, clinging to her earlier promise, "I'll tell you their names!"

I bent to the ground to avoid her desperate attempts to reach for me. She kicked me in the face. My vision was ruined by pain. I bled and spit blood. But I didn't care. This time, I walked behind the witch to avoid her reach. She shrieked everything she could, every possible promise and every threat. I touched the new flame to her dress. The blaze crackled, rising faster than I ever imagined. Like it had always wanted her. The witch became a torch, a flame that rose with her screams. I wanted to walk off, or to at least turn away. But I forced myself to watch. I wanted to make sure she died this time. And it was something I had to do.

# 60

"Are you okay?" my mother asked. I was at my window. "No."
My mother wrapped her arms around my waist and we gazed
outside together. "Is it over?" "Yes." "But you miss them." A tear
streaked down my face. "With all my heart."

# 61

The days after graduation came and went. I was exhausted. Always so tired. I never knew how tiring sadness could be, and a heightened sense of fear was no longer mine to live off of, so I was left only with the grief and nothing else. The sorrow. It was pain. The witch was dead. And I was hollow. Filled only with sadness. Most days, I laid in bed, staring at the corner, with no interest in doing anything else.

Sometimes, I'd drift downstairs to eat a little or just for something to aimlessly do, mostly when my mom was at work or when she was gone for some other reason that escaped me. Most days were spent in my bed or standing at my window, looking out at nothing. Sometimes crying. Sometimes not.

I had nightmares. In them, Stitch Mouth and Balloon Girl died, and not always in the way I had seen. Sometimes it was a pack of wolves, or sometimes they drowned. I could never save them. I was always too late or too far away. Sometimes I dreamt that they didn't remember who I was. Like I didn't matter to them. And sometimes, I dreamt we were together again as the friends we had grown to be. Those were the worst. I'd wake up with a fresh realization of what had happened. Like a wound freshly opened.

When I was awake, guilt plagued me. Thoughts bothered me. It made me think of those flies. Thoughts on how things could have been different. If I had done something sooner. If I had swung the axe. If I had choked the witch just a few more seconds. If I had not been such a coward. If I had just done something. When I still could.

I wanted to remember the sweetest moments, but instead, I forced myself to remember all the ways I had failed them. Those two girls I loved. Remember how you failed them, Sarah. I didn't deserve anything else.

# 62

There was a quiet rapping on my door. I tossed over in my bed, startled by a familiar knock I hadn't heard in two years.

"Sarah?"

"Dad?"

"Can I come in?"

"Of course." I threw my hands through my hair in a desperate attempt to not look like the way I did.

It was strange, seeing my dad. He looked exactly as I remembered him. There were pictures and memories for me to use as reminders of who he was, but pictures and memories didn't capture the subtle way his body tilted to the left, or the nervous way he brushed his shirt as he stepped in, or the gentleness in his blue eyes that questioned whether or not his presence was wanted.

"Dad." I started crying, even as I smiled. "I don't want you to see me like this."

"Like what?" He said, pretending I wasn't a mess.

"Like I'm a sad slob."

"Well, from what your mother told me, you are a sad slob."

"I know," I admitted with a smirk. I wanted to stop crying.

He climbed into my bed to sit beside me.

"I'm okay, Dad."

"I know you are."

"No, you don't."

He nodded. "You're right."

"I didn't mean it like that."

"I know you didn't."

"Did Mom tell you to come?"

"Yes."

"I'm okay, Dad."

"Now you sound like me," he said.

"Like you?"

"Lying about how you are, just so people will leave you alone."

"Well, I have to lie because I haven't seen you in so long, so the last thing I want to do is to start blubbering in front of you. How are you?"

"No, Sarah. I'm not here to talk about me."

"I know."

He closed his eyes a moment. "Sarah, you're my daughter, so if you're hurt or sad, I wouldn't want you to pretend otherwise."

"I know."

"I want to tell you something."

"Okay."

"Something I've never admitted."

"Okay."

He seemed to be building up courage. "After I left you and your mother, shame is the only thing that kept me away from you and her. I wanted to come back, do you know that?"

"No," I answered honestly.

It hurt him. "Well, I did. For a long time, it felt like I had died. My body was just going through the motions because I'd lost the two people who mattered to me more than anything. I wanted to come back every day, but I was afraid the two of you were doing a lot better without me. I didn't want to interfere. I thought it'd be selfish. And so, that's what I imagined, that your life was much better with me gone."

"We never thought that, Dad. We missed you."

"I know. But in a way, it was easier for me to live in misery than to try hard to be good again. Does that make sense?"

"I think so. That's how I feel."

"I know." He nodded. "Why is that?" He was genuinely asking. "Why do we pretend so much?"

I thought about it. It was something I had thought about for days. "Because we feel like it's what we deserve."

He nodded again. He was still the quiet man I remembered. "Your mother told me about everything. About that witch. About your friends."

"You don't think I'm crazy?"

"No." He shook his head and smiled and shook his head again. "Sarah, I've known you for a long time. I still spend a lot of time remembering all of our princess dates and all those times watching you sing. Your voice was always so beautiful."

"So is yours."

He shook his head. "Not like yours. But that's not my point. My point is that you're my daughter and I like to think I know you pretty well, even after being gone all this time. And if someone else told me about witches and strange girls, well, I'd probably think they should be on medications, just like I am."

"You're on medications?"

"I am."

"Why?"

"For my moods," he admitted with a deep sigh. He continued, "But with you, my daughter, I know you're not the type of person to make things up. I believe you. And I'm sorry."

"Thanks, Dad." It meant a lot, though I didn't fully believe him.

"I'm just saying – that hurt – maybe you can learn to let it go. Maybe it would help."

I shook my head. "No. I don't want to," I admitted.

"Why not?"

"I don't want to stop hurting. Hurting helps me remember them."

"I know what you mean," he said. "You don't have to stop hurting if you don't want to."

"I don't?"

"No. That's your choice to make, just like I made mine."

"Are you going to stay for a little while?" I asked.

"I don't think so. I wanted to stop in and see you. I wanted to surprise you for your graduation a couple of weeks ago as well, but it was cancelled."

"You were going to come?"

"Yeah. I wanted to surprise you. And your mom."

"Sorry for ruining it."

"Don't be like that. I got to see you today without anyone else around."

"I'd like you to stay," I said. Having him there with me only reinforced how much I missed him.

"That's up to your mother." I could hear the fresh guilt when he mentioned her.

"I don't think she'd mind."

"She might."

"No," I contradicted. "She wouldn't."

"You think?" He smiled.

"I don't think she'd mind at all."

# 63

Being with my father helped. But the pain remained. That night, I fell asleep crying as always, unable to be anything but pathetic and sad. I thought of what Balloon Girl might say if she saw me like that, baggy eyed and mopey. I could almost hear her saying something perfectly sarcastic, and then Stitch Mouth intervening to stand up for me. After a short-lived smile at thinking about what that might look like, I began crying again, like always. Begging the dark corner to let me see Stitch Mouth and Balloon Girl just one last time. I fell asleep.

A subtle sound woke me. *11:59.*

The room was dark. I peered around, searching for the source of the stirring soft noise. My eyes drifted to the window. A pink balloon rustled at the ceiling. I rushed from my bed and went to it. At the tip of its string, a single piece of purple chalk was tied. I smiled. I untied it. I sketched a door, my heartrate rising like never before. The door opened to golden light.

*Hello, Sarah.*

"Sarah, you came."

# Epilogue

"It's good to see you," Dr. Tariq greeted, his legs crossed comfortably in casual consideration of me. "So tell me. What has happened these past few months since I saw you last?"

"I get to see my dad. He visits once a month."

He nodded, smiled. "Very good. What else?"

"Well, I started school."

"Oh, and what school are you attending?"

"Well, Emma and I are enrolled at the local tech school to take Gen Ed courses before transitioning to a bigger university. We'll probably do that in a year or so."

"That's a great idea. You can save a lot of money that way."

"That's what we were thinking."

"And it gives you time to determine what you want to declare as your major."

"Exactly."

Dr. Tariq tossed his head back with a sigh of exasperation. "Please, Sarah! Enough of such blibber-blabber. Don't tell me you came here to talk about your plans for college."

I smiled and shifted. "No, that's not why I'm here. I wanted to tell you what happened."

His eyes lit up. "Yes. What happened to that witch?"

"Well, I killed her."

"Wonderful." He adjusted his tie. I could feel the excitement in him. "And how?"

"Well, first, I burned down her house. Then she chased me through the woods and her hair got tangled in a tree branch."

"On accident?" He grinned.

"Not quite. I kind of tied her hair there."

Dr. Tariq raised his hands towards the ceiling. "And then she spontaneously ignited into flame?"

"Not exactly."

"How exactly?"

"Well, I lit her on fire."

"Very good." He grinned again.

"You don't think that's wrong?" I asked.

"That what's wrong?"

"That I lit her on fire?"

"Why would I think that's wrong?"

"I just, I guess, it just sounds wrong."

"Well then. It *sounds* wrong."

"Well, yeah."

"Sarah?"

"Yes?"

"What would have happened if you had *not* killed the witch?"

"She would have killed me. Eaten me."

"Yes. Obviously. So why ruin own perfect convictions with a counterfeit sense of guilt?"

"But I did it on purpose."

"Well then. You did it on purpose." He raised his eyebrows. "That's an entirely different matter," he said sarcastically. "Sarah, please, would the witch have *accidentally* lit herself on fire? Would she have *accidentally* died some other way? Would she have stopper herself? No, of course not. Maybe she could have tripped into a lion's mouth or died while hang gliding?"

"Well, no. Well, she could. But it wouldn't be likely."

"And would she have *accidentally* stopped abducting children? Woken up one morning to the startling realization of how filthy and grotesque her tastes had made her? Suddenly developed a conscience, like the one you have?" He rolled his eyes. "I think not. Sarah, you have done what you had to do. You did what had to be done."

"But I killed the other children."

"Yes, yes, those sweet chaste respectable loving wonderful gifted giving innocent children. And if you had released them, they would have circled you with hugs and kisses and eternal thanks, then the lot of you would have gone out for ice cream and roller skating and a late night movie. Enough of this, Sarah. The witch and her children died because it was what they deserved. And if they had not, another child would be suffering right this very second, this very moment, as we speak, suffering at the hands of a witch and children whose fat bellies would be full with *you*."

"I know." I lowered my head.

"Lift your chin, Sarah. I am proud of you. I am happy for you."

"Really?"

"I'd rather see you and have you here than know you had become some stew. Now, tell me, what permitted you to finally make your choice?"

"Well, the witch and her children killed Stitch Mouth and Balloon Girl." I was still calling them by those names, even though I had learned their true ones.

"Yes. Your friends were killed. And only then were you able to make your choice. Tell me how you felt after your friends were killed. And do not tell me you felt *sad*." He frowned at me like a sad clown.

"How'd you know they died?" I asked.

"It's obvious, isn't it?"

"Oh. Well. I guess."

"How did their deaths make you feel, Sarah?"

"Well, I was angry. I wanted the witch to die. And I didn't care if she ended up killing me or not because of what she had done to Stitch Mouth and Balloon Girl. I just wish it hadn't taken so long. I wish I had done something sooner."

"Sarah, your choice came at the perfect time."

"What do you mean?"

"You could not have chosen to be ready any earlier than you were. Nor could you have killed the witch any earlier, even if you convinced yourself otherwise."

"I tried though."

"Necessary as well."

"I think I understand."

"Do you?"

"In order to not be afraid, I had to lose my friends." I hated the idea, even though it was true.

"Yes. But was it worth it?" he asked.

"Was it worth losing them so I could overcome my fear and kill the witch?"

"That is my question."

"No."

"And you say it with such conviction." He raised an eyebrow. "So, you would have gladly kept your fear, and the witch, if it meant keeping your friends from having to die once again."

"Yes. Definitely."

Fixing his eyes on mine to test the truth of my answer, he smiled, then said, "Good."

"Good?"

"Yes. It means you are better than most, Sarah."

"It doesn't feel that way."

"Which is further proof." Then he said, "I am glad it turned out as it did, Sarah, though I am sorry it cost you your friends. But they loved you. They gave themselves for you, and you gave yourself for them."

"I didn't die like they did."

"That is not true. A part of you died in order to do what you had to do for them. You overcame the part of you that feared. A very deep part of you. A very deep part of most people. Not everyone can do that. Some people will even change into monsters just to live among worse monsters, if it means living."

"Like the children of the witch."

"Precisely."

"Dr. Tariq?"

"Yes, Sarah?"

"There's something else."

"Isn't there always."

"Sure. I guess."

"Never mind. What were you going to say?"

"They came back. Stitch Mouth and Balloon Girl."

"They're alive?"

"Yes."

"That is even more wonderful."

"You don't seem surprised."

He adjusted his tie. "Well, I like to think I know you well enough by now to know that if your friends had died and *not* come back, you would have been weeping away to nothing this entire time."

"Oh, I guess that's true."

He nodded.

"Anyway, we hang out quite a bit. And we've met other friends in the third circle."

"Wonderful."

"And other monsters."

"Less wonderful."

I laughed. "But Dr. Tariq?"

"Yes?"

"I have a question. How do you know *things*? You knew that the witch was a witch. Plus, I think you knew the witch was dead and how I killed her. And I think you knew that Stitch Mouth and Balloon Girl had come back. And I think you know their real names."

He smirked. "Sarah, there is much I know."

"But can you tell me *how* you know? Please."

"Well then. You used your manners. I am forced to oblige." His eyes remained fixed upon me, as though considering whether or not he was even going to answer. Then, despite his eyes remaining open, a translucent eyelid winked at me, behind which was a purely golden eye. It disappeared again. Then he laughed and laughed.

– The Brothers Series –

*Late Autumn Trees*
*Haunts of Cruelty*
*The Bear, The Girl, and the Monkey with No Eyes*
Coming Soon: *Stain*

– The Other Stories –

*The Woman in the Window*
*Nibbles*
*Coming Soon: Genevieve and the Skin Face Man*

www.rscrow.com

https://www.facebook.com/rscrowauthor

*Please feel free to leave a review on Amazon.com*

Made in the USA
Lexington, KY
16 March 2018